C. F. Roe was brought up in Scotland and graduated from Aberdeen University Medical School with a gold medal in Surgery. He has practised and taught surgery in the U.S., travelled the world as a ship's surgeon and worked in Afghanistan before becoming a full-time writer. C. F. Roe now lives in London and Albuquerque, New Mexico. Dr Jean Montrose's other cases, *The Lumsden Baby*, *Death By Fire* and *Deadly Partnership*, are also available from Headline.

Bad Blood

C. F. Roe

HEADLINE

First published in 1991
by HEADLINE BOOK PUBLISHING PLC

First published in paperback in 1991
by HEADLINE BOOK PUBLISHING PLC

10 9 8 7 6 5 4 3 2 1

ISBN 0 7472 3696 8

Printed and bound in Great Britain by
Collins, Glasgow

HEADLINE BOOK PUBLISHING PLC
Headline House
79 Great Titchfield Street
London W1P 7FN

Bad Blood

PART ONE

Chapter One

'You girls never get to see the beautiful places right here on your own doorstep,' said Steven Montrose, looking around the breakfast table. Steven was fully dressed, an unusual event at 9 a.m. on Sunday, and the girls knew immediately that their father was up to something. 'I know the places *you* think are exciting,' he went on. 'The Riviera, or the Costa Brava . . .'

'Costa Brava!' said Lisbie, his younger daughter. She tossed the fair hair out of her face. 'Who would want to go there?'

'About eighty-four million people, and all in the same fortnight,' said Fiona, before her father could answer. At twenty, Fiona was two years older than Lisbie. 'And I wish you'd stop tossing you head like that, Lisbie, just because you got a new haircut.'

'Where's your mother?' asked Steven, looking pointedly at the clock.

'She's on the phone to a patient, Dad.' Fiona, dark, slim, and attractive in a more sophisticated way than her sister, was always ready to spring to her mother's defence.

'All right, Fiona, you don't need to sound so aggravated . . .' He turned to Lisbie, looked her over and shook his head. 'Lisbie, I assume you're not coming out dressed like that?'

Most people thought that Lisbie looked like her mother, and she was secretly rather proud of that. Plump, pretty, fair-complexioned, and more rounded than the darker, more elegant Fiona, Lisbie had a small gap between her front teeth which sometimes made her a bit shy with new people, but she soon forgot about it, as did they.

She looked down at her thin, summery pyjamas, and grinned at Fiona.

'Yes, of course I am, Daddy. And Fiona's coming out with just a bra and knickers . . .'

'Just so we don't embarrass you if we stop somewhere for lunch.' Fiona's big, dark eyes twinkled maliciously.

Steven's face flushed slightly as he faced the two girls. 'Get moving,' he said. 'We're leaving in fifteen minutes.'

'Fifteen minutes!' protested Fiona. 'Lisbie won't even be out of the bathroom by then.'

An hour later, everybody was ready.

'What's going on?' asked Lisbie, following her mother down the stairs. 'Why do we have to go out so early?'

'Your father had something done to his car,' replied Jean. 'I think he wants to give it a good tryout.'

Fiona was waiting in the hall. 'Can Robert come with us?' she asked Steven when he came out of the living room. Fiona was wearing a kilt and a green cashmere polo-necked sweater which showed off her attractive, petite figure. As usual she looked as carefully groomed as if she'd spent two hours dressing and making up, rather than just her usual ten minutes.

'No, he can't,' said Steven briskly. He went to the hall table, picked up his driving gloves, pale pigskin ones with holes over the knuckles, and jingled his car keys. 'It would take another half hour to go and pick him up, and anyway, today is family only, if you don't mind.'

Fiona tightened her lips but said nothing more.

Steven looked proudly at his car as Jean and the two girls got in. After the mechanical work had been finished, he'd had it waxed and polished, and the car looked as if it had just come out of the showroom.

While they were still within the town limits, Steven drove sedately enough, but once they were out on the open Blairgowrie road, past the big houses with their grassy gardens sloping down to the River Tay, Steven checked that there was no traffic behind him, slowed right down, then put his foot hard on the accelerator. The surge of power pushed his passengers into the backs of their seats. He did this several times, each time leaning forward to listen to the note of the big Rover's engine.

'Daddy!' said Lisbie, finally. 'Do you have to do that?'

'I put in a new intake manifold,' explained Steven, speaking to Jean, who was sitting beside him. He sounded very pleased. 'You remember how it used to . . . sort of hesitate?'

'Not really, dear,' replied Jean. 'But it seems fine now.'

'I put in a new set of shock absorbers as well,' said Steven after a pause. 'I think we should go out along some of these little side roads . . .'

Fiona and Lisbie looked at each other. Fiona was quiet, sulking because Steven hadn't wanted Robert to come with them.

'Look at the lambs!' said Jean, pointing at a small flock of blackfaced sheep in a field to their right. Steven slowed so that everybody could get a good look, then accelerated hard again.

Steven had certainly picked a good day to take his family out into the countryside; the weather was sunny with high wispy clouds, and with the pure rain-washed clarity seen in Perthshire and in the landscape paintings of van de Velde. The rowans and pine trees along the roadside moved gently with the breeze, the pine needles still bearing the distinctive pale green sparkle of the year's new growth. The traces of the drought that had afflicted the area earlier that summer had vanished as if it had never happened.

A few miles further, Steven turned right off the main road, and after several more turns, came to a cross-roads, then on to a narrow, twisting road that soon led past a series of clean farm buildings, manicured fields with elegant long-legged thoroughbreds and well-fed Aberdeen Angus cattle, their black coats glistening with an opulent silky sheen. Along the roadside, the fields were lined by trees and meticulous white-painted wood fencing.

Steven took a turn rather fast, trying to evaluate the amount of sway the new shock-absorbers allowed.

'Dad,' said Fiona loudly, breaking her silence, 'are you trying to get us all killed?'

'There's nobody ever on this road,' said Steven calmly. 'I came here specially to test the cornering . . .'

'They made the road just for you?' Fiona's voice was sharp. She hadn't wanted to come out, and didn't like being bounced around in the car like that.

'That's enough from you, Fiona,' murmured Jean in a warning tone.

But Steven ignored Fiona; it was doubtful if he even heard her. 'Isn't this the Strathalmond estate that we're going through?' he asked Jean.

'Yes.' Jean looked over to her left. 'The main house is over there, over on the other side of those woods . . . it's huge. You can sometimes see a bit of it from the road in winter, but normally you'd never even guess it was there.'

'It's a *castle*, really, Mum, isn't it?' asked Lisbie as the car swept past the main entrance, a pair of huge pink granite pillars with elegant cast-iron gates set back a few yards from the road.

'Yes, Strathalmond Castle,' said Jean, looking rather apprehensive as the sides of the road rushed past. 'It's beautiful; I went there once. *Steven* . . .'

Jean never criticized Steven's driving, and she wasn't criticizing it now, but she felt he was going too fast considering he had the responsibility of the whole family in the car.

They passed the boundaries of the Strathalmond estate, and came to a straight part in the road, now lined only by scrubby whin bushes and oak saplings. There was a sharp turn at the end, and Jean braced herself, hoping that Steven would slow down. Maybe traffic *was* rare on this little road, as Steven had said, but even he couldn't know what was around the corner, and something might easily be coming the other way.

Steven didn't see the wide patch of oil on the road until he was almost on top of it, and instinctively he braked, knowing the sharpness of the turn right ahead of him. It was the wrong thing to do. The wheels locked, the car slid sideways, and Lisbie screamed while Steven fought to control the heavy vehicle. It bucked and slipped, the front wheels went up on the grassy verge, and Jean put her hands on the dashboard to steady herself, but she was flung against the door as the back swung around and the car slid to the other side of the road, out of control. For a second Steven thought it was going to turn over, but it finally came to rest just at the corner, with two wheels up on the verge, and facing in the wrong direction.

For a few moments everybody sat quite still in the unnatural silence. The engine was off, but it made a loud ticking noise.

'Is everybody all right?' Steven's voice was very subdued. Lisbie started to cry in a muffled kind of way, and Steven turned round to see what was happening. Lisbie, who hadn't been wearing a seat belt, had been thrown to the floor, and Fiona had landed on top of her. Jean got out of the car in a second, opened the back door and helped Fiona to get out. She had a bright red bruise over her left cheekbone, and had also bumped her knee. Lisbie was shaken and dazed, and whimpered for a few moments until Fiona got off her and it was clear that she had suffered no serous injury. Steven got out of the car, and helped Lisbie out of the back.

'Are *you* all right, Jean? I'm terribly sorry. I simply didn't see that oil patch in time.'

'You were going much too fast, Dad,' said Fiona, angrily rubbing her knee. '*That's* why we crashed. You could have killed us all.'

Jean examined the bruise on Fiona's cheek. 'It'll be gone in a few days,' she said, then looked at her knee. 'That's just a bump too,' she said. 'Thank God it wasn't worse.' She hugged Fiona, and Lisbie came over to make it a threesome. Looking over Fiona's shoulder, Jean noticed a flash of red from beyond the bushes and saplings, maybe a dozen yards from the road.

'What's that?' she asked Steven, pointing.

'I don't know,' he replied, glancing around for a second. He stood uncomfortably looking at the three women, feeling

guilty and embarrassed, then got back into the car. The engine
started without difficulty, and he slowly drove forward and
back on to the road, then waited with the motor running
for them to get back into the car.

Jean went around and spoke to him through the open
window. 'Steven, I think you should take a look down
there . . .' She pointed over her shoulder to where she had
seen the patch of red. Steven couldn't see anything, but Jean's
tone made him switch the engine off instantly.

He got out, and while Jean and the girls were getting back
into the Rover, he pushed his way through the thick
undergrowth in the direction Jean had indicated. Then he
saw what had made Jean sound so insistent; it was a car,
a red Porsche, a 411 upside down; the wheels seemed to be
at an odd angle. Steven came closer; the grass was flattened
and the saplings were splintered and broken in the car's path;
it had clearly turned over and slid most of the way on its
roof. The car windows were smashed and crazed, and the
driver's compartment was partly crushed. An arm was sticking
out of the driver's side window; the hand was quite still,
and was a blue, mottled colour.

'Jean?' he called, his voice shaking. 'I think you'd better
come down here. No, not the girls,' he said in a louder voice.
'Just you.'

Jean made her way through the undergrowth to the car,
and the two of them tried unsuccessfully to open the door.
Jean squeezed her hand through the window along the arm,
tried to get a pulse on the neck, but the body was too
crumpled and the head was bent and hidden by the twisted
roof panel. All she could do, by peering between the broken
pieces of opaque, fragmented glass, was to confirm that the
driver was dead and there wasn't anybody else in the car.

'He's been there a while,' said Jean, standing up. 'At least
ten to twelve hours, I'd say.'

'We need to find a phone,' said Steven. He was sounding
very shaken, and sat down on a nearby pine stump.

'Are you all right, dear?' Jean was more concerned about
him than about the crashed car and its occupant. 'Put your

head down between your knees for a minute . . .' She put a comforting hand on his head, then looked back at the silent Porsche. 'There isn't a phone anywhere around here for miles,' she said. 'We'll have to go back to Strathalmond Castle and call the police from there.'

Chapter Two

Fiona and Lisbie were sitting quietly in the car when Steven and Jean got back to the roadside. Fiona had her hand over the bruise on her knee, and Lisbie was looking very pale.

'There's been an accident down there,' said Jean, speaking quietly. She closed the door and fastened her seat belt.

'What sort of accident?' asked Fiona, forgetting about her bruise.

'There's a car back there in the undergrowth,' replied Jean. 'The driver's still there; he was killed. He must have taken that corner too fast . . .'

'That could have been US,' said Fiona, glaring angrily at Steven.

'*We* skidded on a patch of oil,' said Steven, 'and if I had been going too fast, that WOULD have been us down there.' He put the car in gear and it moved slowly forward, then he steered it on to the grass verge again to go around the oil patch.

'We should get somebody to put sand over that oil before somebody else gets hurt,' said Steven. Jean nodded, but she seemed to be thinking about something else.

There was no other traffic on the road, and Steven drove back very circumspectly for about two miles until he came to the entrance to Strathalmond Castle. The gates were still open, and looked most imposing as they drove slowly through; Jean noticed the family crest of the Strathalmonds in the ironwork tracery near the top of the gate. There was no lodge near the gates, so Steven decided to continue on up the drive.

The road was beautifully kept, the gravel even and smoothly distributed over its pink, sandy surface. On each side, huge chestnut trees lined the drive, and far off to the left, beyond a grassy field which sloped gently down, a bend of the River Almond glittered in the bright sunlight.

'Look at that,' said Lisbie, in a very faint voice. 'Isn't that beautiful, down there?'

'Yes, a lovely place for a picnic,' murmured Jean absently, then addressed Steven. 'The house is almost a mile further up this drive.'

'Did you say you'd been here before, Mum?' asked Fiona curiously. 'Is the place open to the public?'

'I've met the Countess a few times,' said Jean. 'She's on the Perthshire Health Committee . . .' Jean hesitated as if she were about to say something more, but just then they turned a corner, and the drive widened into a vast forecourt in front of one of the most magnificent residences any of them had ever seen. The girls gasped, and both of them leaned forward, trying to see as much of the facade as they could.

'You see, girls, it was worth slipping on that oil patch, just to see this place, wasn't it?' said Steven with an attempt at humour.

'I'm sure *Robert* would have liked to see it,' snapped Fiona. 'He doesn't get much of a chance . . .'

'Why don't you ask him over for dinner, then?' said Jean, turning around. 'I'm making a chicken curry tonight, and I'm sure he'd like that.'

Fiona said nothing, but sat back in her seat. Jean turned to look out the window; it wasn't always easy, keeping the peace in this family.

Strathalmond Castle was constructed of dazzlingly white Aberdeen granite, three storeys high, ornate in a way which resembled the great French chateaux of the Loire, with high, slate-covered roofs and wide flag-topped turrets at each end. In the centre of the facade was a great *porte cochère*. The drive continued round each side of the castle, presumably to the stables and garages behind.

'You could drive a double-decker in there,' said Lisbie, wide-eyed, looking at the *porte cochère*.

The gravel crunched under the car tyres as Steven took a wide sweep to approach the entrance.

'Are you going in the front?' Lisbie asked nervously. 'Isn't there another entrance?'

'We're not delivering anything, and we're not servants,' snapped Steven, who had asked himself exactly the same questions a moment before. 'Of course we're going to the front.'

Steven parked under the archway and they got out; Fiona, with her injured knee, made a production out of it. The car seemed tiny and insignificant as they walked over towards the huge, nail-encrusted door.

Lisbie looked up at the great iron lantern which hung from the top of the arch. 'I wouldn't want that to fall on me,' she said, with a nervous giggle.

Jean went up the steps with Steven, and the girls hung behind, overawed by the magnificence of the place.

'Do we ring the bell, do you think, or were we supposed to bring trumpets?' Steven asked Jean out of the corner of his mouth, but as they came up to the door itself, it opened in front of them, and a middle-aged man in a butler's dark suit and with immaculate white hair looked out at them with a polite question in his eye.

Steven explained that there had been a fatal accident down the road, and the police needed to be notified. The butler gravely invited them in.

'A most dangerous turn, there,' he said, leading them into an enormous oak-panelled hallway. The walls were ornamented with claymores, round studded leather-covered Scots shields, and high on the left wall hung a huge painting which Steven thought might be of the Battle of Culloden. A vast crystal chandelier hung from the centre of the beamed and fretted ceiling.

'If you'll excuse me one moment . . .' While the girls gazed at the suits of armour on each side of the double staircase, the butler disappeared through a door to the left of the stairs, reappearing a moment later with a white portable telephone in his hands. After a quick glance at Steven, he handed it to Jean. Everybody stood watching her while she dialled.

'Yes, I'd like to speak to Detective Inspector Niven, please,' she said, and at the same moment they all became aware of someone coming down the stairs. The step was irregular, as if the person were walking with a slight limp.

'His lordship,' said the butler, very quietly.

The man came into view round the bend of the staircase; Jean, who had not met him, guessed he was in his early fifties, slightly built, but very erect and with a military bearing, accented by a dark blue blazer, white shirt and regimental tie. His hair was thin, greying and short over the ears, which were large, but very flat against his head. A bristly salt-and-pepper moustache under a long, aristocratic nose gave him a fierce look that was belied by calm, grey eyes which looked out from under thin, arched eyebrows. He had the calm, in-control look of a man who would be hard to astonish, and seemed neither surprised nor put out to see the small, uninvited group clustered around the bottom of the staircase.

Jean, holding the telephone, smiled up at the Earl, who stopped a few steps from the bottom and smiled rather formally back at her.

'Excuse me just a moment,' she said to him, then turned her attention back to the phone.

'Doug? It's Jean Montrose . . .'

The Earl watched Jean with interest while he waited for her to finish her conversation. His expression, though friendly enough, showed not the faintest trace of humour.

'Doug, there's been an accident . . . I wouldn't have called you, but the man was dead . . . Yes, in a car, a red one; Steven says it's a Porsche . . .'

Jean saw the Earl tense suddenly but wasn't sure if it was because of what she'd said. 'Yes, we're up at Strathalmond Castle — that was the nearest phone . . .' Jean explained to Doug Niven exactly where to find the overturned car. He said it would take him at least half an hour to get to the place.

'We'll meet you there in thirty minutes, then,' said Jean, looking at her watch, then put the phone back in its cradle, which the butler was still holding.

'I'm so sorry to trouble you like this.' Jean's smile was so disarming that the Earl's rather stern expression relaxed visibly.

'I'm Jean Montrose, this is my husband Steven, and these are my daughters Fiona and Lisbie.'

'I'm Calum McAllister,' he said, coming down to the foot of the stairs. He had a deep, well-modulated voice that bespoke Eton and Oxford. He stretched out his hand, first to Jean, then to Steven.

Lisbie laughed. 'For a minute we thought you were the Earl,' she said. 'What a relief!'

'I am, young lady,' he replied, unsmiling. 'The Earl of Strathalmond is my title; Calum McAllister is my name.'

'Oh, I'm sorry . . .' Lisbie was pink with embarrassment, and took a small sideways step to move behind her mother.

'I heard what you told the police,' said Strathalmond, sounding very sombre. He turned courteously back to Jean. 'I very much regret it, but I think I know who the . . . victim may have been.'

'Oh dear . . .' Jean's hand went up to her mouth. 'Not someone from your family?'

'Graeme Ferguson is the only person I know around here who has a red Porsche,' he said. 'He's engaged to marry my daughter Ilona, and he was here yesterday evening . . .' He gave a short laugh. 'But that's silly of me to be such a pessimist; it's probably somebody quite different, somebody who was just passing through . . .'

'Would you like to come back to the car with us?' asked Jean. 'You can't really see the . . . driver, but you might be able to recognize the car. At least it would set your mind at rest, one way or the other.'

Strathalmond was about to answer when somebody else started to come down the staircase. 'Oh,' he said, his voice changing suddenly. 'Here's Marina.'

Marina, Countess of Strathalmond was a striking woman; about ten years younger than her husband, she was almost too slim, elegantly dressed in a black sweater with five or six thin gold necklaces hanging over her chest, and a dark green skirt that came almost to her ankles. She stretched out her hand to Jean; her wrists were long, well-tanned and bony.

'Jean Montrose!' she exclaimed, and came down to give Jean

a rather theatrical kiss. Marina was tall, almost six feet, and made Jean, who was a foot shorter, feel dwarfed. 'I am so glad to see you,' she said. 'Whatever are you doing in our neighbourhood?'

Fiona mumbled something that sounded like 'We're just Sunday slumming . . .' but fortunately only her sister heard her.

'Of course it *can't* be Graeme,' said Marina when she heard the story, but her sudden pallor belied her words.

'Ilona isn't here just now; she's away visiting friends,' she went on. 'She'll be back this evening in time for dinner. Would you . . . would you mind phoning me when you *know*?'

'Of course,' said Jean, and was about to say that the police would surely tell them, but something in Marina's expression stopped her. For some reason, Marina wanted to hear it from Jean.

'Katerine is going to be very upset too,' said Strathalmond in a subdued voice, and Jean noticed that he exchanged a quick glance with Marina.

'Katerine's our other daughter,' explained Marina. 'She's two years younger than Ilona.'

'Eighteen,' said Strathalmond. 'The dangerous age.'

This time Marina's glance at him was decidedly not friendly.

'We'll send Cole down in the Jeep,' said Strathalmond, changing the subject, realizing that he had aroused Marina's ire. 'If it is Graeme, he should be able to identify the body.'

For the next several minutes Marina talked almost exclusively to Jean; she spoke fast in a rather high-pitched voice, and her hands fluttered a lot. Jean was surprised; if this was the *real* Marina, she was quite different from the rather aloof lady who came once a month to the offices of the Health Board.

As they left, Jean happened to glance back up at the balcony, and she caught a brief but disconcerting glimpse of a young woman peering down at them from the balustraded landing at the head of the stairs. It couldn't be Ilona, she knew that, because she was away visiting friends; that meant it had to be Ilona's younger sister Katerine.

It was only after they'd all got back in the car and were making their way back to meet Doug Niven that Jean began to understand; Marina had indeed been very glad to see her; in fact, she had been in a state of acute agitation throughout their brief visit.

'How long do you think he's been dead?' asked Doug. He arrived at the same time as the Montroses, and Jean had walked back with him to the crashed Porsche while Steven and the girls waited in the car.

Jean tried to bend the arm projecting from the window. 'At least twelve hours,' she said. 'Dr Anderson should be able to give you a better idea . . . I'm assuming you'll get a post?'

They heard the sound of a car coming down the road. It slowed, then a door slammed and a few moments later Mr Cole came stepping very carefully through the undergrowth towards them.

'That's Lord Strathalmond's butler,' Jean told Doug softly as he approached.

'His lordship wishes me to view the corpse,' he said in his precise, almost accentless voice when he came up to them. 'I happen to know the young gentleman . . . By sight only, of course.'

'Help yoursel',' said Doug, his Glaswegian accent particularly pronounced. 'Careful you dinna get those fine shoes of yours dirty.'

Cole was indeed wearing a pair of gleaming patent-leather black shoes. He smiled patiently at Doug, then walked around the car. He bent down to peer inside, but couldn't see any better than Jean or Doug. The head was of course upside down and was twisted in a way which made it impossible for the face to be seen.

Cole straightened up, and arranged the crease on his trousers. He looked suddenly pale, and for a moment Jean thought he was going to faint. 'I'm awfully sorry, sir,' he said to Doug, 'but I can't tell you whether that's the young gentleman or not . . .'

'Can you recognize the car?'

'Hardly, sir,' said Cole. 'All I can say for sure is that Mr Ferguson owned a very sporty red car . . .'

'That's a' right, then,' replied Doug. 'You can go back to polishing the silver. I'll be in touch if I need you.'

Cole didn't wait to discuss the matter further, and picked his way back to the road.

'Why were you so rude to him?' asked Jean after the Jeep had gone. 'He didn't do anything . . .'

'All that aristocratic stuff sticks in my gizzard,' replied Doug, venting the life-long antagonism he felt towards the upper classes. 'And their lackeys are just as bad or worse, they take on all those airs, just as if they were earls themselves.'

'Well, then, I think I'll be going,' said Jean. 'Unless you can think of anything else I can do . . .'

'We'll need a statement,' replied Doug. 'But I can stop by this evening and get it. There's no need for you to come to the station.'

Jean made her way back to the road; Doug heard the door slam and the Montroses' car driving off. There was a complete silence now, and Doug prowled around the Porsche again, trying to ignore the eerie presence of the body inside the car. Because of the broken and crazed windows and damage to the bodywork, there wasn't much more he could do in the way of examination; there was nothing in the victim's one accessible pocket, and Doug couldn't reach anything else that might help to identify him. He looked at the tyres on the car; they were almost new Michelins. He touched the tread of one tyre, then looked at the grey patch of oil on his finger. All four tyres had oil on the treads.

Doug went back to his car and called in the Porsche's registration number on the radio. He didn't have long to wait. The owner of the car, they told him, was one Graeme Ferguson, aged thirty, address, 5, Lintock Gardens, Perth. He had no record of vehicle-related arrests or fines within the last three years.

While he was getting out of his car again, he heard a heavy vehicle approaching from the direction of Perth. It slowed for the corner, then nosed cautiously around. It was Perth's largest police breakdown truck, with a powerful crane on the back and enough space in the bed to carry a vehicle that couldn't be towed. Doug guided the driver as he backed the vehicle down the bank into the bushes. It took almost an hour for them to winch the Porsche back to where the crane could reach it. Doug helped the two men put heavy canvas lifting straps around the car, and slowly, very slowly, they lifted it over the truck bed, and gently eased it down. While the men fastened the vehicle down with chains, Doug pulled a tarpaulin over the arm projecting from the window. There seemed to be no way they could extract the body until they got to the garage; the mechanic thought they might have to cut the bodywork away from around it.

'D'you have any sand?' asked Doug.

'In the back.'

Doug helped the men lift out the drum of sand, and they covered the oil patch that had caused one fatality, and almost taken the lives of the entire Montrose family.

After the breakdown truck left, and had cautiously made its way back around the corner, Doug Niven walked up the road and looked hard at the big patch of oil. It covered almost the entire width of the road, with trickles running down on each side of the camber. How had it got there? Had some vehicle lost its sump cover and leaked all its oil in that one spot? There was no trail of oil along the road to support that idea. Maybe a can had fallen off a lorry or a farm vehicle and burst . . . Doug looked in the long grass at the roadside and in a few moments came back with a yellow plastic can of tractor oil. It was dented and split, and still contained a small amount of oil. Satisfied, he threw the container further back into the bushes.

All the time they had been there, not a single car or tractor had come by. After giving the breakdown truck and its gruesome load a fair start, Doug started up his car and headed for the police garage, adjacent to headquarters. Graeme Ferguson's name had certainly rung a very loud bell, but of course, just because Ferguson owned the Porsche, it didn't necessarily mean that the body inside it was that of Graeme Ferguson.

Chapter Three

A portion of the police garage had been temporarily roped off for the unloading; the crane whined, and slowly picked up the Porsche and swung it away from the salvage truck. The car didn't seem to be as badly damaged as Doug had originally thought. When it turned over, the hardtop had caved in on the driver, but that, plus a few dents and scratches and all the broken glass, seemed to be the extent of the damage.

'Four, maybe five thousand, that's all it would cost to fix up,' said Steve Webb, the foreman, to Doug. He had one hand guiding the Porsche as the crane slowly swung it towards the tarpaulin-covered examination area. 'That's not including any damage to the steering or suspension . . . OK, lower it down!' The roof touched the tarpaulin and the next five minutes were spent righting the car. 'Maybe the insurance company'll sell it to you cheap,' he said, panting with the exertion. 'Even like this, it's still better than that old Austin of yours.'

Douglas was not listening. The windscreen of the Porsche was smashed but still in position; there was something odd and opaque about the glass. He slid his hand in and touched the inside of the windscreen. It was tacky, so he scraped at the film with a fingernail. When he withdrew his hand and looked at it, he could see that there was blood, but that wasn't all . . .

They needed the hydraulic equipment to pull the door open before they could get at the body to remove it. It was stiff, and in a jack-knifed position. There was a lot of blood, mostly around the head, presumably where he'd struck it on the steering post.

'God, look at that face,' said Steve Webb as they laid it on two side-by-side stretchers. 'It looks as if somebody'd taken a meat axe to it.'

'We can't get him into a bag, let alone into the freezer,' said Terry, the mechanic, looking at the rigid, flexed corpse with its right arm sticking out at the side. Terry was young, a slim, tow-headed boy, and at this moment was looking quite sick. 'What do we do, Steve?'

'We just put a cover over him and take him over to the morgue,' replied Steve nonchalantly, trying to sound as if he did this kind of thing every day. 'He'll loosen up while he's waiting for Doc Anderson.' He grinned. 'Most of his patients do, eventually.'

Doug went through the pockets, jacket and pants, not forgetting the little watch pocket in the front of the pants, and checked the inside of the car. He put everything he'd found into a plastic bag and took it to the detectives' office. There he spread it all out on the counter while the secretary stood by with a notebook and made a list of all the items, which he signed and she countersigned. Then he put them back in the bag and took it up to his office, went in and closed the door.

He reached into the bag, pulled out a wallet, a very elegant one made of snake or lizard skin, a long black comb, two rubber bands, a slim address book made of the same material as the wallet, six small plastic envelopes each containing some whitish powder, a gold Cross pen and pencil, a gold and platinum Rolex Oyster wristwatch, a packet of Marlboro cigarettes, and a rectangular gold Dunhill lighter. And that was it.

The name in the wallet, on all the credit cards and on the thin stack of business cards was Graeme Ferguson. Sighing, he picked up the phone, and dialled the first number on the business card.

'Crossman Securities,' said a pleasant female voice. 'We are closed for the weekend but if you would like to leave a message . . .'

Doug tried the second number.

'This is Detective Inspector Niven,' he said. 'I'd like to speak to anyone related to Graeme Ferguson.'

This was the part he hated more than almost any; it was usually some innocent person who answered, and as bearer of the worst possible tidings, he was often the recipient of their very last cheerful 'Hello?'

But this woman's voice at the other end was cautious, even suspicious.

'May I ask what this call is about?'

Doug took a deep breath and gripped the phone tight.

'There was a car accident last night, involving a vehicle belonging to Graeme Ferguson . . .'

'Is he all right? This is his mother . . .'

'A person was killed in his car,' said Doug cautiously. 'We don't know for certain who it is, and I'd like someone from his family to come down and help us to identify the body.'

'Oh my God . . .' The voice became tight, censorious. 'I told him he should never have got a car like that . . . he didn't come home last night, but he doesn't always, he might have stayed over at a friend's house . . .' The woman talked on, postponing the onset of her grief and shock. She *knew* that her son had been in the car, Douglas was convinced of it, and he understood from the flatness and from the bitter, resonant edges of her voice that this woman, Graeme's mother, was accustomed to pain, the kind of pain inflicted by people she loved. And had she been able to harangue Graeme, Doug thought, he'd never have heard the end of it for having the heartlessness to upset her once again with his death.

'His brother Roderick is here,' she said finally. 'I'll ask him to go down and identify the body.' And then she said in a different voice, 'Inspector, was this a . . . normal accident? Or was he killed?'

'Mrs Ferguson,' replied Doug, startled, 'as far as I know the car slipped in a patch of oil and went off the road, probably at a fairly high speed. We're treating this as a normal traffic death, but if you have any information to the contrary . . .'

'No, of course not,' she said hurriedly. 'Roderick should be down there in fifteen minutes.'

As soon as they got home, Fiona went to the phone and spent

about half an hour talking to Robert, until Steven told her firmly that until she got a phone of her own, it had to be available for everyone. Robert accepted the invitation for dinner.

'You've got it bad,' said Lisbie down in Fiona's basement room.

'I can't stand it here,' said Fiona. 'Dad specially. I can't even talk to Robert on the phone without him pulling the phone out of my hand. I think I'll get myself a flat in town somewhere. There's a time for every girl to leave home, and for me I think it's now.'

'I'll miss you,' said Lisbie. She had always been the more emotional and easily upset of the two of them, particularly when it came to domestic matters. Normally, Fiona would have yelled or thrown something at her for blubbering, but now she got up off the bed and hugged her. Lisbie clung to her sister and wept.

Later, everyone felt the tension in the house gradually rising, although nobody could have said exactly how. It was clear that much of it seemed to be coming from Steven. Not that he really did or said anything in particular; he spent most of the afternoon sitting in the living room with his *Independent on Sunday*. But they all knew him well, and the unspoken emanations from him were powerful.

Roderick Ferguson appeared at the station about twenty minutes later, and was taken up to Doug's office by Constable Jamieson. Roderick appeared to be in his early thirties, stocky, with a good-looking and slightly florid face. His hair was brown, thick, and styled in a smooth wave over his forehead. Even though it was Sunday he was formally dressed in a striped shirt with a dark tie, all tidily tucked into a pin-stripe business suit which fitted him like the skin on a sausage. He struck Douglas as someone who liked to get his own way, but there was a trace of petulance and weakness around his mouth.

'Would you look at these items and tell me if you recognize any of them?' Doug pointed at the wallet and the other possessions laid out on his desk.

'May I touch them?'

'Of course.'

Roderick picked up the wallet, then the address book, and looked at the rest. 'Those objects are all Graeme's,' he said. His tone was very formal, almost stilted, as if he had rehearsed the words.

'Thank you.' Doug started to put the items away in the plastic bag.

'What's going to happen to them?' Doug saw him eyeing the wallet and the address book.

'They'll be returned to the next of kin in due course,' replied Doug. 'By the way, are you aware of any drug use, or drug . . . involvement your brother might have had?'

'No, certainly not!' But Roderick's eyes shifted, and he replied too fast and too emphatically.

Douglas might not have noticed, because his voice became quiet and sympathetic. 'Now, I'm afraid the next part is going to be unpleasant. The face of . . . the victim has been badly damaged in the accident, and may not help you in the identification.' Doug opened the door, and Roderick followed him out, then down two flights of concrete stairs to the mortuary in the basement.

On the way down, Doug called to Roderick, 'Does your brother have any identifying marks on his body you would recognize, moles, scars, or tattoos?' His voice was loud to overcome the ringing echo in the stairwell.

'Yes, he does,' replied Roderick. The tone of his voice seemed strange, but that could have been from the distorting acoustics.

The body had been put against the white wall of the mortuary's waiting area, positioned on two stretchers because of the rigid flexion of the body. Roderick's nose twitched at the odours of ammonia and formalin. 'He's got a scar on his chest, on the left side, about three inches long,' he said.

Doug didn't want to subject Roderick unnecessarily to the sight of his brother's mangled face, so he lifted the sheet over the chest. The body was already showing bluish mottled marks on the skin, and it took Roderick a few moments to find the scar.

'There it is,' he said. He pointed the scar out to Doug, then took a deep breath and in a loud, rather blustery voice said, 'I hereby identify this body as being that of my brother Graeme Ferguson.'

'Thank you, Mr Ferguson,' said Douglas, nodding to the attendant who slowly manoeuvred the covered corpse towards the white swing doors of the autopsy room.

'By the way,' he asked as Roderick was leaving, 'how did he get that scar?'

Roderick paused in mid-step and turned to face Douglas. 'That scar was made with a kitchen knife,' he said. 'In my mother's house. I was holding the knife.'

Chapter Four

Dr Malcolm Anderson didn't particularly like working at weekends but occasionally an extra heavy caseload, or a problem with the central pathology facility in Dundee would result in his doing autopsies or other forensic work at unscheduled hours. On this particular Sunday, he had been called in to do an autopsy on a week-old child who was thought to have died of meningitis.

He was taking off his long red rubber gloves when the stiff, angled body of Graeme Ferguson was rolled in, balanced precariously on the two stretchers, and placed against the wall.

Douglas came in right behind the stretcher.

'Dr Anderson! I was just going to leave a note on your desk. Do you have a minute to take a wee look at this man here?' He explained briefly what had happened. 'There was a lot of blood, considering the situation, but you'd know better than me if that was normal.'

Anderson pulled back the sheet, and looked at the torn and distorted face. He felt the temples, and his hand slid over the vertex of the skull. 'Feel here, Douglas, laddie . . . aye, and slide your hand over, push in there . . . what do you feel?'

Douglas put his hand where Dr Anderson told him, and was puzzled. The skull felt soft almost, spongy . . . Dr Anderson went to the other side of the stretcher, and looked at the back of Graeme's neck. He had worn longish hair, now matted with blood, particularly over the front. 'Aye, here it's . . . Come around to this side, Douglas, so I can show you.'

Douglas moved round the stretcher; Anderson was pointing at the back of Graeme's neck where it met the skull. For a moment Douglas couldn't make out what the pathologist was showing him, then he saw the small dark opening, with a rim of grey around it.

'Aye, this lad was shot, Douglas. I knew that from the feel of his skull.'

Douglas waited for the explanation. Sometimes he felt that the real detecting in his cases was done by other people, and all he really did was assemble the fruits of their wisdom.

'Somebody held a gun right up against this lad's heid and pulled the trigger,' said Dr Anderson. 'That caused a sudden huge rise in pressure inside the closed skull . . .'

'Which exploded all the bones in his skull,' said Douglas, as if he'd known it all along. 'That's why it feels all spongy like that . . .'

Malcolm Anderson grinned good-naturedly at him, then took an ordinary lead pencil out of his pocket and pushed the rubber end through the bullet hole. It entered the skull easily. Anderson moved the pencil around inside the hole. 'I would guess a .38,' he said, after a moment. 'Low-velocity, non-expanding bullet probably from an automatic.'

Doug looked at him with some awe. He knew Malcolm Anderson was pretty good, but this display of forensic virtuosity left him open-mouthed. 'How could you tell all that with just a pencil?' he asked.

'Well, the pencil's a bit thicker than a .22 bullet,' he said. 'If that had been the weapon used, I couldn't have got the pencil in. I could move it around a bit in there, so a seems about the right size. Low velocity because there's no exit wound, and an expanding bullet would have taken his entire face off. Automatic because that's what most .38s are.'

Doug's face was a picture.

'I suppose with a ball-point pen you could have told his entire fortune as well,' he said.

'I don't need a pencil or a pen to tell you that puir laddie's fortune,' retorted Anderson, looking down at the corpse.

'Thanks, Malcolm. I'll remember this demonstration.'

'There'll be no charge,' said Malcolm, grinning. He wiped his pencil on the edge of the sheet, put it back in his pocket and walked out, anxious to get away before something else turned up.

Douglas moved fast; he sent Constable Jamieson out with the forensic team to cordon off the area where the Porsche had been found, and with instructions to comb the entire section until they found the murder weapon.

'I wouldna be surprised if it was a .38 automatic,' Douglas told Jamieson, who was suitably impressed by his boss's uncanny ability to predict such things.

Doug went back up to his office to phone a report of the case to his direct superior, Chief Inspector Bob McLeod. His wife answered; Bob was having a nap, she said, and went off to fetch him. When he came to the phone, Bob rather grumpily told him to carry on, but if Grampian TV or the *Courier and Advertiser* happened to get wind of the case and wanted an interview, Doug was to phone him back.

Fiona cheered up a bit as the afternoon progressed, and helped her mother prepare dinner. Jean was concerned about her elder daughter; Fiona had had plenty of boyfriends, few of whom lasted more than a couple of weeks, and although Jean made a big effort to keep up, she sometimes lost track of their names. But this was different, there was no doubt in Jean's mind. Right from the beginning, Fiona had known that Robert was not just the next in a long string. She'd met him at a party a couple of months before, and their eyes had met across the crowded room . . .

'Fiona, how much cumin, do you think?' Fiona, in spite of her work as a trainee manager for a big chain of stores, had a strong domestic streak in her, and loved to cook. She had become the household authority on Indian cuisine.

'A bit more, Mum. And more cayenne, or it'll taste like baby-food . . .'

'Your father doesn't like it too strong,' said Jean, and Fiona knew that was what would ultimately determine the strength of the curry.

'Mum, why does everything have to revolve around *him*? It's always what *daddy* wants, what *he* likes, what doesn't agree with *him*.'

Jean sighed. All Fiona's resentment of her father seemed to be recent, and had arisen soon after the advent of Robert; Jean rather sadly recognized the signs; Fiona was in the process of transferring her allegiance from the dominant male in her life to his successor.

'Well, Fiona, he's still the one who brings home the bacon.' Jean stood on tiptoe looking for the packet of shredded coconut. 'Here, girl, you're taller, can you reach that coconut for me?'

'And he hates Robert . . .' said Fiona. Jean watched her daughter stretch up for the package. She was so slim and pretty, it made Jean feel suddenly sad, just for a second. She had *never* looked like that.

'Of course he doesn't,' replied Jean. 'He just feels you've been very snappy with him ever since Robert came into your life.'

'*That's* got nothing to do with Robert.'

Oh dear, sighed Jean to herself, Fiona's angry again.

'Mum, I think it's time I got myself a flat. I'm old enough, and I make enough money.'

'If that's how you feel, dear . . .'

'But Mum, I don't want to break up the family . . .' Fiona's words came out in a rush, and she put her arms around her mother, hiding her tears.

'Well, of course not. It's not as if you'd be moving to America.' Jean stroked Fiona's head. 'Now let's get on with this fine dinner we're making. I never remember if you're supposed to wash the lentils first, or do you just throw them in?'

Robert had just arrived when the telephone rang; Fiona went into the hall to pick it up. 'It's for you, Mum!'

Doug was calling to tell Jean that the body in the Porsche was indeed that of Graeme Ferguson, and that he had been shot in the back of the head at close range.

Jean was shocked by the news, and felt terrible that she had had to be *told*. How could she have missed the signs, when she was right there at the site of the accident? Surely by now she had enough experience to tell the difference between a simple vehicular accident and a murder with a gun?

She went back into the kitchen and put the plates to heat in the oven. Steven liked his plate to be hot, and it certainly made sense. Jean thought about Fiona's cool reaction to Doug Niven's phone call. Usually when he phoned, Fiona leapt around her like a gazelle, trying to listen in on the conversation, sighing, and saying how wonderful he was. Jean smiled, feeling very tender towards Fiona. Real love, she thought, leaves room for only one man in a girl's heart.

After leaving the mortuary, Doug Niven came back to his office in the police headquarters off the Caledonian Road. The building was a fairly modern, depressing multi-storey grey block of prestressed concrete. Doug's office on the second floor was small, with barely enough room for his green metal desk, chair, and two filing cabinets. A second chair for visitors was positioned strategically against the wall opposite the desk. Doug went to the window and looked down at the garage and yard below. Today it was chilly, and the heating system didn't work very efficiently; it always made the room either too hot or too cold.

Doug sighed and flopped down behind his desk. He was just as surprised as Jean about the Ferguson business. He had heard about Graeme, of course, from the narcotics people; he was basically a user, but had recently gone into dealing to finance his extravagant life-style. Doug also knew that Graeme's brother Roderick who'd come down to identify Graeme was a lawyer who worked in one of the bigger firms in Perth. Like his brother, Roderick was an ambitious man, and had been widely touted as a possible candidate for the next Parliamentary elections.

Doug pulled a lined notebook and a pencil out of the top drawer of his desk and tapped the paper with the point. He felt pretty sure that Graeme's murder was drug-related; the bullet in the back of the head had the hallmark of professional gang killing. But Doug still had to talk to the various people

Graeme had been involved with, at home, at work . . . and of course his fiancée, Ilona McAllister and her folks.

Doug's lip curled as he wrote on his pad in large letters; *The Earl and Lady Strathalmond*. Or was it *Countess* Strathalmond? All that mumbo-jumbo about titles annoyed him out of all proportion. There was nothing really different about those people, he knew that; Doug had felt the same way with the Lumsdens when he was investigating the death of their baby, and Jean Montrose had to remind him at that time that those aristocrats weren't any smarter or better looking than ordinary folks. Doug just couldn't make himself act naturally around them and that annoyed him enormously. He wrote a list of names of all the people he would need to talk to, then put his pencil down and stared at the large-scale map of Perth on the wall opposite him.

He picked up the phone to call his opposite number, Inspector Ian Garvie, in the narcotics section. Ian was at home, and sounded interested to hear of the death of Graeme Ferguson. 'Well, that *is* a surprise,' he said. 'Maybe the big boys in Glasgow heard we were on to him, and wanted to cover their tracks. Those boys play rough . . .'

Doug sat back, wondering if he should hand the case over to the narcs. It certainly seemed to belong well and firmly in their bailiwick, and he already had more work than he could properly handle. But somewhere in the back of his mind, intuition plus experience told him the case wasn't going to turn out to be just a simple drug killing. He went back to his list and reached for the phone again. It rang just as he was about to pick it up.

'This is Marjorie Ferguson, Inspector. I'm Graeme Ferguson's mother, if you remember,' said the voice. She sounded angry and frightened. 'I think I need to talk to you.'

Chapter Five

The phone rang in the middle of the Montroses' dinner, and it was a welcome interruption. Usually Fiona was on her feet before the second ring, but tonight she sat tight, protectively close to Robert. Steven, for some reason known only to himself, was not being the gracious host.

'Well, Robert,' he was saying, 'how are things at work? Exciting? Stimulating?' His smile seemed friendly enough, but his sarcasm was lost on no one, and certainly not on Robert.

Lisbie went to pick up the phone in the hall, and came back in a few seconds. 'Mum, it's for you . . .' She looked at her mother oddly. 'It's a Mrs McAllister.' Then Lisbie's eyes went wide. 'Oh my . . . that's the lady from the castle . . .'

Jean excused herself from the table, but not before giving Steven a rather tight-lipped look.

'Jean?' Marina's voice was high, on the brink of panic. 'I just got a phone call from a Detective Inspector . . . Oh, I can't remember his name . . .'

'Niven?' suggested Jean.

'That's the one.' Marina's voice seemed to be going faster than she could keep up with. 'He wants to see us all here tomorrow, he's coming in the morning at eleven . . . He said that it *was* poor Graeme that got killed in his car, and he said . . . he said . . .'

'I know,' replied Jean. 'That is such a tragedy. How is Ilona taking it?'

'Ilona?' The Countess said the name as if she'd never heard it before. 'Oh . . . yes, well, she's very upset, of course. You know the wedding was only five weeks away, and all the preparations were under way. The marquee people were coming tomorrow to see where to set it up . . .'

'Did Inspector Niven say why he wanted to talk to all of you?'

'Well, no, and that's the part that's worrying me. I asked him, because I was surprised that he needed to talk to us all, but he wants to talk to *everyone*, even Cole, he said, and when I asked him why, he just said routine, Ma'am. You know the way they talk, those policemen, they scare you but they actually tell you nothing, absolutely nothing . . .'

'I'm sure it'll be all right,' said Jean, turning an ear towards the dining room, from which only an ominous silence was coming. 'I suppose it's because you all knew him, and the incident happened near your home.'

'I hope he doesn't think any one of us might be . . . involved. I don't think he does, do you?'

'I really don't know . . .'

Jean could hear Steven's voice from the dining room, and she recognized the tone.

'Marina, I'm sorry, but we're having a dinner party, and I really have to get back . . .'

'Yes, of course . . .' There was a moment's silence, then Marina said, 'Jean, could I ask you a huge favour?'

'Yes, of course.' In the dining room, Fiona was saying something, and her voice sounded angry.

'Would you . . . Would you be kind enough to be here tomorrow when that policeman comes? I'm terribly nervous about it, and . . .'

'I don't know, Marina. I have a surgery at nine, but it should be a small one . . . But surely you don't need me? Doug Niven's very nice, and he won't give you any problems, I'm sure.'

'Jean, if you could *possibly* . . .' Her voice trembled, and she sounded close to tears.

'All right, then, Marina, I'll try . . . But maybe Inspector Niven might not want me there. After all, he's . . .'

'*Please!*'

'I'll phone him, and if he doesn't mind, I'll come,' said Jean firmly. 'But if he has any objections . . . I'll phone you, all right?'

'Thank you, Jean,' said the Countess of Strathalmond, recovering her dignity, 'I am most grateful to you.'

Jean put the phone down, squared her shoulders and went back to the fray.

Steven was looking as grim as Jean had ever seen him. She looked from one face to another; to her astonishment, there were tears in Lisbie's eyes.

'Well, Jean,' said Steven, crossing his arms in front of him, 'I hope your phone call was as interesting as what you missed here. First, Fiona tells me that she's leaving home and getting herself a flat. Second . . .' Steven paused as if he couldn't believe what he was going to say, 'she now tells me that she and Robert have decided to get married.'

Doug Niven decided to go to see Mrs Ferguson rather than have her come to the station, not to save her the trouble, but because he thought she might talk more freely in the familiar surroundings of her own home. Not only that, but Douglas was convinced that he always got a better idea about people if he saw them in their natural habitat. And, as an additional bonus, he might also see Brother Roderick, as Doug now thought of him, and possibly even have a talk with him.

Douglas decided to wait until after dinner, again not for his own comfort, and even less for Marjorie Ferguson's, but because it would give her more time to stew over whatever it was that was bothering her; it would come out purer for the wait.

It was getting dark when Doug got to 5, Lintock Gardens. The house was in the best part of town; Lintock Gardens was a cul-de-sac and number five was at the end, a large square red sandstone house standing in its own grounds, with a short, curving driveway up to the front entrance. Doug left his car on the street, and walked up to the steps and rang the bell.

He could hear its chiming sound through the thick door, but didn't hear the footsteps.

'Mrs Ferguson?' he asked the woman who opened the door. She was in her early fifties, he guessed, very plainly dressed, getting heavy in the hips, and with a flat, pale face devoid of

any makeup and a stubborn, sulky mouth. Her eyes were red
from weeping, but she seemed otherwise well under control.

'Come in, Inspector.' She led him through the hall, past an
elaborate hat and coat stand, a large bevelled mirror above
an ornate Victorian oak table bearing a silver salver.

Silently she opened the door to the living room and Doug
followed her in. It was large, with a high ceiling decorated with
ornate plaster mouldings. A fine Adam-type fireplace was
partially hidden behind a large Oriental screen, and faced by
a leather-covered sofa with matching easy chairs on each side.
The room smelled airless and musty.

'Do sit down,' she said. 'Would you care for a cup of tea?'

'That would be lovely,' replied Douglas. He didn't really
want any, but it would be a welcome change from his wife
Cathie's recent fad for Chinese tea.

While she went out to the kitchen, Doug looked around
the room. There was a large, rather threadbare, pink-looking
Persian rug on the floor, and a console TV to his left. The
pictures on the walls were all by Scottish artists of the stag-
at-bay school, and appeared to be originals. A few silver-
framed family photos were dotted around the room, on the
mantel and on a roll-top bureau opposite the TV console.
Doug got up to look at them; they were mostly of the two
boys, Graeme and Roderick at various stages of their
development, in short pants at the beach, in school uniforms,
one with their mother. On the wall to the right of the
mantelpiece was one of all three of them, dressed up in their
Sunday best outside a church. Graeme looked extremely
handsome, with strong, regular features of almost film-star
quality. Doug remembered the swollen, destroyed face, the
stiff, bent body on the stretcher in the mortuary. Marjorie
came back into the room wheeling a two-tiered trolley with
a cosied tea-pot, milk, sugar, two cups, and plates of cakes
and biscuits on the bottom.

'Very nice,' murmured Doug, 'but there was no need . . .'

'This is Sunday, and not working hours for you,' she replied.
'It's the least I could do.'

She poured, and they sat down.

'You sounded very concerned on the phone,' said Doug, taking a piece of fruit cake off the trolley.

'I was,' replied Marjorie, her lips tightening, 'and I still am.'

Doug took a sip of his tea, then looked in the cup. It was pale yellow, and tasted just like Cathie's.

'I knew something like this was going to happen,' said Marjorie. 'Graeme was mixed up with the wrong people . . .' She looked at Doug, who nodded encouragingly. '*Really* the wrong people,' she said. 'They scared me . . .'

'You spoke to them?' asked Doug.

'Once they were here with Graeme, just a few days ago. I came home early, and I heard them shouting. I went into the living room and made Graeme introduce them . . .'

'Would you know them again, do you think, Mrs Ferguson? I mean from photos?'

Marjorie hesitated, and Doug had the feeling that she was trying to tell him something, but couldn't quite summon up enough courage.

'Maybe,' she answered. 'I was upset at the shouting, so I might not . . . There was one of them, big, with freckles and red hair . . . I don't remember the other one at all. They didn't want to talk to me, obviously, and they were furious that I was there at all, me, in my own house . . .' Marjorie's voice became high and indignant again. 'Anyway they left immediately.'

'What do you think they wanted with Graeme?'

'I don't know,' said Marjorie, but her eyes would not meet Doug's. Her face showed conflicting emotions; anger at the men involved in her son's death, and fear; Doug thought she might be afraid of implicating herself. There was another source of fear there too, and Doug soon found what it was.

'Is your son Roderick here?' he asked. 'I'd like to speak to him too, if I may.'

A strange expression came over Marjorie's face.

'Roderick doesn't know *anything* about this. In fact, he wouldn't be at *all* happy if he thought I was talking to you . . . Anyway he's out right now. He went to some political meeting . . . Did you know he has ambitions to be an MP?'

Again, Marjorie's face showed a disconcerting variety of emotions; pride and love fighting with sadness and anger.

'Will he be at his office tomorrow? I can call him there.'

'I'm sure he'd rather get in touch with *you*,' replied Marjorie quickly. 'I'll tell him you phoned.'

Douglas stood up, as if the interview was over, and she seemed to relax. 'Thank you so much for your help, Mrs Ferguson. I hope we'll be able to find whoever was responsible for Graeme's death.' He took a few steps towards the door, then turned round as if some minor thought had just occurred to him. 'By the way,' he said, 'have you talked to the Strathalmonds since the tragedy? They must be very upset, Ilona especially . . .'

'I don't know about Ilona,' said Marjorie, sounding taken aback, 'but I'm sure the rest of them are delighted. I don't think they much liked the idea of a commoner marrying into their family.' She opened the front door, anxious to get him out.

'Did you know them pretty well, the Strathalmonds, I mean?' Doug wasn't about to let her get away with such a vague answer.

'I've been over there a few times. Calum's always been very nice to me. Marina looks at me as if I'd crept out from under a stone . . .' There was a flash of such strong antipathy in her eyes that Doug was taken by surprise.

'How about the girls?'

'Ilona seemed all right,' said Marjorie, grudgingly. Then her voice hardened. 'As for that little . . . that little *whore* Katerine . . .' Marjorie spat out her name with venom, and Doug wondered what Katerine could have possibly done to elicit such a response.

'Do you think any of them might have had anything to do with Graeme's death?' he asked in a sombre voice.

'I don't know. There's a lot of hate in that family . . . The women were jealous of Ilona, and the father . . . Well, he's pretty self-contained, but he wasn't too happy with the situation, as you can understand.'

'What situation do you mean, Mrs Ferguson?'

Marjorie looked at the hall clock.

'I've talked too much already, Inspector, and Roderick'll be home soon. I just wanted to tell you . . . about Graeme . . .'

Marjorie's eyes filled with tears, and again Doug had the impression that there was something else she wanted to tell him, but simply couldn't.

'Well, thanks again, Mrs Ferguson, and thanks for the tea. I'll get in touch with you about coming to look at some photos you might be able to identify. And I'm really sorry about Graeme . . .'

He shook hands with her, thinking how he would have hated to have a mother like that. He felt sure there wasn't much Graeme or Roderick could have ever done right in Marjorie Ferguson's eyes.

As he walked down the path to the gate, he heard the front door close behind him. Who or what was she so afraid of? There was something very suspicious and watchful about that woman. And she was a loner, unable to share anything, even with her sons . . .

Doug looked back as he opened his car door. It was dark now, and there were very few lights on in the big house; in the short space of time since Douglas had entered it, the Fergusons' home had somehow acquired a very sombre, almost menacing look.

Chapter Six

Next morning Jean got to the surgery fifteen minutes before she was due to start seeing patients. Eleanor, the secretary she shared with Helen, her partner, was there already.

'Morning, Dr Jean,' said Eleanor. She was wearing a loose flowery dress under her white coat, and as usual there was something sloppy about the way she looked that never failed to irritate Jean. 'There's some messages for you on your desk. Would you like a cuppa?'

'That would be lovely,' replied Jean, feeling ashamed of her harsh thoughts concerning Eleanor. 'And a couple of biscuits, if you have any . . .' She smiled guiltily. She was supposed to be losing weight, and knew as well as anybody that eating biscuits wasn't exactly the best way to go about it.

'Inspector Niven called a minute ago,' said Eleanor, the disapproval clear in her voice. 'He said he'd tried you at home.'

'Did he want me to phone him back?'

'No, he said he'd be out of the office a lot, and he'd call back.'

'OK . . . How many patients do we have this morning, Eleanor?' Jean looked at the clock. It would take her at least thirty minutes to get out to Strathalmond Castle, at the moderate speed she liked to drive.

'Twelve. There's no new ones today. Dr Helen only has seven.' Eleanor looked to see how Jean took that piece of information. In the tiny kitchen behind Eleanor's desk, the electric kettle whistled.

'Give me three minutes to look at the mail and drink my tea,' said Jean, 'then we can start.' She opened the door to her office. 'Oh, and ask Dr Inkster . . .'

At that moment, Helen Inkster came through the front door like a gust of wind. She was big-boned, athletic-looking, bluff, and jovial, with a ruddy outdoor complexion unsullied by makeup. Helen was the perfect partner for Jean; erudite, up-to-date in medical matters, she could often put her finger on complicated diagnostic problems, whereas she often relied on Jean to explain the more subtle psychological and social interactions among their patients. Helen didn't have the patience to fuss with all that stuff herself, but realized their importance in the kind of family practice they ran.

Some of their patients preferred Helen's no-nonsense, this-is-what's-the-matter-with-you-and-this-is-what-you-must-do approach; others appreciated the fact that Jean always had time to listen, was gentle with old people, and took the time to think about her patients' families and work situations. People who were in serious trouble for any reason, Eleanor had noticed long ago, usually wanted to see Jean.

'I heard on the radio that you discovered a body,' said Helen, coming up to the desk. Her voice was like her appearance, big and booming. 'I really don't know about you, Jean . . .' She went behind Eleanor into the little room to switch off the electric kettle, and went on speaking over her shoulder. 'For a quiet, generally inoffensive person, you always seem to be in the centre of trouble.'

The telephone rang, and Eleanor answered it.

'It's him again,' she said, looking away. She handed Jean the receiver.

Jean listened for a few moments. 'Doug, I told her I'd only come if you didn't object,' she said. Out of the corner of her eye, she saw Eleanor mouthing 'Inspector Niven' to Helen. 'I don't know. She called me yesterday evening, at home . . . All right, then. I'll see you up there.'

She put the phone down.

'Helen, I promised to hold somebody's hand this morning . . . She has to talk to Inspector Niven, and she thinks he's going to push splinters under her fingernails.'

She gave Helen a quick grin. 'Do you mind? I can cover for you tomorrow . . .'

Helen hesitated. 'That's fine with me, but only on one condition.' Helen was looking very stern.

Oh dear, thought Jean. She thinks I'm taking too much time off . . .

'And that is that you tell me the whole story when you get back. All right?'

'The highlights,' said Jean firmly. 'I might have to leave out some parts to protect the guilty.'

'Deal,' said Helen. She stumped off towards her office. 'Tea, please, Eleanor. No milk, no sugar.'

'No milk, no sugar,' grumbled Eleanor when Helen had closed the door to her office. 'Twelve years I've been here, and she's still telling me how she likes her tea . . .'

An hour later, Jean was examining Ailsa Farquar, a woman who hadn't been to the surgery for over a year. She seemed very nervous, and was complaining about a mole on the outside of her left leg.

'Has it been getting any bigger, Ailsa?' asked Jean.

The woman shook her head. 'I don't think so, doctor.'

Jean looked at her, puzzled. The mole had been on her thigh since she was a child, and only now had Ailsa thought it was a problem. But the woman was obviously concerned.

'Has it changed colour, or got darker?' Then Jean remembered seeing an article on melanomas in the *Perth Courier and Advertiser* the week before, and since then several patients had come in to the surgery and asked to be checked.

'No . . .' Ailsa was as tense as a spring.

Jean stared at her for a second; there was something about the woman that aroused her clinical suspicions.

'I think I'll give you a general check over,' she said. 'Take your blouse and your skirt off and lie down on the table, Ailsa. I'll just take a minute.'

Ailsa did what she was told without protest. She was about fifty; big, flabby, with a paunch that hung down over the elastic of her panties. Jean took her blood pressure, listened to her lungs, made her breathe deeply, then listened for any abnormality in her heart sounds. Everything seemed to be all right.

'Undo your bra and lie back for a minute,' said Jean. 'I'll

just check your breasts and tummy.' Ailsa had small breasts for her size, and it took Jean just a minute to find the lump on the left one.

'How long have you had this?' she asked Ailsa quietly.

'About three months,' said Ailsa, and a huge sob escaped her as if she'd been storing it inside herself for all of those three months. 'I've been worried sick . . .'

'Why didn't you mention it?' asked Jean.

'I was too scared,' said Ailsa simply.

Jean checked under the woman's armpit, looking for enlarged lymph glands.

'There never was anything the matter with that mole on your leg, was there?' she said finally, putting a reassuring hand on Ailsa's arm.

Ailsa shook her head, and a tear flew on to Jean's white coat.

'Well, you certainly have a quite a lump there in your breast, and we have to get it taken care of,' said Jean when Ailsa was dressed again. 'I'm going to send you to see a surgeon . . .'

Ailsa started to weep quietly, and Jean wondered once again how people could stand the fear and the apprehension when they knew they had something serious the matter with them, and yet delayed seeking help and treatment for so long.

'It won't be so bad,' said Jean. 'Nowadays they can just take the lump out, and probably give you some radiation treatment . . . Anyway the surgeon will tell you . . .' Jean reached for the phone; she finally tracked him down at the hospital and had a brief conversation with him.

'He can see you tomorrow afternoon, Ailsa,' said Jean, putting the phone down. She smiled reassuringly. 'His name is Peter Jones. You'll like him—he's very nice.'

Jean escorted Ailsa back to the waiting room, made a return appointment for her, and found that she had been her last patient.

Jean's car was parked in her usual spot on Williams Street, near the corner. She unlocked it and got in, feeling annoyed with Marina for dragging her all the way out to Strathalmond Castle just to calm her fears of Douglas Niven.

Doug had been a bit sarcastic—'Would you do that for

somebody up in the council estates?' he'd asked. But Jean had been able to answer confidently in the affirmative; she didn't pay too much attention to social class; if somebody needed her help, she did her best to give it.

By the time she got past Bell's Distillery on her left, with the long rows of barrels ageing out in the open air, Jean had put in a cassette and was half-listening to Mahler's Resurrection Symphony, a work which always gave her the shivers with its grandeur. Her thoughts were mostly about all the different times she'd gone out this road; it was off the beaten track as far as her work was concerned. Theirs was an urban practice, and most of her patients lived within the city limits. As she went round the big roundabout, she caught a glimpse of Steven's glassworks through the trees, and it occurred to Jean that when she wasn't coming this way to visit Steven, it was usually trouble that brought her out in this direction. The Lumsden baby . . . Jean shuddered at the recollection. About ten minutes later she passed the fateful Lossie Estates far to her right, then a couple of miles further on she slowed down for the bad turn before the turn-off to the private school where Morgan Stroud had been a teacher . . . Another six miles, and she came to a cross-roads; she turned right, and a few minutes and several turns further on, Jean slowed again for the sharp bend in the narrow road that led to the gates of Strathalmond Castle. The oil patch was still visible, although Doug had sent out a road crew to wash it down with a detergent and resand it.

The gates were open, and Jean went slowly along the immaculate drive towards the castle, past the manicured fields and the view of the bend in the River Almond. This time several cars were parked along the side of the castle. Doug's police car stationed at a respectful distance from Lady Marina's green Bentley, and a very clean-looking dark blue Land Rover was parked on the other side of the *porte cochère*. Jean came to a stop behind the Land Rover, and looked at her watch. Twenty past eleven. They must surely have started by now. Well, she couldn't help it. She had to take care of her patients; that was her job, first and foremost.

Cole was waiting for her, or so it seemed, because the huge studded door opened as she came up the two wide granite steps.

'Dr Montrose,' he said.

'That's me,' smiled Jean, then immediately felt she must have sounded frivolous to him.

'If you'll follow me, madam . . .'

They went through the long hall, and this time Jean noticed a huge embroidery of a tree hanging the full length of the high wall. As she approached, she saw that it was in fact a most elaborate genealogical tree, with dozens of names and dates embroidered in red on white at the ends of the branches.

'A remarkable piece of work,' murmured Cole, seeing Jean's interested glance. 'His Lordship has been able to trace the family antecedents back to the thirteenth century . . .' Cole spoke in a tone of reverent pride. 'Inspector Niven is using the first-floor drawing room,' he went on. 'Her Ladyship insisted that they wait until you arrived.'

The wide stairway was rather incongruously carpeted in thick beige all the way across, and Jean felt that if she accidentally stepped out of her shoes she might never find them again.

From the landing at the top of the stairs Jean could see the entire, vast hallway below her, with its military souvenirs, suits of armour, and paintings of great battle scenes hanging from the walls. The two long, stained-glass windows opposite the main door would have done credit to St. John's Church in Perth.

She followed Cole, feeling very tiny, down the panelled and portraited corridor till he stopped outside a large double door of light-coloured carved oak, in the shape of a Gothic arch.

He slipped in, then opened one leaf of the door for her from the inside.

The room was huge, with three ten-foot windows on the side overlooking the river. The facing wall displayed four ancestral portraits, two on each side of a six-foot high marble fireplace, surmounted by an ornate, gilt-framed mirror which extended all the way up to the ceiling. In contrast, the furniture was rather nondescript and looked tiny, distributed around a vast Kashan rug in the centre of the floor. A few leather armchairs were spread around the room in a haphazard way; an oval pedestal table stood in front of a full-length bookcase against the end wall.

In the middle of the room, sitting behind a small table, was Douglas Niven, looking more apprehensive and uncomfortable than Jean had ever seen him.

'I'm glad you're here,' he said almost in a whisper as Jean made her way into the room.'This place gives me the creeps; it's like sitting in the middle of King's Cross Station.'

Cole had come in soundlessly behind Jean, and neither of them had noticed him. When he spoke, Doug jumped.

'Sir, shall I intimate to her Ladyship that you are ready?'

'No, just *tell* her,' answered Doug abruptly.

Doug watched Cole walk back to the door. 'How do these people nae make ony noise with their feet?' he asked Jean, his Glasgow accent heavy on him.

The door opened again, and Marina, Countess of Strathalmond came in, dressed this time in a grey-blue cashmere jumper which came down over the top of a long grey skirt. The hem swirled around the tops of her elegant, high-heeled leather boots whose colour matched her jumper.

Doug jumped to his feet, furious at his own alacrity.

Marina ignored him, and came towards Jean with both hands outstretched. 'It's so good of you to come!' she said.

'Do you mind if we get on with this, Ma'am?' Doug's voice sounded high-pitched and irritated. He looked at his watch, and Marina gazed at him coolly with her dark, deep-set eyes.

'Of course. Would you like to start with me?' Jean thought she sounded under good control now, as if she had successfully nerved herself up for the ordeal.

Cole had brought up two chairs and placed them facing Doug's table, but Jean asked him to move hers to one side. Cole placed it, to form an equilateral triangle with the other two chairs. Jean nodded a thank you to Cole; if she *had* to be there, she didn't want the position of her chair to imply whose side she was on.

Marina swirled her skirt and sat down facing Doug, her hands folded in her lap, her long legs slanted sideways. She looked at him with a cool gaze that made an effort not to appear supercilious, but Doug thought he knew what she was thinking; she could buy him and the whole Perth police department with the loose change in her purse.

Chapter Seven

Roderick Ferguson sat at his desk that morning, thinking hard. People had been coming in and out of his office expressing their condolences on the death of his brother.

'A great tragedy,' said Edward Imrie, his senior partner, looking Roderick firmly in the eye. 'Graeme was a fine chap with a great future. We're all most terribly sorry . . .'

Listening to them all, Roderick had trouble keeping his composure, and several times that morning he'd wondered if his wild elation had shown. Didn't these fools know what bullshit they were talking? Didn't Imrie, who was pretty bright and kept a close eye on what was going on around town, didn't he know that Graeme Ferguson, the pride of the international currency exchange team at Crossman and Kennedy, Graeme Ferguson, who thought of himself as the *Admirable Crichton, Scotus Mirabilis*, 'paragon of his own sex, paramour of the other', was in fact Graeme Ferguson the treacherous druggie, the dope peddler, welsher, womanizing thief . . .

'Mr Macdonald is here to see you,' said his secretary, poking her head in the doorway.

'Thanks, Elizabeth, send him right in, please.'

Roderick's eyes rested on Elizabeth for a second before she ushered the visitor in; she was new to him, having worked for another partner until a week ago, and he hadn't really noticed her before. But she looked rather nice, young, and had a good shape. It occurred to him that he could certainly use a little light entertainment at this point in his life. He'd keep an eye on that girl.

Mr Macdonald came in, large, beefy, red-faced. He was a cheerful-looking man, the kind one might expect to see sitting at the bar at the local pub, surrounded by friends, loud, ready to laugh, but always making sure he was at the centre of attention.

Roderick got up out of his chair, a beaming smile on his face. 'Well, hi, Bill! I didn't . . .'

'Let's get right down to it,' said Mr Macdonald, his smile vanishing as soon as the door closed. He walked up to the desk and sat down in the visitor's chair, his knees spread. He had a loud, haranguing voice. 'I heard about your brother on the news,' he said. 'They said there was some question of drugs, that they'd found some in his car?'

Roderick sat back in his chair, trying to look calm and dispassionate. 'Rumours, Bill, just rumours. Graeme was pure as the driven snow . . .' Roderick suddenly realized that he couldn't have chosen a worse simile. 'What I mean is that there's no truth to that whatever. I personally saw everything that was in his pockets and in his car, and I can assure you . . .'

'You know that the focal point of our entire political campaign is against the use of drugs,' said Bill. 'And we can't afford for our candidate to be associated in *any way* with drugs, you understand that?' He glowered at Roderick. 'Jesus, your *brother* . . . do you know what our opponents could make of that?'

'I entirely agree, Bill, but luckily it's not true . . . Cigarette?' He opened the big box on his desk and offered it to his guest. Bill reached forward with a grunt, took a handful of the expensive, gold-tipped cigarettes and shoved them in the pocket of his jacket.

'I talked to my committee this morning,' he went on, 'and this is what they say . . .'

Roderick wondered how many of the election committee members had been able to get a word in edgewise, or even if they knew what they had decided.

Bill kept on talking, making no effort to disguise his view that the other committee members were merely the necessary tail to his comet.

'We'll give him ten days,' said Bill, scratching the inside of his thigh. 'Ten days, that's what they said. They said if the

rumours have all died down, and there's not the slightest breath
of drug activity scandal around you, you're in. You're our
man, our next MP. Otherwise, if by then you're not as clean
as a bishop's collar, it's goodbye Charlie. For ever. Got it?'

'Well, Bill, I can tell you right now . . .'

Bill heaved himself out of the chair and went stiff-legged
towards the door.

'Good luck, Roderick!' he said, without looking back. He
left a strong odour of mint behind him.

Roderick licked his dry lips, then pressed the intercom
button. 'Elizabeth? Would you come through for a moment,
please?'

Fiona had set off that morning, flinty-eyed, to find a flat. She
had made a list of all the ones that looked even marginally
suitable from the ads in the paper, but they turned out to be
either disgusting or far too expensive.

The bored lady from the estate agency, who sounded as if
she'd much rather be selling a million-pound estate to a rich
Arab, wasn't able to do much better, until Fiona pointed out
one of her listings which sounded perfect. 'Small cottage, 2
rms, elec, tel., all mod cons.' It was a few miles out of Perth,
said the agent, a mile off the Glasgow road, and yes, it might
actually be quite suitable . . .

They drove out in the agent's car, and although the cottage
was situated next to a chicken farm, Fiona fell in love with
it instantly. There was a little garden at the front with a
few straggly geraniums on each side of a crooked wooden
gate. Inside, it wasn't very damp, the lights worked, the water
ran and the toilet flushed, and Fiona was quite certain that
this was it. She stood in the tiny bedroom and thought about
how wonderful it would be here with Robert, just the two
of them.

They drove back to the agency office on South Street and
went in to complete the formalities. Even though Fiona had
a good job, the woman wanted Fiona's father to countersign
the lease, but she backed down immediately when Fiona started
to yell at her. Fiona paid the deposit and the first month's rent,

and feeling totally depleted both of cash and energy, drove home.

There was nobody in the house; a huge wave of loneliness hit Fiona when she got down to her room, with all its familiar furniture. She looked sadly at her bed and books and clothes and stuffed animals, and felt a prickling at the back of her eyes. A moment later, Fiona lay down on the bed and wept, something she hadn't done for years.

Doug moved restlessly on his chair, glanced at Jean, then at Marina, whose steady gaze showed no sign of nervousness. He looked down at his list of prepared questions.

'Now, your Ladyship . . .' Doug swallowed. 'The pathologist estimates the time of Graeme Ferguson's death at between ten p.m. and midnight on Saturday. Can you tell me what you know about his movements that evening?' Doug knew he was using his 'for the gentry' voice and it was driving him wild, but he couldn't help it.

'Well, he came around nine, after dinner . . . I didn't actually see him, but I heard his car, and Cole let him in . . .' She gave a slight smile. 'It's very quiet around here at night.'

'Did you hear him leave?'

'Yes, but I can't tell you the time. I was already in bed so it must have been after ten thirty.'

'Who else was in the house at that time?'

'Calum, me, Ilona, Katerine . . . Cole has an apartment in the service wing, behind the kitchen. The other servants live out.' Marina was beginning to sound edgy and she looked over at Jean.

'No guests?'

'You mean staying overnight? No.'

'Had anybody else visited that day, that you know of?'

Marina thought. 'Nobody that I know of. But there must have been tradesmen, people like that.'

Doug's hypersensitive ear told him that she meant people like *him*; peasants, rabble, lowly creatures unworthy of her notice.

'Do you know of anybody who might have wanted to kill

Mr Ferguson?' he asked, gritting his teeth.

Again Marina hesitated, but longer this time. 'He certainly was a man who stirred up passions around him,' she said, and Jean stared at her and wondered what exactly she had meant.

Marina glanced at Jean, but Jean avoided her eye and stayed studiously impassive, interested in the way the questioning was going.

'Passions?' asked Doug brusquely. 'What passions? Whose passions?' He stared hard, almost insolently at her.

'What I meant was . . .' The Countess was certainly getting flustered now, and Douglas felt a grim smile growing somewhere inside him. 'What I meant was that he . . . He's an interesting . . .'

'Aye, ma'am . . .' The sarcasm in Doug's voice was so obvious that Marina stopped talking, and looked from him to Jean.

Then, with what seemed a major effort of will, Marina came back at Douglas. 'If you persist in treating me as a suspect, Inspector, instead of as someone who is trying to help you, you'll never resolve this case.'

Her eyes were flashing, and Jean saw that her hand was clenching and unclenching on the arm of the chair.

Douglas grinned at her, but there was no friendliness in his eyes.

'Let's leave this . . . *passion* business for a wee while.' Doug spoke the word 'passion' as if it were an obscenity. 'Do you know if anybody left the house earlier that evening? Between the time Mr Ferguson arrived and the time he left?'

'I suppose anybody could have gone out . . . I really don't know.'

'Phone calls? Did anybody make or receive any?'

' Quite possibly, but I don't know.' Marina waved a hand. 'It's a big house.'

'How many phone lines do you have coming in?' persisted Doug.

'Several. You'd have to ask Calum. He has two in his office for business calls, Cole has one, and there must be two or three more . . .'

Douglas shook his head in amazement. It was hard to imagine living in a place so big you didn't know how many phones you had. He'd have to remember to tell that to Cathie.

He leaned forward. 'Tell, me, ma'am . . . Graeme and Ilona were going to get married . . .'

'In five weeks. She was going to wear her great-grandmother's gown . . .' Tears appeared unexpectedly in Marina's eyes.

'How were they getting along? Was everything just rosy? Were they having arguments? Fights? After all, he had quite a history, didn't he, Graeme?' Douglas' voice remained polite, but there was an unmistakable harshness in his tone.

Jean watched Marina's reaction with interest. She seemed to be fighting for control over herself, but Jean got the feeling that Douglas still hadn't said anything that had really rocked her, and she wondered if Marina would fall apart if he happened to press the right buttons.

'They seemed to be getting along all right,' she said carefully. 'I suppose they had their disagreements . . . Ilona is a very headstrong person, you know.'

'Had she a lot of . . . beaux? I mean before Graeme?'

'There was his brother Roderick for a little while, and before that was a young man . . . Denis something . . . Oh yes, Denis Foreman.'

Douglas thought Marina had deliberately pretended to forget Foreman's name. He wrote it down in big letters.

'Serious?' he asked. 'I mean with Foreman?'

Marina smiled tolerantly. Yes. He was the love of her life,' she said, 'but you know how young girls are . . . Anyway, her father would have none of it, and sent him packing.'

'Why was that, your Ladyship?' Douglas almost choked on the title.

'He thought Ilona was too young, for one thing, and secondly . . . Well, he was a nice enough young man, and apparently very successful . . . He was Graeme's boss, you know, but his father was a tavern-keeper, or something of the sort . . .'

Doug's pencil splintered with the pressure he was using, and he had to get another one out of his briefcase.

While Doug's head was down, Marina looked questioningly at Jean as if to ask how she was doing, and Jean smiled non-committally back. Privately, Jean thought she was doing just fine.

'Now let's get back to the subject in hand, if you don't mind,' said Doug, as if she had been responsible for bringing up the topic of Ilona's early love-affairs. 'How about Graeme Ferguson? What was he like?'

There was a brief silence, and Jean, who was watching Marina very carefully, had the instant impression that she'd felt more about Graeme than might be expected from a future mother-in-law.

'Very handsome, elegant, well-mannered . . . He had a way with him that everybody liked . . .' She caught herself. 'Well, almost everybody.'

'Who, for instance?'

'Who..? I'm afraid I don't understand.'

Yes you do, thought Jean, yes you do.

'Who didn't like him? I mean in this household?'

Marina hesitated.

This is a rather clever lady, thought Jean. She's making this interrogation go the way she wants it to go.

'Well, I heard him having a very . . . strong argument with Katerine, and she's said a few really nasty things about him . . .'

'Such as?'

'That he was marrying Ilona for her money and her position . . .'

'Was that true, do you think?'

Marina hesitated again, and there was a strange gleam in her eye.

'I think that was her opinion.'

Douglas paused, then put his pencil down and sat back. 'Thank you so much, your Ladyship. You've been most helpful.' His voice was relaxed; the interview was over, and Marina relaxed too. She got up.

'Could I see his Lordship now?' asked Doug, shuffling his papers.

'He had to go down to one of the farms,' said Marina looking at her watch. 'He should be back in half an hour or so. Would you like to talk to anyone else first?'

'Yes,' said Doug. 'Is Ilona available?'

'Yes. Everybody is . . . I'll send her in.'

Marina went quickly towards the door, looking relieved and anxious not to be called back.

Doug called after her. 'By the way, your Ladyship, do you happen to own a gun?' asked Doug suddenly.

'Good heavens, no!' replied Marina. 'What ever would I want with a gun?'

'I don't know,' said Doug, watching her. 'Maybe to shoot an ex-lover, something like that.'

Two angry red spots appeared on Marina's cheeks, and she came back towards Douglas. 'If you're suggesting . . .'

'I'm suggesting nothing, ma'am,' said Doug sharply. 'I'm trying to find out who committed a murder. And the first thing I'm looking for is motive.'

Jean looked at the floor, embarrassed.

When Marina had gone, Doug looked over at Jean. His voice was thoughtful, but his eyes had the look of a boy who's successfully stolen an apple out of the hand of the local witch. 'That finally got to her, don't you think?'

But Jean felt that Marina had not only survived the ordeal, but got through it without a single scratch.

Chapter Eight

The sun shone misty yellow on his well-tended fields and farm buildings as Calum McAllister, twelfth Earl of Strathalmond, bumped along the estate road in his Range Rover on his way back towards the castle. He had been down checking cattle weights with Bert Reynolds, the livestock manager, and had to make a decision; he had 200 head of Aberdeen Angus ready for market within the next week, but according to his computer printout, beef prices were down almost two pence a pound, probably only a temporary sag in the market. Should he hold on to the cattle and absorb the extra price of feed, or sell now at the lower price? Bert thought he should sell.

Calum drove round the east side; the vehicle's wheels juddered on the rounded cobblestones outside the kitchen entrance; he set the brake and climbed stiffly out of the vehicle. He walked over to the outside tap and washed his boots down, holding one leg out after the other into the splashing stream of water. He stamped the water off, then went inside; everything looked dark to him after being all morning in the bright sunshine. He stepped past the double doors that led to the kitchen, then opened another door into a large, linoleum-floored room with several large washing and drying machines along the wall. Near the door, opposite the machines, he found a pair of clean socks and his loafers, set as usual before a low stool covered with a small square of McAllister tartan.

Calum felt oppressively tired; some days the weight of his responsibilities felt like a load of lead on his back. He pulled his boots off and sat down. Sounds of clattering pans came through from the kitchens but he didn't hear them.

Cole came soundlessly through the door. 'The gentleman

from the police is here, your Lordship, in the person of
Detective Inspector Douglas Niven. He is in the east wing
drawing room as per your earlier instructions, and has already
interviewed her Ladyship . . .'

Calum nodded. There were so many more important things
he had to think about and deal with. 'Who is he seeing next?'

'He has sent for Miss Ilona, in your absence, my Lord,' said
Cole, with a respectful inclination of the head. He bent to pick
up the boots, and placed them tidily against the wall.

'Tell Katerine to go next, after Ilona,' said Calum. A frown
accentuated the deep lines on his face as he mentioned his
younger daughter's name.

After Marina, Countess of Strathalmond had left, Jean stood
up and straightened her skirt. 'Well, I suppose I can go now,'
she said. 'I didn't promise her I'd stay all day, and I have work
to do.'

Doug hesitated. 'You can certainly stay if you like . . .' His
hands fiddled with the pad in front of him. In fact . . .' He
tried to look nonchalant. 'To be quite honest, I'd be very glad
if you *would* stay.'

Jean looked at her watch and sighed. 'Well . . . maybe for
the next one. I'd better phone Helen, though.' She knew how
uncomfortable Doug was with these upper-class people; they'd
discussed it before. To him they seemed to come from another
world; everything he'd learned about human nature, about the
way people reacted under different situations, all that seemed
to be of no value when it came to dealing with these aristocrats
who talked at him from behind an impenetrable screen of
wealth and privilege.

'Just remember, Doug,' she said quietly, 'these people are
basically just like us. They're no cleverer, and have the same
passions . . .' Douglas looked suspiciously at Jean, thinking
that she was maybe making fun of him and what he'd said
to the Countess, but her smile was as disarming as usual.

Doug stood up rather precipitately when Cole came into the
drawing room with Ilona, and his chair almost fell over. With
an unobtrusive move of surprising swiftness, Cole caught it and

righted it. Red in the face, Doug asked Ilona to sit down. She
was more regal than beautiful; even Douglas could see how right
she would look with a coronet on her head. Very erect with a
smooth, even skin, Ilona had a good figure, and her big, dark
eyes regarded Douglas with the same kind of cool self-possession
her mother had shown. But Ilona had also a look of controlled
sadness; Jean wondered for a moment if she had any theatrical
training. Doug surveyed her with some trepidation and gripped
his pencil tightly. Of all the people he'd met so far in this strange
environment, Ilona struck him as the one who was most
different, most . . . aristocratic, although somehow she didn't
appear to present a threat to him. He surveyed her for a
moment, taking in her elegant but understated grey skirt and
dark green sweater, and almost decided he *liked* this young
woman, until a stern inner voice told him to forget about likes
and dislikes, and to get on with his job. But still, he felt he could
deal with her all right, even if she was the daughter of an earl.
He glanced at Jean, and to his surprise, she was looking at him
with a tight-lipped expression which said 'Don't you bully this
girl, or you'll have me to deal with too!'

He started off gently enough.

'I'm sorry to have to question you at this time,' he said,
'but I'm sure you're as anxious as we are to find the persons
or persons who killed your fiancé.'

Ilona nodded, her eyes fixed solemnly on him, but Doug
had the weird impression that she hadn't really heard him.

'Can you tell me about the evening before his death? I
understand he was here with you . . .'

'Yes, he was,' said Ilona after a slight pause. 'He'd just come
back from a business trip . . .' Her voice was rather low, very
attractive, and quite devoid of the bleating upper-class tones
which could set his teeth on edge merely by thinking about
them.

'Do you happen to know where he went?' asked Doug, his
pencil poised.

'London,' she replied. 'He was giving a seminar on
international currency exchange . . . He was very good at his
work, I'm told.'

'Were the two of you on good terms?'

'Yes, of course. We weren't married yet, remember . . .' Ilona didn't smile, but both Jean and Doug felt a quick tug of friendliness and sympathy towards her.

'Did he seem concerned or scared at the time he left this . . .' Doug waved his hand to indicate the castle. '. . . Here?'

'Not at all,' she replied. 'We'd been talking about our honeymoon . . . He wouldn't tell me where he was going to take me, and we got into a minor discussion about that . . . He left soon after eleven.'

Doug wrote all this down in his laborious script.

'Do you know of anybody who might have wanted him dead?'

Ilona shook her head. 'No . . . But that doesn't mean that he didn't have enemies.'

'For instance?' he prompted gently.

'Well,' said Ilona. 'We could put them into three categories, work, domestic, and . . .' she hesitated. 'Other.'

Doug's eyes opened wide for a second. Without even realizing it, he'd decided that because Ilona was attractive, rich, and an aristocrat, there was absolutely no need for her to be intelligent too. In fact, it might detract a lot from her charm . . . Doug glanced at Jean; she was looking straight ahead of her, but seemed more relaxed; there was maybe even the trace of a smile lurking somewhere there . . . Whose side is she on? he wondered, feeling a little bit aggrieved.

'All right, then,' he said to Ilona, turning to a fresh sheet on his pad. 'Let's start with the enemies Graeme had at work.'

'Don't you think you might be better off starting with the ones here?' asked Ilona mildly. 'You see, I can tell you more about them.'

Doug took a deep breath. 'Very well,' he said. 'Let's start with his enemies *here*.'

Ilona moved on her chair.

'This is not going to be easy for you,' she said, and her eyes were full of a gentle concern for him. 'Because you'd have to know the people, and understand that love and hate is all tied up here.'

Doug sat stolidly and said nothing. It wasn't often that the people he was interrogating felt compassion for him, and he found it unnerving.

Ilona folded her hands together. 'And I said *domestic*, and that doesn't necessarily mean here.'

'Well, who would you like to start with?' To his surprise and annoyance, Doug found himself willy-nilly handing over the reins of the interrogation to this young woman.

Ilona smiled suddenly, and Doug saw what it was about her that had attracted Graeme . . . and probably many others.

'I think that if I first gave you an outline of the situation here it might be helpful,' she said diffidently, and Douglas finally realized that the best thing he could do in this situation was to keep quiet and listen.

'You see, it's not very easy being in my position.' Ilona smiled again. 'People like or dislike me for the wrong reasons . . . probably even you, Inspector.'

Doug blushed and mumbled something; he felt like a little boy whose mother had unnervingly told him exactly what he was thinking. Ilona's smile was at once insightful and without malice. 'When one is an heiress, one has severely to modify one's attitude to men.'

Doug's mouth opened slightly and stayed that way.

'About a year ago,' Ilona went on, 'I was going out with Roderick Ferguson, Graeme's brother. He was very keen on me, but as you might guess, for all the wrong reasons. Poor Roderick; his eyes had dollar signs in them every time he looked at me.' Ilona shook her head. 'To tell you the truth, I'm not sure that he knew it himself. You see, part of Roderick's problem is that he doesn't have an iota of humour in him.' She looked up at Douglas with a serious, questioning look, as if asking him whether that really mattered. 'Maybe I did the wrong thing . . . maybe one day he *will* be Prime Minister, but I doubt it.'

'Was he very angry when Graeme . . . When he . . . took over?'

Ilona looked at him sadly. 'Yes, he was VERY angry. Can you imagine *me* being the cause of such an emotional upheaval?' Her expression showed mild astonishment. 'But in case it crossed your mind that he killed Graeme in order to regain his wicked hold over me . . .' She shook her head, and Douglas thought that money or no money, beauty or no beauty, this was a woman he would run away from as fast as his legs would take him. Clever women made him almost as nervous as aristocratic ones.

'No, when Graeme came on the scene, it was the *coup de foudre* . . . for me, anyway. He was just beautiful . . .' Suddenly Ilona's lip trembled, and to his complete astonishment, and in spite of his immediately preceding thoughts, Doug wanted to come around and put a comforting arm around her shoulders . . . With a quick, irritated movement, Ilona wiped a tear away with one finger.

'I'm sorry . . .' said Douglas gently.

'No,' said Ilona. 'It's probably just as well.' She tried a smile, but couldn't quite make it. 'You see, Inspector Niven, a girl chooses the man she wants by his good characteristics . . . But he brings other ones too, that may not be as desirable.'

She looked at Doug, and the tears in her eyes revealed their unusual depth and lustre. She was quite an extraordinarily beautiful woman, Douglas realized with almost a shock.

'Graeme had so many good points,' Ilona went on, as if it were only now that she could look sensibly at him. 'But he also had some . . . less good ones. Two, in fact.' She paused. 'Do you think I'm cold and heartless, thinking about him like this?'

'No, I don't,' replied Douglas quietly. 'I think you're being very realistic.'

'Graeme was an incredible spendthrift . . . He made a lot of money, but he never had a penny. Extravagant . . .!' Ilona shook her head. 'The other thing, the only other thing, was that he . . . he liked women too much. Even here, in my family . . .' She tried to smile, but her upper lip was quivering and that made it difficult for her.

'I don't want to say anything more . . . Graeme's dead, and whatever he did . . . I don't want to drag him—or his or my family— through any more dirt.'

'I assure you that's the last thing we want to do,' said Douglas earnestly. 'I'm only interested in . . . all that if it can help us find the person who killed him.'

Ilona looked at Douglas, then at Jean, who smiled and nodded almost imperceptibly at her.

'It would have been a marvellous wedding, though . . .' Ilona's voice was strangled, but she recovered herself quickly. 'Of course I knew that after that I would have a terrible problem keeping him faithful to me . . .'

Jean was listening to Ilona with rapt attention; Doug, astounded, wished Cathie could have heard her say what she'd just said. She wouldn't have believed it.

'Then why ever did you want to marry him?' he finally got out.

Ilona glanced at Jean as if only she could understand what she was saying. 'I loved him,' she said simply, 'and above everything, I wanted to have children. You know,' she said, facing Doug again, and now under better control, 'there's only one way for a woman to feel *really* beautiful, and that's to have children. They *know* you're beautiful, because you're their mother . . .'

Doug leaned slowly back in his chair.

'Miss McAllister, you were going to tell us about your fiancé's enemies . . .'

'Well, Inspector, I've just changed my mind. As you know, that's a woman's privilege . . .'

She smiled at him, then got up with an air of finality. 'Graeme's dead, and there's nothing I can do to bring him back. If you want to amuse yourself trying to find out who did it, good luck to you. As you can guess, I now have to think of other things . . .'

'Well, of course,' said Doug, standing up also. 'That *is* your privilege. 'By the way,' he said, almost apologetically, 'do you still hear from . . .' He looked at the name he'd written on his pad, 'A Mr Denis Foreman?'

Ilona shook her head, surprised.

'No,' she said smiling. 'Denis . . . he was a long time ago. It was beautiful, but . . . Well, I suppose a girl's first love affair is *supposed* to be beautiful, isn't it?' She smiled at Douglas, and again he felt an inexplicable tenderness for this young woman. He forced himself to ask the second question. 'Miss. Ilona,' he said, and Ilona smiled at the way he used her name, 'what was the relationship between Graeme and your mother?'

Ilona stood straight up, and for the first time her eyes flashed angrily but not, Jean thought, at Douglas. 'They were . . . naturally very fond of each other,' she said, tightlipped, and Douglas knew that he wouldn't get another word out of her on that subject.

'Thank you very much for your help, Miss McAllister,' said Douglas. 'That'll be all for now, but as the investigation proceeds, I may need to speak to you again . . .'

Ilona nodded regally; there was a breathtaking grace about her as she walked back towards the door.

'My God,' said Doug in an awed voice when the door had closed behind Ilona. 'Have you ever seen or heard anything quite like her?'

'She's really something, that young lady,' said Jean quietly, and there was admiration in her voice. 'She was so attractive and fascinating that I almost forgot to listen to what she was saying . . .' She bent down to pick up her handbag. '. . . but not quite.'

Jean got up and straightened her skirt with a twist. Douglas was still sitting, his elbows on the table, looking straight ahead into the distance.

'Yes, she strikes me as a most remarkable young woman,' continued Jean, looking directly at Doug. 'Not only that . . .'

Doug was shaking his head, and Jean stopped speaking.

'The only way to feel *really* beautiful is to have children . . .' he was repeating, talking almost to himself.

At that moment, he wasn't thinking about Ilona but about his wife Cathie.

Chapter Nine

Katerine McAllister turned in at the gate and roared up the drive towards Strathalmond Castle in her restored MG TD, scattering sand and gravel as she went. She was returning from a shopping trip to Perth, and feeling particularly irritated. It had turned out to be one of those mornings when no clothes fitted, the shop assistants were rude and uncaring, especially that impertinent girl in the photo shop . . . In her mind, Katerine was composing an indignant letter to the owner of the store, when she saw a rabbit in the grass on the side of the drive just ahead of her. Without even thinking, she drove up on to the verge to run it down, but the creature hopped out of the way just in time. Katerine could feel how her lips had drawn back from her teeth during her moment of leporicidal fury, and she steered back on to the driveway in a bumpy cloud of dust and rattling gravel.

Coming round the corner, she saw the strange cars parked at the front and remembered that the police were supposed to come that morning. They were coming about Graeme . . . Well, she could tell them a thing or two about that situation that would pin their ears back . . .

Katerine slammed on the brakes as she turned the wheel in the middle of the courtyard, and the car slid around, wheels locked, finally stoping at an angle outside the portico, leaving two wide black gouges in the white gravel behind her.

She jumped out, took a long cardboard tube out of the tiny passenger compartment and marched along the walkway of flagstones that lined the front of the building. She turned the corner and headed for the small side door which led to her apartment. Her high heels clicked on the stones. There was no one around, and she let herself in with a key she took from her purse.

Katerine had a first-floor suite of three large rooms at the end of the east wing of the castle. Her apartment was situated above the library, and in addition to the stairway which led down to the outside door, it joined the east wing gallery with its tall mirrors, family portraits and vast windows which looked out over the courtyard and the wooded park beyond. At the central end of the gallery was a long balustraded landing, from which the double staircase curved down to the main hall.

Katerine went up the stairway and let herself in. She went through the sitting room to her bedroom and into the en-suite bathroom, dropping the cardboard tube on the bed as she passed.

The intercom phone buzzed. Katerine hesitated, then picked it up.

'All right,' she said grudgingly. 'I just got in. It'll take me ten minutes to get cleaned up . . . Well, they can just wait.' She slammed down the phone. That goddamned mealy-mouthed Cole . . .

There was no real hurry, so Katerine took her time; she showered, then changed into a tight black silk body-shirt, black tights, and a very sexy and very expensive white leather skirt which her father had rather briskly described as barely more than a wide belt. She turned and looked at herself in the full-length mirror for a few moments. Nice legs, she thought, twisting around, and a dynamite pair of boobs . . . She twisted the body-shirt a bit tighter. That should take the policeman's mind right off his work.

Before leaving the apartment, she picked the cardboard tube off the red and black bedspread and pulled out a long roll of photographic paper. In order to straighten the roll out, she put it on the floor, set a pair of heavy walking shoes on the top, and then rolled it down. She kneeled on the lower end and stared at the enlarged photo for a few moments, unconsciously putting her thumb in her mouth and biting on the edge of the nail. Then she giggled, a bubbly, hoarse giggle, before standing up. She straightened her skirt, and adjusted its lower edge to be exactly level with her crotch. She replaced the life-size photo into the tube, and dropped it back on the bed before heading for the door and her interview with Douglas Niven.

'I really have to get back,' said Jean, getting to her feet. She'd called Helen on the portable phone Cole brought her, and although Helen assured her everything was under control and to stay as long as she wanted, Jean was feeling guilty at leaving her partner with the full load of the practice on her shoulders.

Douglas, feeling much more at ease after his interview with Ilona, was about to say goodbye when Katerine came sashaying in.

'My God,' muttered Doug. 'Please, Jean . . .' After one look, Jean had already sat down again. She wasn't going to miss this for anything.

And Katerine was really quite exquisite to look at, in an incredibly sexy, and, thought Douglas, incredibly vulgar way. She was small, slim, with pale makeup and a pretty, slightly pouting expression. Fascinated, both Douglas and Jean watched her approach; she had a cat-like way of walking, a kind of jungle prowl, and came towards them with a self-assurance that, along with everything else, took Doug's breath away. It was left to Jean to introduce them.

Katerine sat down, unsmiling, her chin up in a provocative pose, her silky knees aimed directly at Douglas.

'We are here to investigate the matter of Graeme Ferguson's death,' said Douglas through dry lips.

Katerine crossed her knees, and he gave Jean a glance that verged on desperation; but she was enjoying all this by-play enormously and ignored him.

'Miss McAllister, were you at this location on the evening prior to the deceased's demise?' he asked, unable to improve on his pompous terminology, the very sound of which made him furious.

'You mean was I here last Saturday?' Katerine's voice was soft, but it had a hoarse, earthy quality to it.

'Aye, that is the time and place I'm referring to.'

'I was here, yes, but not with *them*.' Katerine's pout hardened for a moment. 'Do you mind if I smoke?' She pulled a cigarette from a red-and-white packet of Marlboros and lit it. Douglas instinctively reached for his own pack in his shirt pocket. It had held one cigarette from the time he'd stopped smoking some months previously, and it had been taken out and put back so many times that it had a tired, wilted look. He shook the packet, confirmed its presence, and put it back.

'Were your sister and Graeme alone?'

'I suppose so.' Katerine smoked her cigarette as if she were making erotic love to it. 'Not that they needed any chaperoning . . . She wouldn't let Graeme *touch* her.'

'But they were engaged, weren't they?'

Katerine laughed. Douglas thought it was not a nice laugh at all, and Jean wondered why Katerine was going to the trouble of putting on this elaborate act.

Doug felt increasingly out of his depth with this young woman, but he couldn't help what his eyes did when Katerine crossed her elegant legs, particularly as she did it a lot more often and more slowly than was necessary. Jail-bait, he thought indignantly, that's all she is . . . Then it occurred to him that there were quite a few men who lived and worked in and around Castle Strathalmond. He smiled at her.

'How did you get on with the deceased?'

'Graeme? Well, of course, I knew what he was up to, and I told him so. He didn't like that too much . . .' Katerine did her bubbly laugh again. 'What he didn't know was that Ilona is a lot smarter than him.' Katerine emphasised the word 'Ilona' with a little shrug, as if it were an obvious and inevitable conclusion. She put her thumb up to her mouth; it was a curiously child-like gesture.

Doug nodded, not wanting to interrupt her train of thought. 'He wanted to marry Ilona for the money and stuff,' Katerine waved a hand vaguely in the air. 'But Ilona was really using *him* . . .'

Douglas desperately wanted to ask Jean whether he should take this young woman seriously, but Jean was sitting back,

watching and listening quietly; Doug wondered whether
Katerine had even noticed that she was there.

'And how did the other members . . . the others who live
here get on with him? Did your parents approve of the
marriage?'

'As far as I know. Ilona says my *mother* certainly did . . .
and that she'd have approved of anything as long as Graeme
stayed around . . .' Katerine's big, heavily mascaraed eyes
stared unblinking at Doug. 'The blissful pair was going to live
here after the wedding, and Ilona was *not* happy about that,
as you could imagine . . .' Katerine grinned a private grin and
her thumb went back into her mouth, up to the first joint. Her
jaw moved as she nibbled on the nail.

Douglas felt a throbbing between his temples; either this
young woman was completely mad or deliberately trying to
confuse everything . . .

'How about your father?' he asked, more to give himself
time to think than because he wanted an answer.

Katerine shrugged her narrow shoulders; Doug could see her
nipples pointing under her body-shirt, and he stared hard at
her face, willing his eyes not to move down.

'Well, of course, Ilona is Daddy's little girl,' replied Katerine
with a malicious pout. 'He loves her, and believes whatever
dear Ilona says to him . . .'

'What I meant was, what did he think about the marriage?'
said Doug sharply. He didn't want to hear about Katerine's
petty jealousies.

Katerine stared at him, and again it crossed Douglas's mind
that the girl might not be playing with a full deck.

'Why don't you ask him?' she said. 'How should I know?'

Douglas' irritation and contempt for the nobility was never
far below the surface, and his lip curled at the obvious
degeneracy of this particular member of the Strathalmond clan.

He forced himself to be objective and to stay open-minded
and fair.

'How about the . . . help?' Doug wanted to say minions,
or slaves, but he knew that Jean would instantly get after him
if he said any such thing. 'Did they have anything to do with

Graeme? Any resentments . . .?' Doug let the question hang
in the air.

'Cole hated him, of course, because he saw what was going
on. He knew Graeme was trying to get off with me, and he
knew how my mother felt about him . . .'

Doug's head was throbbing now with some intensity, and
he wondered if there might be a couple of aspirins somewhere
in this castle. He couldn't tell whether this girl was completely
psychotic and a prey to delusions, or whether she was actually
reporting the truth as she saw it. Jean would know . . .

'I think that will do for now, thank you, Miss McAllister.
I may need to talk to you again, but if so, I'll let you know.'
Doug's mouth was dry, and he was dying for something to
drink, anything as long as it was wet.

Katerine got up with alacrity.

Just as she turned to go, Doug spoke sharply. 'Miss
McAllister, do you own a gun?'

Katerine shook her head, her thumb back in her mouth and
watched him with a strange expression.

Doug persevered. 'Did you follow Graeme Ferguson out of
here last Saturday evening and shoot him while he was trapped
in his car?'

Katerine looked startled for a second, then a look of childish
cunning came across her face. 'Sir,' she said, slurring the word
out, 'I've never followed a man in my life.' She cupped her
breasts in her hands for a moment and stared at him in such
a provocative way that Douglas gasped. 'I always let them
follow *me.*'

Katerine wiggled her way out and the door closed behind
her.

'My God!' said Douglas, wiping his brow. 'When you think
that one's the same age as your Lisbie . . .!'

'She's not nearly as sure of herself as she'd like you to think,'
said Jean.

'Is she crazy, or what?' asked Doug, putting both hands to
his temples. 'Can I take anything she said seriously, or do you
think she made all that up?'

'I'm sure you've met people like her before,' replied Jean,

looking at her watch. 'She hears isolated comments or conversations, takes them out of context, then mulls over them to the point that she constructs a fantasy world around herself. I suppose it has to do with the isolation up here at the castle . . . She's hardly had what you would call a normal upbringing.'

'And I suppose she'd misinterpret looks, like from Graeme, thinking they meant more than they really did . . .'

'Probably. But behind all that, there's quite likely more than a grain of truth to what she said. As you say, it's how it's interpreted. And that, Douglas Niven,' she said, standing up, 'is your job to sort out. Now I really must go; Helen's going to kill me for being so late.' She smiled a little maliciously at him. 'Good luck!' she said from the door.

In fact Helen had not even noticed Jean's absence; when Jean got back to the surgery, everybody seemed to be in a tizzy; Mrs White, an old patient of Helen's had just tripped on the step on the way out of the surgery, Helen and Eleanor were trying to help her to her feet, and several patients had come out of the waiting room to help.

'She's a wee bit shaken,' explained Helen when Jean came in; she was puffing with the exertion of supporting the woman. 'If you could get the wheelchair . . .' They kept a folding wheelchair for such emergencies in a cupboard with the bucket and the vacuum cleaner. Jean hurriedly fetched it and pushed the chair behind Mrs White, who was looking shaken and pale, standing with her weight on one leg, then just before Helen eased the old lady into it, Jean said, 'Hold it just a minute . . .' She knelt down and put her hand up under Mrs White's long skirt and felt around the top of her thigh. There seemed to be a little swelling there, and just to make sure, Jean rotated the knee just a little. Mrs White grimaced, then yelled with the pain.

'I think she's fractured her hip,' said Jean. She stood up and pushed the wheelchair out of the way. 'Let's put her down on the exam table. It'll be easier for the ambulance people . . .' She didn't need to mention that if they had sat the old lady down in the wheelchair it could have caused displacement of the fracture.

'Call the ambulance,' Jean whispered to Eleanor, and took over the arm she was holding. Eleanor went over to her desk and picked up the phone.

Helen and Jean helped Mrs White to the table and eased her on to it as gently as they could, although she shouted with the pain when her hip was moved.

Once they had Mrs White lying down, Helen saw that the foot on her injured side had turned outward. 'You're right about her hip,' she said to Jean in her gruff voice. 'As usual.'

After the ambulance people had come and taken Mrs White to the hospital, Jean and Helen got back to work and finished their surgeries about the same time.

'I'll stop by the hospital on my way home to see Mrs White,' said Helen as they sat together in Jean's office. 'How was it up at the castle?'

'Very interesting,' replied Jean with a smile. She told her partner briefly about Ilona and Katerine. 'Doug said he'd stop by tonight to let me know how the rest of the interviews went . . .'

'I know about that Katerine,' rumbled Helen. 'She's a promiscuous little besom if I ever saw one.'

'It must have been difficult growing up in that environment,' murmured Jean.

'Well, Ilona grew up in the same place,' retorted Helen, 'And look at her. She's a really wonderful young woman. Interested in the estate, works for charities, doesn't put on airs . . .'

'It's all a matter of heredity, I suppose,' said Jean thoughtfully, then she smiled. 'That's what their father thinks, anyway.'

'Who else does Niven have to interview?'

'Well, there's the Earl himself, of course, and Cole, the butler, I suppose . . . that's about all. There are other servants, but they all live out, and of course people who work on the estate farms and so on.'

'Cole the butler, huh,' said Helen, grinning. 'If this was a mystery story, Inspector Niven wouldn't have to look any further to find the guilty party, would he?'

Helen went off, and Jean stayed on for a while doing her paperwork, filing long reports on all kinds of seemingly unimportant matters. Jean worked away, feeling increasingly irritated; all this form-filling was becoming a larger and larger part of the work of the practice. If it went on increasing like this, she reflected, eventually she wouldn't have any time left to see her patients.

Chapter Ten

Calum McAllister, Earl of Strathalmond, came in to the room, shook hands, and sat down in the chair opposite Douglas. He was dressed in a check shirt and dark green tie under a beautifully cut lovat green suit, and his immaculate brown brogues completed the image of a perfect country gentleman. He looked calm but Douglas could tell from the way he moved that he was a busy man who didn't have time to waste; it was a big estate and he had many responsibilities to discharge. Calum's eyes were watchful, but had an odd lack of lustre, Douglas thought, the kind of look old prisoners have, or people who have suffered some terrible tragedy in their lives.

Douglas mumbled something unnecessary about being sorry to have to take up his time, and finished up flushed and tongue-tied. The Earl gazed at him with the beginnings of impatience, and Douglas tried again.

'I have been led to understand that Graeme Ferguson was here at this location on the evening he was killed,' he said heavily.

'Yes . . .' The Earl hesitated, and Doug's pencil stopped twirling. 'Although I didn't actually see him myself. When they're here, the children usually stay in their own quarters, except, of course, at meal times.'

'Can you tell me a bit about Mr Ferguson?' asked Douglas. 'Did you know him well?'

'He seemed a fine enough young man,' the Earl said, relaxing his military bearing a fraction. His long hands were placed flat on his thighs, and the fingers of his right hand slid forward to grasp his knee. 'He seemed to be very fond of Ilona, and she of him.'

'Did you feel he was a suitable person to . . .' Douglas looked around. 'To take all this over, eventually?'

'Actually it will go to Ilona,' replied the Earl, his voice softening. 'And she's learning a great deal about estate management. She's really very good — she could take over now, actually . . .' He smiled. 'So it would be up to her how active her husband was in running the estate.'

'Let's come back to last Saturday evening,' said Douglas, feeling he'd exhausted the possibilities of that line of questioning. 'If I may ask, where were you, I mean in what part of the castle, sir?'

'I spent the early part of the evening in the office I use for estate work . . .'

'And whereabouts might that be?' interrupted Doug, his pencil poised.

'On the ground floor. You may have noticed a door at the end of the main hall, opposite the entrance . . .'

Doug had to prevent himself from shaking his head; he tried to imagine himself saying to Cathie 'And yes, my dear, have the butler serve tea this afternoon in the west wing estate office . . .' It seemed so ludicrous, but these people really did live like that.

'And later that evening?'

'I beg your pardon?'

'Where did you spend the later part of the evening, sir?'

'In my work room. I call it the genealogy room, my family call it the g-room, for short.'

'You were there until . . .?'

'Oh, about midnight, I suppose. I usually get tired about then.'

'And where were . . . the children that evening?'

'Ilona and Graeme would have been in the television room . . .'

'And where might *that* be, if I may ask?'

'The one they use is between Ilona's and Katerine's apartments . . .' The Earl waved a hand in the general direction of the east wing.

Douglas, feeling lost in the geography of the place, decided to change his tack.

'Do you know of anybody who might have wanted to kill Graeme Ferguson, sir?' he asked abruptly.

Calum stared calmly at him, with the look of a general who makes it a fetish never to be flustered.

'I can't say that I do, Inspector,' he replied.

'What were his relations with the other members of your family?' Douglas watched the Earl's face very closely; these were dangerous waters he was venturing into, he knew it, but he felt sure that Calum McAllister would know what was going on in his own home, big though it was.

Douglas was disappointed. He could almost feel the curtain of well-bred reserve come down; it was soft, silky, and quite impenetrable.

'Everybody seemed to like him,' replied Calum, bland as a press secretary. 'No problems that I know of.'

'You didn't actually see him on Saturday evening, then?' asked Doug, reverting to his previous line of questioning. 'And if you didn't see him, you can't really confirm that he was here?'

The Earl hesitated for only a moment. 'Actually I heard his voice . . .'

'From the east wing? Surely . . .'

'When he left, he came down the main stairway, and that's not too far.' He smiled faintly.

'Even then, he must have been speaking very loudly,' insisted Doug.

'Yes. I think there was an argument,' said the Earl uneasily, and Doug sat back, feeling that finally he was getting somewhere.

'Did Ilona happen to mention it later?' asked Doug. 'Did she say what their argument was about?'

'Well, as a matter of fact,' said the Earl unwillingly, 'it wasn't Ilona he was arguing with. It was Katerine.'

Jean was not expecting the large, plainly dressed woman who stepped hesitantly into her office. Although she was a registered patient, she was an infrequent visitor.

'I thought it was time for me to get a PAP smear,' said the woman hesitantly. 'I was reading a bit in *Cosmopolitan* that said all women should have them done every year.'

Jean smiled. It was amazing how much money the government spent on health education, and yet it was an article in a newspaper or a magazine that women paid attention to. Maybe all that money would be better spent elsewhere . . .

'All right, Mrs Ferguson . . .' Jean consulted her records. She had never had a PAP smear done in the past. 'If you'd step into the examining room, I'll get Eleanor to set you up.'

Five minutes later, when Eleanor had got Marjorie Ferguson up with her feet in the stirrups, Jean came in and pulled on her latex gloves.

'How are you doing?' she asked, very sympathetically. 'Poor Graeme; his death must have been a dreadful shock for you.'

Marjorie said nothing, but started to sob, quietly.

'I think I know who killed him,' she said. 'I don't know what to do . . .' Her sobs shook the table.

Jean, shocked, sat down on the wooden chair by the table and put a hand sympathetically on Mrs Ferguson's shoulder.

'I think maybe you should talk to Inspector Niven,' she said. 'He's in charge of the case, and . . .'

'I *can't*!' replied Mrs Ferguson. 'It's not just Graeme I have to think of . . .' Eleanor came into the room, and Jean shook her head warningly. After a curious glance at Marjorie, Eleanor went out again, closing the door gently.

'It's Roderick I have to worry about; he's all I've got now.' There was a kind of desperate fierceness in Marjorie Ferguson's voice; Jean got the strong impression that Roderick was the only one she cared about even when Graeme was alive. 'You know he wants terribly to get into Parliament . . . If there was any kind of scandal, he'd never get elected, not around here; the other candidates would crucify him, especially if it had anything to do with drugs . . .' Her words tumbled out like a pile of logs that had overbalanced.

'But Inspector Niven . . .'

'NO!' Marjorie tried to sit up, then sank back. 'I did tell

him a bit, but Roderick was furious. He says it would get into all the papers . . .'

'Let me get the PAP smear done,' said Jean. 'You can give it some more thought while I'm doing it.'

She positioned her stool and inserted the speculum, then the specially shaped wooden spatula. 'Take a big breath . . . push down . . . That's good . . . Hold it . . . OK, that's it.'

Jean smeared the material onto a labelled glass slide, which she then put on the table beside her. She said nothing, waiting for Mrs Ferguson to speak.

'Graeme was into drugs,' she said, now reverting to her normal tone. Her face was sullen, defeated. 'I didn't tell Inspector Niven, but I think he knows. Graeme owed the big dealers a lot of money, and he couldn't pay them.'

'Did Graeme tell you that?' asked Jean. Mrs Ferguson didn't seem the kind of mother a grown-up son would confide in, particularly about any illegal activities he might be involved in.

'No, of course not. He thought I didn't know what he was up to . . .' She put her hand up to her head. 'Could I have a glass of water?'

Jean pulled a paper cup out of the rack by the sink and filled it from the tap.

'He lived at home, like Roderick, and of course I do all the housework . . .' An expression of weary self-pity spread over her face. 'He kept his stuff in a suitcase on the shelf above his clothes cupboard. It was always locked, of course, but one time he accidentally left the key on the dresser . . .'

Jean took Mrs Ferguson's feet out of the stirrups and helped her to sit up.

'And a few days ago, two men came to see him . . . I came home when they were leaving, and Graeme was shaking. He was so frightened . . . But then he was never very brave. After they left, he asked me for money . . .' Mrs Ferguson's lower lip started to tremble again.

Even though she felt very sympathetic about the loss of her son, Jean couldn't help feeling that nothing would ever go right for Marjorie Ferguson.

'It was a huge amount, twenty thousand pounds . . . And I told him no, that he would have to straighten out his own financial affairs. He was always in debt . . .' An expression of anger and contempt came over her face. 'Graeme was just like his father, no control over anything.'

There was no mistaking the difference in her attitude to Graeme and Roderick. She couldn't stand even the memory of the one, and idolized and depended on the other.

'I could have given it to him, of course, but it would have been wrong, wouldn't it? It would have just gone straight into the hands of those drug people, wouldn't it?' Marjorie was almost begging for Jean's approval.

Jean looked away. What would *she* have done? To get one of her own children out of that kind of deadly trouble, she would have got a second mortgage on the house, sold anything she possessed, done anything . . .

'Roderick said I did the right thing . . . How were we to know they would *kill* him?' She started to sob again, a hopeless, almost soundless shaking of her shoulders.

'Maybe Roderick's partly to blame, but I don't think so,' Marjorie continued. 'I suppose you know that he was going with Ilona before Graeme came on the scene. He wanted to marry her, then Graeme snatched her away. Graeme was always a lady's man, very smooth . . . I'm sure you know the kind, Doctor. Anyway Graeme got her away from Roderick, who would have been *perfect* for her. Rod and Graeme used to get on well enough, but after that, you can imagine what it was like at home . . .'

'I think Inspector Niven knows about the drugs,' said Jean, after a pause. 'If you help him, he might be able to find the men who killed Graeme.'

Mrs Ferguson's upper lip started to quiver. 'All right then,' she said hesitantly. 'I'll tell him . . . As long as you don't think it would get Roderick into more trouble.' She turned her heavy body and slid down from the table. 'Dr Montrose, could you give me a prescription for some sleeping pills? I can't sleep, and when I do sleep I've been getting terrible nightmares . . .'

Outside the surgery, Mrs Ferguson blinked in the sunlight

and went down the short flagstoned path to the street. She
was feeling exhausted and depressed. Everything in her life
weighed on her, and there seemed no end to her unhappiness.
And Graeme was the cause of as many problems now as when
he was alive. It was just one thing after another — first their
disgraceful father, and now Graeme, just like him, bringing
shame on the family and maybe even destroying Roderick's
fondest aspirations . . .

At the back of Marjorie's mind was the grey, threatening
thought that she could have saved Graeme's life with a sum
of money that would not have ruined her by any means. But
how could she have known . . .? She turned the corner on to
King's Place, but she didn't see the trees and grass of the South
Inch or the old people playing on the velvety bowling green
across the street. For many years Marjorie Ferguson had been
so immersed in her own problems that she saw little else around
her. She felt so alone . . . Maybe she'd done the wrong thing
with her husband Victor . . . She shook that thought from her
mind. It had been even worse when her husband had been at
home, with his drinking and everything . . . Anyway that was
years ago, and she tried never to think about him now. In the
old days, she'd occasionally go to visit him, but of course the
children had never been allowed to see him again. It was bad
enough having a chronic alcoholic for a father without their
having to see the dreadful end results of that disease. And it
was his fault; he hadn't even *tried* to stop, not until it was too
late.

Marjorie stopped after walking a few yards; where had she
left her car? It took her almost a minute to remember on which
side street she had left it. She turned and retraced her footsteps,
shaking her head. She was getting to be as bad as Victor. The
only thing she could think about now, the guiding principle
of her existence, was to protect Roderick from harm, even if
it meant she'd have to brave his anger, or worse.

The Countess of Strathalmond, née Marina von Schwenke,
left the drawing room after her interview with Inspector Niven,
and stumbled on the carpet outside. Cole, who had been

standing outside the door, caught her elbow with his instant
and effortless reflexes, and steadied her.

Marina barely noticed; she walked quickly away, as if
hurrying from the scene of an accident she'd rather not have
witnessed. Cole watched her go a little unsteadily down the
long corridor to the west wing apartments that she and the
Earl used; she was incredibly tensed up; he'd felt the quivering
muscles when he caught her arm. Cole hoped that the
policeman would not take too long with the others, then he
wondered if the Inspector would want to speak to him.

Cole smiled his secret smile, knowing that anything he had
to say would only add to the Inspector's obvious confusion.

Marina couldn't wait to get to the sanctuary of her room.
She was oblivious to the vast, dark paintings of highland scenes
from the last century which lined the walls, and to the great
silver wall sconces reputedly selected by Lord Byron and bought
in Italy by his friend, an ancestor of the Earl's. The double
doorway to the main apartment of the castle was shut, and
she twisted the door handle with a violent gesture and slammed
it behind her. Graeme, Graeme . . . The name shouted at her
from inside her head until she thought everybody around could
hear it. How could everything have gone so wildly, dreadfully
wrong? He *couldn't* be dead . . . She remembered the warmth,
the life, the vibrancy of his body and moaned aloud in the
agony of her loss. Maybe Ilona had found out . . . or else that
little monster Katerine. How had she ever borne such a child?
Even as a toddler Katerine wasn't happy unless she was hurting
something or somebody; her favourite occupation was finding
earthworms and slicing them up with a knife.

'More than six pieces and they stop wiggling, Mummy,' she
said once, bringing in the fruits of her scientific experiments
from the garden on an old china plate. Marina was having a
tea-party that afternoon for one of her charities, and the ladies
saw and heard it all . . . Marina shuddered at the recollection;
even then, Katerine knew exactly what she was doing, with
that little malicious, triumphant pout of hers . . . And it didn't
matter how hard she spanked Katerine, how many hours she
made her spend in a dark cupboard, how many suppers she

missed. *Any* punishment . . . Marina's lips compressed as she thought of some of the more imaginative ones she had imposed. They just seemed to make the child worse, more stubborn, more vicious. And now, what was the girl doing to torment her? Somewhere, somehow Katerine was involved in all this horror, Marina was sure of it, and a wave of unreasoning hatred welled up inside her. The child had already poisoned her motherhood, and was now trying to destroy everything she had left. When she looked in the mirror at her own suffused face and clenched fists, she was shocked.

She sat down on the padded stool in front of her mirrored dresser. The interview had left her shaky, as if she'd had several cups of coffee too many. How had it gone? Had she pulled it off all right? She knew there would have been no point in trying to implicate Katerine, or even pointing the detective in that direction. They would have just thought she was trying to divert attention from herself.

And at this point Marina was also very frightened; she knew that violence begets violence, and that it didn't always come from the same direction. Sometimes, it only needed a hint, or an example.

And then Marina felt a surge of gratitude to Jean Montrose; she didn't think she could have survived the ordeal with that dreadful policeman without Jean's steadying presence beside her.

PART TWO

Chapter Eleven

Douglas Niven left his car in the cobbled no-parking zone outside the offices of Crossman Securities and got out, followed by Detective Constable Jamieson. The offices were in the end house of a block of three big houses that had been renovated and converted from private houses into high-class commercial property. The middle house, Doug already knew, held the offices of Roderick Ferguson's law firm. An interesting apposition, he thought. Constable Jamieson walked with him up to the door; they both briefly enjoyed the bright sunshine. Doug could feel the warmth on the top of his head, and wondered if his hair was thinning.

'What was the name of Graeme Ferguson's boss again?' asked Doug, pausing with his hand on the polished brass doorhandle. His memory tended to be erratic; he could easily remember the names of people involved in cases of years ago, but try as he might, he'd usually forget the name of somebody he'd been introduced to only a couple of minutes before.

'Denis Foreman,' replied Jamieson instantly. Doug's boss, Chief Inspector Bob McLeod, had an easy explanation for Jamieson's facility with names; there was nothing else inside his head to compete for the space.

'Right . . .' Doug stepped inside. The air was cooler in the hallway; this must once have been a very elegant private home, thought Doug, looking around at the high ceilings and tall windows. From the hall, he could see through an open doorway into one of the offices. They had a wonderful view out over the North Inch and the river.

The receptionist was small, with big dark eyes, a triangular face and a great mass of tightly curled brown hair. She had

a charming smile, and, as Doug noticed when she got up to
take them upstairs, an impressive figure inside a neat white
blouse. Doug watched her appreciatively as they followed her
to the foot of the stairs. She had difficulty walking up the steps
because of the tightness of her long grey skirt.

Denis Foreman's office was off the first-floor landing; his
name was on a brass plate fixed to the door at eye level. The
girl knocked, then opened it and let them in with a smile before
disappearing back towards the head of the stairs. Doug briefly
hoped she wouldn't fall and break her neck on the way down.

Doug introduced himself and Jamieson. There was
something about Jamieson, maybe his size, that always added
to the impact of their entry. Doug often wondered if he'd get
the same effect with a German Shepherd.

Foreman remained seated behind his desk. He was in his
early thirties, dressed expensively in a grey suit and red silk
tie. His cuffs were precisely the right length, barely exposing
a pair of obviously very expensive gold links. Above his square,
healthily tanned face, Denis's thick curly hair was meticulously
groomed. Regular eyebrows, a straight nose and a strong jaw
added to the impression of strength and sincerity. Denis
Foreman also had the ready smile and quick, calculating eyes
of an insurance salesman.

Douglas glanced quickly round the office; it was well-
appointed, with a good Persian rug on the floor, three
comfortable, padded, brown leather chairs for visitors, and
a bookcase full of volumes that didn't look as if they were
there to be read. There were several photos on the walls and
desk, mostly of Denis with various local politicians. Doug
glanced at one on the wall nearest to him, and recognized the
smiling face of Roderick Ferguson between Denis and Graeme;
the photo was apparently taken at some official function,
because all three men were in evening clothes.

'You've come about Graeme Ferguson,' he said, pointing
to the chairs in front of his desk. Doug and Jamieson sat down.

'Yes, sir,' said Douglas. 'I understand you were his direct
supervisor.' Doug always tried to make his first comment
something the interviewee had to agree with. It sets the tone,

as he explained several times to Jamieson, who nodded but didn't really understand.

'Well, yes, I suppose so, but actually his operation was quite distinct and separate.' Denis Foreman emphasized the last few words. 'Actually, we were more friends than colleagues, him, his brother Roderick and me. We knew the same people, and, you know, we moved in the same circles . . .' Foreman shook his head, as if he couldn't believe that Graeme was dead.

'Can you tell us something about him?' asked Doug. Again, vague leading questions were the best, he always said. The answers could be far more revealing than the responses to a specific question.

But Denis Foreman was not taken in. 'I'll try to answer any questions you have about him,' he replied, and sat back. The high leather chair creaked, approving his cleverness.

'How long had he been working with your company?' asked Doug, looking out of the corner of his eye to see if Jamieson was ready to take this down. Indeed, Jamieson had taken out his notebook, undone the two rubber bands which kept it closed, licked the tip of his pencil and was busy writing.

Denis opened the buff personnel file in front of him. 'Almost three years,' he replied. 'His anniversary would have been in two weeks.'

It took Doug a moment before he realized that this was corporate-speak, and wondered how many 'n's Jamieson would put into the word 'anniversary'. As it turned out, Jamieson merely wrote 'employed three years'.

'Was he doing well?'

Denis moved cautiously in his chair, and Doug prepared himself for some more evasive action.

'He specialized in foreign-exchange transactions,' said Denis. 'That can be a very risky operation, and yes, he did . . . very well.'

Doug had read in various magazines about the spectacular amounts that could be made and lost in the foreign currency markets.

'Is that what you all do?' he asked. 'I mean does the whole of Crossman buy and sell marks and yen and dollars?'

Denis smiled faintly, and turned his head momentarily to look out of the window. His profile was impressive; the very image of a youthful corporate mogul. 'No. We deal mostly in less exotic fields.' He put his hands together and rubbed the tips of his index fingers. 'Only a small group dealt with currency exchange . . .'

'*Dealt*?' asked Doug. 'Not any more? Was Graeme Ferguson the only one?'

'Almost,' said Denis. 'The main thrust of this company is in investments in corporate stock, both in Europe and the US . . .'

'So Graeme's operation was a bit out of line with what the rest of the company was doing?'

'Somewhat . . .' Denis was beginning to look uncomfortable, and passed his hand through his hair. 'To some of us, it was only marginally within the company's proper field of interest . . .' He grinned. 'Graeme and I had many a good fight over that. Is there anything more I could help you with, concerning Graeme?' He put the slightest emphasis on the last two words.

'No, thank you, Mr Foreman, I think that'll be it.'

Douglas got up slowly, and Jamieson followed his cue by snapping the elastic bands on his notebook with a reassuring finality. The interview was over, and Denis seemed surprised, and even, for a moment, a little uneasy.

'Any time,' he said affably. He looked Doug straight in the eye, shook hands with well-practised strength and directness.

'Oh, and by the bye,' said Doug, turning at the door, and aiming one of the Parthian shots for which he was justly renowned, 'Was Graeme Ferguson in any way a threat to you? I mean professionally?'

Denis stopped dead. 'Of course not,' he said, 'I've been here for ten years, and I've been in charge of a section for the last three . . .'

'Crossman Securities is a big firm, isn't it?'

'Yes, we're quite a good size. Mr Crossman's built it up to be one of the biggest in Scotland, actually, and we're expanding into Brussels and Bonn . . .' Foreman hesitated, then couldn't resist it. 'Mr Crossman's going to be retiring soon, and . . .'

'Congratulations,' said Doug. There was only a hint of sarcasm in his voice. 'Oh, and just one other thing. You used to be friendly with Ilona McAllister?'

Denis stared at him for a second, then laughed. 'Yes, but my God, that was ages ago. She's gone a long way since then, and to be quite honest, so have I.'

Douglas opened the door. 'We thank you, sir, for your assistance.' Not that it was a damned bit of help, he thought. Well, that's police work. Most of the herrings eventually turned out to be red, although they didn't usually change colour until it was too late to matter.

Jamieson followed Doug down the stairs, his weight causing them to creak alarmingly. From behind her desk, the little receptionist watched them approaching. She was still smiling, and Douglas wondered if she washed the smile away at night with the rest of her makeup.

When they were exactly opposite her, she said, very quietly, 'Everything all right up there, Inspector?' Doug stopped and smiled at her. 'Just fine, Miss . . .' He peered at the name plate which lay almost horizontally on her chest. '. . . Miss Arnold. Why did you ask?' His friendly tone seemed to reassure her.

'I suppose he suggested you talk to Sam Braithwaite?' she said with a strange emphasis. Her smile didn't waver one iota.

'Actually . . .'

'Ten twenty-five, sir,' said Miss Arnold, looking at her watch. She was still smiling. Then Doug saw that Foreman had come part way down the stairs and was watching them from the landing with a quite peculiar expression.

When Marjorie got home from Jean's surgery, the phone was ringing in the kitchen. She ran in, leaving her key in the lock; Roderick hated to be kept waiting and could be very sarcastic if she took too long answering.

'Yes?' she said breathlessly. 'Roderick? I'm so sorry, I was out . . .'

'Mrs Ferguson?'

Marjorie was so startled she almost dropped the phone. The
voice was loud, common, with a Glasgow twang.

'Yes,' she replied stiffly. 'I thought . . . Who am I speaking
to?'

'This is about Graeme . . .' The man's voice sounded distant
and purposely distorted, but the tone held an unmistakable
threat. 'He had some unfinished business with us, and we need
to get it off the books. We know you've got it . . . You could
have saved everybody a lot of trouble if you'd come up with
it the first time.'

The line seemed to fade for a few seconds, and a thin beading
of sweat formed on Marjorie's forehead, then the voice came
back again. '. . . You don't want any more trouble, Mrs
Ferguson, do you? You have one son left, now . . .' The man
laughed, and the sound chilled Marjorie's blood.

She made a moaning, desperate sound in spite of herself.

'You know how much Graeme owes us. Twenty thou . . .
Get the cash from the bank. We'll phone you tomorrow and
tell you exactly what to do. Meanwhile, if you talk to anybody
about this, there'll be another death in the family.'

The phone clicked and Marjorie stood there, still panting
from trying to get quickly to the phone. Then the fear hit her,
and she sat down, thinking she might faint. The phone was
still in her hand, and she looked in her phone book and dialled
Doug's number; her hand was shaking so badly she had to
try three times before she got it right.

Jean Montrose was really tired, but nobody would have known
it. She had stopped at the tiny neighbourhood Indian grocery
store on the way home. Indian cooking was the current rage
at the Montrose house, and that night they were going to have
a chicken biryani.

'I'm looking for some almonds and some black
cardamoms,' she said to the owner, Mr Singh, gazing up at
the tall shelves. The place had a cosy, warm smell of oriental
spices. Mr Singh came out from behind the narrow counter
to help her. Everything was so cramped that she had to move
to let him pass. Mr Singh was tall, impressive, with a spotless

white turban and a thick beard, dark in the middle and white at the edges.

'Let me get them down for you, lady doctor,' he said with a grave, sing-song courtesy. He had a deep, rather melodious voice, as if he had once sung baritone. He reached up for the items and with both hands put them into her basket, as if offering a ceremonial sacrifice. 'Is there anything else you might need?'

'That should do it, thank you,' smiled Jean. 'I'm so glad you're open late.'

'At your service,' said Mr Singh, bowing, then he hesitated, and smiled rather sadly. 'Next month, we start closing at eight,' he said. 'There are hooligans in this town who take pleasure in robbing helpless shopkeepers such as me . . .' He shrugged. 'When my son takes over, he can be strong, and work late. But I, I am getting old . . .' He shrugged. 'No matter. For you, Doctor, I would come from my home, open my store to serve you at any time . . .'

'Thank you, Mr Singh, you're very kind . . .' Jean smiled, paid for the groceries, and a few moments later she was on her way, hurrying homewards, hoping that Fiona had marinated the chicken and that there would be enough rice.

There was.

Steven was only moderately fond of Indian food, but both Lisbie and Fiona were so enthusiastic that any objections would have been overcome by a storm of protest, so wisely he didn't do more than grumble briefly to Jean in the kitchen before dinner.

According to family custom, Jean placed the steaming dish on the trivet in front of Steven, and he ladled it out on to the plates.

'Put my rice separately, *please*, Dad!' cried Lisbie, who didn't like mixtures.

'I'm sorry, but it's already mixed in, Lisbie,' murmured Steven. He too preferred the rice on one side of his plate and everything else on the other.

'How was your visit to the palace?' Fiona asked her mother in a slightly sarcastic tone.

'A palace is a *royal* residence,' said Steven, sounding a bit pompous. 'Strathalmond Castle is . . . Well, it's just a castle.'

'They should all be abolished,' said Fiona, who was very anti-aristocracy. 'And that goes for Buckingham Palace too. It could make a fine museum that *everyone* could visit.'

'What about the Queen?' asked Lisbie. 'And the Duke of Edinburgh and all the rest of them? That's their home.'

Fiona had plans for each member; Steven and Jean couldn't tell if she'd thought about it before or was just talking off the top of her head.

'The Queen and Prince Philip,' said Fiona, 'should be retired. We'd give them a little pension, and a flat in a council estate somewhere . . . They'd have time to have some fun for a change, go to the pub on Friday nights, and have picnics and outings and stuff. Nobody'd bother them any more.'

'Wonderful,' said Steven, sarcastically passing the plates of hot biryani. 'And what would you do with Prince Charles, pray?'

'Easy. We'd send him to architecture school, provided he worked as a labourer on building sites during the holidays. And Diana'd go back to teaching kindergarten, but she could make some extra money modelling for toothpaste advertisements.'

'I don't think you should talk like that, Fiona,' said Jean, shocked. 'The Royal Family is very hard-working, and they do a lot for our national esteem . . . Lisbie, is the chutney down at your end?'

'You were going to tell us about your visit to Strathalmond Castle,' said Steven.

Lisbie snatched the jar of chutney from Fiona. 'Your mother asked for it first,' said Lisbie, making a face at her sister.

'It was really interesting,' said Jean, glancing at her daughters. 'Do either of you know the younger one, Katerine?'

'She drives around in an old MG,' said Fiona. 'And she looks like a spoiled, bad-tempered bitch.'

Steven threw her a warning glance. He didn't tolerate any kind of bad language at home, and 'bitch' was getting close.

'When you're in your own place, Fiona,' he said pointedly, 'you can say what you like.'

'Sandra Watt says she's just *awful*,' said Lisbie. 'She wears clothes that nobody around here would dare to be seen in. She's into photography, and she gets her films developed at Boots where Sandra works. They all talk about her. Everybody thinks she has a screw loose.'

'Well, you should have seen what she wasn't wearing today,' smiled Jean. 'Doug Niven's eyes almost popped out of his head.'

Normally this would have elicited a comment from Fiona, but Doug had been replaced in her affections by Robert; Lisbie grinned tauntingly at her sister but didn't get any response.

There was a few moments' silence after that; everybody was thinking rather sadly about Fiona's impending departure to live in her rented cottage.

Just as they were finishing dinner the doorbell rang, and automatically everybody waited for Fiona to leap for the door. They all knew it was Doug from the way he rang the bell.

Fiona got up very leisurely and put her napkin on her plate. 'I'm going down to my room,' she said, nose in the air and deliberately nonchalant.

Lisbie went to open the door.

Steven sighed, and listened to the murmured conversation as Lisbie showed Doug into the living room.

After a few moments, Jean got up and started to put the dishes in the hatchway between the dining room and the kitchen.

'I'll do that, dear,' said Steven, getting up in turn. 'Go and talk to him. I'm going upstairs to watch the news.'

So he didn't hear Doug tell Jean that he'd got some vital new information about Graeme Ferguson's murder, and now had not only a motive but also a strong suspect.

Chapter Twelve

'It all turned out to be relatively simple,' said Doug. He was sitting sprawled in Steven's big armchair, in the relaxed attitude he adopted when things were going well and he felt confident and in control of a situation. He was also smelling strongly of whisky, to Jean's surprise and mild disapproval.

On the basis of an anonymous tip, he told Jean (not quite accurately; there was nothing anonymous about the shapely Miss Arnold) he had gone back to the station with Jamieson and made a phone call to a young man by the name of Sam Braithwaite, who had been Graeme's assistant at Crossman.

Doug and Sam had met later in the upstairs lounge of the Isle of Skye Hotel. Sam Braithwaite was tall, in his late twenties, and, in Doug's eyes, rather sloppily dressed in wide baggy grey trousers and a loose-fitting shirt and jacket. Doug expected white-collar workers to be dressed like Denis Foreman, and the name Armani meant nothing to him. Sam had a thin, intelligent face and eyes that moved restlessly around all the time he talked. He looked like a runner.

'Glen Grant, a double,' he said in response to Doug's invitation. 'The one with the *oval* label,' Sam added to the barman who was reaching up for the Grant's blended whisky. 'It's always the same,' he said, his eyes moving quickly back to Doug. A sprouting of black chest hair stuck up above the widely open sports shirt. 'They never *listen* to what you say. I hate that blended shit. To me it tastes like medicine, not like a real single malt whisky.'

'Just a plain Dewar's for me,' said Doug deliberately, after the barman had measured out Sam's two nips. *He*, Doug, didn't mind drinking blended whisky, but then what did he, a lowly, ill-paid pleb, know about single malts . . .

Doug led the way to a booth by the window overlooking the river and the new bridge. It was early, and there were only a few people in the lounge.

Doug didn't waste any time.

'I hear Graeme Ferguson was a real hot-shot at work . . .'

'Right. *And* at play, I can tell you that without any breach of confidentiality.' Sam leaned forward, his eyes twinkling, as if imparting a secret of momentous importance. He had an easy, relaxed way about him, and didn't seem at all concerned about talking to a detective inspector. Doug found that rather refreshing.

'Miss Arnold suggested that you might have some important information concerning Graeme . . .' said Doug, not quite accurately. His voice deliberately sounded diffident.

Sam shook his head, then took a sip of Glen Grant.

'Miss Arnold, huh . . . A really grand pair of tits on that girl . . .' Sam was watching Doug carefully.

Doug looked startled at Sam's deliberate crudeness, but had the honesty to remember that he'd had the same but unexpressed first impression of Miss Arnold. He smiled with complicit male bonhomie.

'Right, my feelings exactly . . .'

Sam was looking calmly at him out of his pale blue eyes, and grinned. Somehow he made Doug feel as if he'd been testing him in some way.

'Anyway, she suggested that you . . .' Doug deliberately stumbled over his words, and Sam interrupted.

'Let me tell you what was going on at Crossman,' he said, holding his glass in both hands and staring into it. 'Graeme was good. In fact, he was so good at his job he made the rest of us look like a bunch of amateurs . . .' Sam took a long drink, then looked surprised, and stared resentfully at the empty glass.

'You want another?' he asked Doug.

Doug quickly emptied his own glass and nodded. He watched Sam go over to the bar; the man had an odd, sloping way of walking, as if he were fighting a strong side wind. But he was smart, Doug knew that already; and he felt pretty sure a few more double Glen Grants would really loosen him up.

Sam came back with a glass in each hand and smiling. Doug suddenly took a liking to this rather odd young man. Especially as he had a strong feeling that in the next few minutes Sam would tell him all he needed to know about Graeme Ferguson, and maybe more.

Sam sat down, his knee banging against the table and almost spilling the drinks.

'Och, that was a near tragedy averted,' said Doug, grinning, after his hands flashed out to steady both glasses.

Sam hadn't noticed. 'Graeme was making pots of money, although God knows what he did with it all, because he never had a penny to his name. After a very strong two years, though, Denis Foreman wasn't too happy about that whole operation,' he said, leaning forward again. 'He wanted to shut it down. Currency exchange was far too risky in the long term, he said, and it wasn't until a week ago that Graeme figured out exactly why.'

'Why should Denis want to shut it down if Graeme was doing so well?'

Sam drained his glass and got up without answering. He went over to the bar and reordered. Doug watched him from the booth with a mixture of emotions. It didn't seem fair, these young kids earning maybe ten times what he made, and not seeming to be ten times smarter or ten times as hard-working. Sam was looking back at him, drumming his fingers on the top of the bar. Outside, it was getting dark.

By the time Sam came back with the drinks, Doug was already feeling a pleasant buzz; he wasn't drunk, by any means, but he knew he had as much Dewar's in his system as was good for him. Douglas felt a great urge to let it all go, forget about his work, forget about being a policeman, about Graeme Ferguson, and just sit there and get thoroughly drunk and enjoy Sam's company. Although he'd only known him a few minutes, he felt an instinctive ease with Sam, an absence of the confrontational feeling Douglas often had in male company.

Sam put the small glass down in front of Doug. It was half
full of amber liquid, darker than Sam's pale yellow Glen Grant.

'Thanks.' He waited until Sam had sat down before
repeating his question. 'Why should Denis want to shut down
the foreign exchange business if Graeme was doing so well?'

Sam took a big sip of whisky. Doug got the impression that
he probably knocked back pretty big amounts on a regular
basis.

'Last week,' he said, leaning forward and speaking very
quietly, 'Graeme told me, confidentially, that Denis Foreman
was doing a computer fiddle on *his*, that is Graeme's foreign
currency accounts. It's too complicated even for me to fully
understand, and I was his assistant, mind you, but according
to Graeme, who spent *weeks* of computer time trying to figure
out what had happened, good old Denis had found a way to
alter a few of the transaction prices, only by a tiny fraction
of a per cent, and only a very limited number of them. But
as the total amounts were often in millions, it all added up
to a very tidy sum, and Denis was automatically transferring
it to separate dollar accounts he'd opened, but Graeme hadn't
been able to figure out where. It would take at least another
three hours of computer time, he said, and even then, he'd
have to get lucky.' Sam sat back, feeling relieved that he'd
told someone about the problem. It had been on his mind since
Graeme's death.

Douglas was all ears. He'd already had too much Dewar's
to absorb fully what Sam was saying, but it was quite clear
that if Sam was right . . .

'Could you prove it?' he asked.

Sam shook his head. 'No. Well, maybe . . . If I had nothing
else to do for three months except track down the details of
all these tens of thousands of transactions. Good old Denis
is pretty swift with the computer, and apparently covered his
tracks pretty well.'

'What was Graeme going to do?'

'He was really upset, because he and Denis were such good
friends. The two of them used to hang around together, them
and his brother Roderick, until Graeme stole his girl . . . The

thing that upset Graeme as much as anything was that after that, Denis Foreman seemed to have ganged up with Roderick. Apparently the two of them spent a lot of time together; you know our offices are next door to each other, and Graeme found out they were partners in this scam.'

Douglas listened hard, and tried to concentrate through the gathering alcoholic haze. Roderick Ferguson's name seemed to be turning up more frequently in this investigation than just by chance.

'You were going to tell me what Graeme was going to do about it.'

'Well, a week ago he told me confidentially that as soon as he had all the data he was going to blow the whistle. And he finally got it all together, or at least enough to be quite sure, on Thursday.' Sam took another sip from his glass. 'The damn fool . . . It just didn't occur to him that . . . Anyway, he confronted Denis with all that on Friday, about the worst possible time, because it gave Foreman all weekend to figure out a solution.'

'Are you saying . . .'

'All I'm saying is what I said,' replied Sam carefully. 'If you want to draw any conclusions from that, that's your business.'

They had another drink, then Sam said he had work to do and left. Doug stayed for another ten minutes, wondering whether he should call somebody to drive him home. He would have called Cathie, but she didn't drive. Finally he got up and tested himself by walking unobtrusively along a line on the carpet. Being both examiner and examinee, he passed with flying colours. On the way home, he decided to talk it over with Jean; she was the soul of discretion, and Doug had the all-too human failing of wanting to share his triumphs with someone whose respect he needed.

'That's the hardest part of this kind o' case,' he said, after telling Jean the story. He was feeling very relaxed and a bit pontifical in Steven's comfortable chair. 'Once you *ken* who the perpetrator is, *then* you can start tae dig. I mean, looking for murder weapons, a' that kinda thing. A jury needs solid evidence . . .'

'Sit still and I'll make some coffee for you,' said Jean, getting up a little stiffly. She had had a busy day and it wasn't getting easier these days getting out of her deep chair.

While Jean was out of the room, Douglas looked around. There was something slightly different from the last time he'd been there. The furniture was the same, the long, glass-topped coffee table still bore the big book on Venice, the black upright piano was still in its normal place . . . Just as Jean came back in, he noticed the large new framed colour photo on the wall above the china cabinet. It showed a proudly smiling Steven being presented with a wood and silver plaque by an equally smiling Duke of Edinburgh. In the photograph, Jean was standing beside Steven, slightly out of focus, wearing a smart blue dress with an elegant lace collar.

'That was Steven's Award for Industry,' said Jean proudly. 'Doesn't he look nice in the picture?'

'Yes,' said Doug rather vaguely. 'I read about it in the papers.' He stood up and peered at the photo. 'It's a shame they didn't get you focused right,' he said.

'Well, it wasn't supposed to be of me,' replied Jean, smiling. 'Now here's your coffee . . . You're getting it strong and black, my lad!'

'Thanks . . . Do I get some sugar?'

'Aye . . .' Jean laughed. There was something rather touching and helpless about Doug when he'd had more to drink than he should.

'How are the girls?' asked Doug, sipping his coffee.

'Fine,' replied Jean. 'And you've been replaced in Fiona's heart, as you've probably guessed. She has a new boyfriend . . .'

'Serious?' asked Doug, watching her over the edge of his cup.

Jean smiled. 'Yes, I suppose you could say that. They're going to get married in six weeks.'

'Well, that's great!' Doug waved his cup in the air, and Jean felt sure some of the black coffee would finish up on the carpet.

Doug got up to go a few minutes later, apparently quite sober enough to drive. Usually, Fiona would have been hanging around to say goodbye, and he missed her pert prettiness. Jean stood on the step, watching him go quite steadily down the short path; she was thinking about what he'd said, and knew that although all that stuff about Graeme finding out about the scam a couple of days before his death might well be true, it still wasn't going to be such an easy case to solve as Doug seemed to think.

Chapter Thirteen

Roderick Ferguson opened the front door and walked into the spacious but dark hallway of his mother's house.

'Rod?'

'Who else, Mother?' he answered irritably. 'Were you expecting somebody?'

'No, of course not, dear.' Marjorie Ferguson hurried through from the kitchen, wiping her hands on her apron. She reached up to kiss Roderick on the cheek, and he pulled away and wiped it brusquely with the back of his hand.

'Did you have a bad day at the office?'

'Not more than usual.' Roderick was not in a communicative mood.

'Well . . . I had a terrible problem here, Rod . . .' Marjorie stood before him, her big ringless hands twisting together. Roderick turned away. He didn't want to hear about her tiresome problems.

'They phoned, Rod.'

It was more the tone of her voice than what she said that stopped him as he headed towards the cupboard where he kept a bottle of vodka and one of vermouth in spite of her strenuous objection.

'Who phoned, Mother?' At home, Roderick had a puny, whining kind of voice quite different from the strong, capable-sounding voice he used in the office and to address political meetings.

'Those people . . . Graeme's friends . . . Well, not his friends, really, it was those people who came here asking him for money last week . . .'

Roderick became very still. 'What did they say, Mother?'

'They want the money they say Graeme owed them. He said unless I paid up there would be terrible trouble.' Marjorie took a deep breath, almost a sob. 'Roderick, I'm really frightened . . .'

'What did you say to them, Mother?' Roderick took a step forward and caught his mother by the shoulders. 'WHAT DID YOU SAY?' His voice was loud and menacing, and he shook her hard.

'Oh Rod, don't . . .!' Marjorie had tears in her eyes, and cringed as if expecting a blow.

Roderick let her go and stood back.

'Well?' he asked.

'He's going to phone again tomorrow,' said Marjorie. She'd decided to go ahead and pay the money and get it over and done with. There was no reason for Roderick to get involved, and if he did, he'd just blame her. She sat down heavily on an embroidered chair. 'It's a lot of money . . . Twenty thousand pounds.'

Roderick looked at her with an expression of contempt but didn't interrupt. 'He said if I called the police or anybody else they would kill you . . .'

'Kill ME!' squealed Roderick. 'Why me? Why not you?'

'They must have known *I* wouldn't mind dying,' replied Marjorie listlessly. 'Not after all I've had to go through in my life, all the things I've had to put up with, starting with your father . . .'

'For God's sake, don't start that all over again,' cried Roderick. He sat down in the matching chair, facing her. He put his head down between his hands. 'This is the worst thing that ever happened to me,' he muttered. After a moment he raised his head. 'Mother, I'm afraid you're just going to have to pay them.'

Marjorie stayed silent, and Roderick realized that she had taken the matter into her own hands. Slowly he got up, not taking his eyes off her face.

'What did you do?' His voice was like a hiss; he moved, and stood threateningly over her. 'You called the police . . . You phoned Inspector Niven, didn't you?'

Roderick's face suffused with rage; deliberately he raised his hand and slapped his mother hard across the face. Then he called her a name which made her gasp with shock; the house shook when he slammed the door on his way upstairs to his room.

When Doug got home his wife Cathie did not seem too happy to see him.

'Fit's the matter with you the day?' she asked. 'Fit wye did ye nae phone to let me know you'd be late?' Cathie's Western Isles accent always became stronger when she was upset. 'Your dinner's been in the oven now for almost two hours.'

'Well, that's fine, as long as it's no' in the fridge,' replied Doug, making an attempt at humour. 'Here, gie's a kiss.'

'Ye're nae gettin' nae kisses fae me,' repied Cathie tartly. 'You've likely been out getting all the kisses you need!'

'Now come on, Cathie,' protested Doug. 'I was working; you know that. What's more, quine, I think the case of Graeme Ferguson is solved, as a result of some rather smart dee-tective work tonight by yours truly.'

'You're drunk,' said Cathie.

'Aye, maybe a wee bit . . .' He smiled broadly; Douglas was indeed feeling no pain. He reached up to the cupboard above the sink, and brought down a half-bottle of Dewar's, poured a generous amount into a glass and sat down at the table. Cathie flashed him a surprised, disapproving glance, but Doug wouldn't have cared even if he'd seen it.

She put Douglas's plate down in front of him with a bang. The two fried eggs had contracted to the size and shape of golf-balls, yellowed, with edges like brown lace. The chips were dark brown, and looked like broken, pencil-like pieces of mahogany. 'You'd better put on some ketchup,' said Cathie, looking doubtfully at the semi-carbonized meal.

Doug could not have cared less, and attacked the eggs with a knife and fork. 'Fine, this,' he muttered, half-way through the meal, his mouth full. Cathie winced at the noise of cracking chips; from the sound, they could just as easily have been Douglas's teeth.

'By the way, there's a message for you,' she said after Douglas had wiped his mouth, belched, and loosened his belt. 'It's from a Mrs Ferguson who said she talked to you earlier today, and she'd like you to phone her back as soon as you can.'

Calum, twelfth Earl of Strathalmond, sat at the huge angled drawing-table in the genealogy room in the central part of the castle, above and behind the entrance hall. Pinned securely to the surface of the table was a vast sheet of tracing paper upon which was drawn an extraordinarily detailed family tree, which had as many branches, twigs and leaves as one of the giant rhododendrons in the formal gardens of the castle.

On the two long sides of the windowless room, loaded bookshelves stretched up to the high ceiling. Another glass-fronted bookcase to the right of the door contained full sets of *Debrett's* and *Burke's Peerages*, all the *Almanachs de Gotha*, the *London Gazette* and some lesser known reference books on British and European nobility.

Calum spent at least three hours every day in this room, and if it weren't for the demands of running the estate, he would probably have rarely been seen outside it. The family history of the Strathalmonds was admittedly an obsession with him; he had developed a three-dimensional system of keeping track of his far-reaching family tree, with a set of parallel transparent perspex sheets and inset lights controlled by a small switchboard, but it was cumbrous, difficult to change or add to, and almost impossible to demonstrate adequately to visitors, even those as intelligent and interested as Jean Montrose.

Normally Jean would have refused the Countess Marina's invitation to come out to the castle for tea, but it happened that the practice was in one of its infrequent quiet periods and there was something in Marina's voice that had slightly alarmed Jean. In addition, Jean had her own reasons for wanting to return there.

The day was sunny and bright as Jean set off in her little white Renault; the Perthshire countryside seemed to have completely recovered from the devastating heat wave which

had afflicted the area in the earlier part of the summer, and
was lush and leafy-green again.

When she came to the fatal turn in the road near the
Strathalmond estate, Jean slowed, and after carefully
negotiating the bend, drove on to the verge and stopped the
car. She sat there for a moment, not quite sure if she wanted
to get out, but finally undid her seat belt, opened the door,
slid out and walked back to where Graeme Ferguson's Porsche
had gone off the road. She came to the place where the car
had finally come to rest, then looked back at the road,
estimating the distance. She thought it would be about a
hundred feet. Graeme must have been travelling at quite a clip
when it went off the road, but his car was very aerodynamic
and could have slid a good part of that distance upside down.
But the very fact that it had gone so far off the road, and also
that in its final resting place it would have been quite invisible,
particularly at night, made Jean feel certain that this murder
had been carefully premeditated and planned.

Bits of broken glass twinkled in the sunlight as she walked
slowly back to where the car had lain. Shattered saplings, fallen
branches with white, splintered stumps, scrapes of red paint
on stones and deep ruts in the ground showed where the vehicle
had been dragged back to the road. Jean walked back to the
road, past her car to where the oil patch had been. The dark
outlines were still visible; it had covered most of the road, was
roughly pear-shaped, the long end extending to the sloping
right-hand verge. The main puddle was slightly more to the
left, the side Graeme would have come down the road on. If
the oil had merely come from a leaky container on a vehicle,
surely it would have made a long trickle along the road . . .
Unless a full container had fallen and been burst by the tyres
of a passing vehicle . . . Jean spent a few moments looking,
and quickly found the bright yellow plastic oil container in
the long grass at the side of the road. She noted the dent and
the long split in the side. There was still a small amount of
golden oil inside. Jean wondered briefly about fingerprints,
then just as Doug had, abandoned the thought and threw the
container back into the grass.

Jean's last mile to the entrance to Strathalmond Castle was slow and very thoughtful.

Cole led Jean soundlessly and deferentially up to the morning room where Marina was writing letters on a large, leather-covered table. She got up instantly, and came towards Jean with her arms outstretched in a welcoming if rather theatrical manner.

'Jean! How nice that you could come! It's so difficult, living out here in the back of beyond . . . I'm always amazed that anyone ever comes here to visit!'

Jean murmured some suitable response.

'I don't believe I've ever shown you around, have I? Let me take you to see the sights . . .' Marina smiled and took Jean's arm. 'Cole, would you serve us tea in the conservatory, in about half an hour?'

Half an hour later, suffering from severe cultural indigestion, Jean sat down opposite Marina in the centre of the vast conservatory, a humid, glass-domed hot-house of a place with great twining and hanging creepers, orchids with their sweet, close, fetid odour, meaty-leaved tropical plants and palm trees which reached almost up to the glass roof. There was a faint but to Jean a disturbing smell in the air, a smell which made her think of old age, of putrefaction . . .

Somewhere in the background was the sound of running water, a fountain perhaps. She tried not to think of what it would cost to run and heat this place, especially in winter.

Marina glanced around as if she expected somebody might be hiding behind one of the low Sabal palmettos.

'You must be wondering why I asked you to come up when Inspector Niven was here, and also now . . .'

What Jean was actually thinking at that moment was that she would really like to get out of this oppressive atmosphere and into a cold shower.

'Yes,' she said.

'Jean, to tell you the truth, I'm a bit afraid . . .' She gave a slight laugh to cover her embarrassment; it did sound silly, the way she said it.

'Why, Marina?'

'Because I'm afraid that what happened to Graeme might happen to me.'

'Did you tell that to Inspector Niven?' asked Jean, watching her carefully, and trying to figure out how scared Marina really was. Her expressed fear might be a device to turn suspicion away from her. 'Doug's a very good man.'

Marina was already shaking her head. 'No, Jean, I couldn't do that. It wouldn't help . . .' Marina's face was pale, and the skin seemed stretched over her cheekbones; the more she watched her, the more Jean felt that Marina's fears were to be taken seriously.

Cole appeared with a silver tray loaded with tea things and two plates of biscuits. He put them down, and was about to start pouring when Marina waved him away.

'You see, Jean . . .' Marina's hand was shaking as she poured from the silver tea-pot. 'There are a lot of things you need to understand about this family . . . About my husband, about Ilona, and of course Katerine . . .' Her long face wore a sombre expression; Jean thought she looked like a Modigliani painting. Marina's gaze moved to somewhere over Jean's right shoulder. 'And you should know that my relationship with Graeme Ferguson was . . . well, it wasn't quite . . .'

'Marina . . .' started Jean, feeling that she was about to hear something she didn't want to hear, but her training stood her in good stead. If Marina was really afraid, she had no doubt carefully decided in advance what she would have to tell Jean.

'Graeme was killed, but he wasn't the only one who died,' continued Marina. Her voice was strong, but sounded forced. Jean could see what an effort it was for Marina to speak of him, and understood her middle-European rhetoric. 'There's a great deal of . . . emotion here at the castle, but most of it's under the surface; there's some love, but there's a lot more hate.' Marina took a deep breath. 'Jean, I'm really scared . . .' She put out her hand and put it on Jean's arm.

'Now, Marina, if you're scared, I'm sure you have a pretty good idea of who . . .'

Jean heard the noise as the glass conservatory door opened, and Calum appeared through the thick green leaves.

Marina smiled up at him. 'Would you like some tea,
darling?' she asked.

'No thanks.' His voice was polite but distant. He smiled at
Jean. 'I came to see if Dr Montrose would like to take at look
around our demesne.'

'I've already shown her the galleries and a bit of the gardens,'
said Marina. 'But of course, I didn't show her the genealogy
room. I'm sure she'd love to see it.' Marina's voice had changed
almost imperceptibly.

'*Would* you?' he asked Jean, after a glance at Marina.

'Certainly,' replied Jean, I'd love to.'

She got up, glad of the interruption; she had an
uncomfortable feeling that Marina wanted to tell her a lot more
about her personal life, and Jean had no desire whatever to
hear it.

Chapter Fourteen

Calum took a step back when Jean got up; on their previous visit, Jean had noticed that he liked to keep a greater-than-usual physical distance from other people, and she respected that. Jean thanked Marina for the tea, and followed Calum out of the conservatory into the blissfully fresh air of the rest of the house.

'Awful atmosphere in there, isn't it?' Calum was walking fast along the corridor which led back to the main hall, and didn't look round when he spoke.

'It *was* a wee bit warm,' agreed Jean, panting after him.

She followed him up the vast main staircase and along a short corridor, then Calum stopped outside a high double door.

'After you . . .' He held one side of the door open for her.

The room, like so many in the castle, was vast, and made the furniture look Lilliputian.

Jean noticed the huge chart on the drawing table, with what seemed like hundreds of interconnecting lines and tiny squares.

'That's my working tree,' explained Calum. 'I work out the details of a particular branch there, then transfer it to the computer . . .' He pointed to a desk which held a desktop computer, a colour monitor and a telephone. 'That's a laser printer,' he said, indicating a light beige machine next to the desk. He walked to the other side of the room where a series of about forty vertical perspex plates about six feet tall by four feet wide were separated from each other by space of a couple of inches.

'This was made for me by a Swedish firm to my design,' he said, unable to hide the pride in his voice. He went over to a wall panel and pressed one of an array of buttons. The plates separated in the middle like slowly opening pages of a book. Calum pressed some more buttons, and the now visible inner surfaces lit up with a complex interconnecting network of lines and colours.

'It's not quite finished,' he said apologetically. 'But the basics are all there.'

'What do the different colours represent?' asked Jean, fascinated by this extraordinary display.

'There's a different colour, or combination of colours, for each hereditarily traceable factor.' Calum's eyes were shining with fervour. 'There are several genetically determined characteristics we can follow through multiple generations,' he said. He came closer to Jean and turned his head. 'You see the little bump on the rim of my ear?' He pointed, and Jean looked. 'As you probably know, that's called a Darwin's tubercle . . .' He went back to the wall panel and pressed more buttons. A number of small green squares lit up instantly in several of the plates. Calum pushed a larger button marked 'p' and a noise came from the printer, which then extruded a long sheet of paper. 'The printer just put out a complete list of all known family members with a Darwin's tubercle, and a list of those who might have been expected to possess it. My great-grandfather was the first really to take an interest in these hereditary traits . . .'

As Jean watched, Calum pressed some more buttons, and the display lit up again, this time in dotted blue. 'These are the family members with blue eyes,' he explained. 'You can examine each individual one here, or have it printed out also . . .'

The display changed again, and what was evidently the most recent data lit up. Jean put on her reading glasses. The display showed the living members of the family; there was a square for Marina, Calum, each of the girls, and the spouses and offspring of his two brothers, one of whom, Calum said, was an officer in the Scots Guards, and the other now a landowner and farmer in Australia. Jean looked, awed by the technology.

'Are Marina's ancestors in this too?' asked Jean.

'Yes, but they're not particularly interesting,' said Calum

dismissively. He paused. 'If you're interested, I can show you my mother's family tree . . .' To Jean's surprise, he had moved quite close to her, and put a hand on her arm. 'Yes,' she replied. 'I'd love to see it.'

'My mother is actually related to several of the European royal families,' said Calum. His voice had changed, and he was looking oddly at Jean. He made some further adjustments at the panel, and the plates closed and reopened at a different place. A few moments later, a series of little interconnected squares, some with a red outline, lit up.

'Her family is originally from the Saxe-Coburg-Gothas,' said Calum. He pointed to a point high on one of the two facing plates. 'That square up there represents the Princess Irena Katerine, a sister of Princess Mary Louise Victoria . . .' He glanced at Jean to see if she knew what he was talking about. 'Princess Mary Louise Victoria married Edward, Duke of Kent, and from that union, one fine spring day, on May the 24th, 1819, to be exact, in one of the apartments of Kensington Palace, was born no less than . . .?' He paused to give Jean time to answer, but Jean didn't have the faintest idea who he was talking about. 'Queen Victoria!' he finished with a triumphant flourish, both hands in the air.

'Oh my!' said Jean, looking closer at the series of boxes, only some of which were coloured red, including the one representing Queen Victoria herself. 'Does that mean . . .' But Calum, in his enthusiasm, was already back at the buttons, and for the next twenty minutes he showed her some of the bewildering variety of information he'd accumulated about his various ancestors.

'For months, I used to almost *live* in Somerset House,' he said. 'But after they moved, it was different . . . It's all on computers now, and they don't like you to handle original documents . . .' His voice dropped with obvious disappointment.

'Don't you have all you need here?' she asked, indicating the shelves with the thick, bound volumes of *Debrett's* and below them, those of *Burke's Peerage*.

Calum waved a dismissive hand. '*Debrett's* only goes back

to 1802,' he said, 'and as for *Burke's* . . . well, they're even more recent, first published in 1826 . . .' He spoke scornfully, as if they were newly trumped-up publications hardly worthy of mention. 'Now *this* is a bit more substantial,' he said, taking Jean's arm and leading her across the room. He stopped in front of a second tall, glass-fronted bookcase separated from the first by a high, old-fashioned wooden filing cabinet. '*The Almanach de Gotha*,' he said proudly. 'This is a complete set . . .' he pointed up to the first thick, leather-bound volume. 'That's number one, dated 1764 . . .' None of them looked very new, and Jean noticed that the last one was dated 1944. Calum, watching her, smiled. 'I know what you're going to say . . . But that's it, my dear, every one that's ever been published. There were no more *Almanachs* after 1944, by order first of Adolf Hitler, then Josef Stalin, then Konrad Adenauer . . .' Calum shook his head sadly, then smiled, rather a strange smile. 'But it's still a magnificent resource . . .' He sighed, and carefully closed the glass doors.

'I feel that I'm a voice in the wilderness, Dr Montrose,' he said, turning his back to the bookcase. 'You see . . .' He glanced sharply at Jean, surprised at his desire to confide in her. 'There are two things that I respect above all,' he said, slowly, still not entirely sure he wanted to discuss this with Jean. 'One is the hereditary aspects of existence . . .' He waved vaguely at all the paraphernalia and the books in the room. '. . . Because *everything* depends on it, our physical appearance, our intelligence, our behaviour . . .'

Calum was losing a lot of his reserve with her, Jean noticed. He was making more hand movements, and his expression showed the almost fanatical absorption he had in the genetic history of his family.

'What's the other?' she asked.

He stopped. 'Other . . .?'

'I'm sorry; you mentioned there were two things you respected . . .'

'Oh, yes . . . Honour,' he said. 'That's the other thing, family honour. Did you see the chainmail suits, the suits of armour in the hall? Those were worn by my ancestors, defending the honour of the Strathalmonds, and some of my forebears died for it . . .' Calum's eyes were really flashing fire now, and he took up his military posture as if he'd like nothing better than to enter the lists under a great banner with his coat of arms on it.

There was a faint sound behind them, and Jean turned. Marina was there, looking from Calum to her with an astonished expression. It took a moment for Jean to realize why she was so surprised; Calum was standing only a few inches from Jean, well within the distance he liked to keep between himself and other people, and even more astonishing, in his enthusiasm he had firmly taken her by the elbow.

'It's all quite awe-inspiring, isn't it?' said Marina, indicating Calum's books, computer, and the giant perspex genealogical display with a limp wave of the hand. 'To think that my grey eyes and Calum's long nose can be traced back to some obscure medieval copulations . . .' Her nose wrinkled, and she smiled at Jean, who smiled back; Marina certainly didn't share her husband's obsessive interest. But what *did* they share, if anything?

'Have you shown Jean everything?' Marina's voice was carefully considerate. 'Because if you have, I'd love to show her the maze, and the peacocks,' said Marina. 'Calum pulled you away before I had a chance to tell you about them . . .'

Jean was about to say she had to get back to her surgery, and indeed she'd already spent longer than she'd expected at the castle. But Marina insisted, and Jean knew that Marina had something she was very anxious to tell her. Also Jean hadn't found out everything she wanted to know, on her own account.

The boxwood maze was a wonder; set a good five minutes brisk walk away from the house, beyond the formal gardens and stables, its eight-foot walls rose on the edge of a sparsely wooded, hilly area where, Marina said, pheasants were bred and raised to be shot later for sport. The entrance to the maze was merely a small hole in the dense hedge. 'Calum says that the maze in the gardens of Versailles was a copy of this one,' said Marina, smiling, as they stepped into the first cool passage of the maze. 'But who knows . . .' Jean soon felt hemmed in by the high green walls, and hoped that the visit wouldn't take too long. Then it occurred to her that here in the middle of the maze, anything Marina said to her was unlikely to be overheard, and maybe that was why they were there.

Sure enough, after a few more minutes of walking, Marina stopped and faced Jean. 'There's something I need to tell you . . .' she said, but before the words were out of her mouth, a sudden loud explosion, repeated four times, crashed out not very far from them. Jean and Marina looked at each other for a second, and the blood drained visibly out of Marina's face.

'Shots!' realized Jean after a stunned moment. 'My God, Marina, get us out of here . . .' They ran for what seemed an interminable distance, turning, slipping at the corners . . . Marina fell once, and when Jean helped her up she could feel every muscle in Marina's body quivering, but then hers were too. Marina knew the way, and had no doubt where the shots had come from.

'Over there, by the trees!' she said, and started to run towards the clump of tall pines about forty yards away. Jean wondered how Marina could be sure that she wasn't going to get shot at herself, but she followed, breathless with the exertion. When they reached the trees, they leaned up against the pinkish trunks and panted for some moments until they got their breath back.

Marina was looking around, trying to figure where the shooting could have come from, when the sound of a voice very close to them almost made Jean jump out of her skin.

'You wanna try?' The high, affected, bubbling voice was Katerine's. She came from behind a tree, dressed in a skintight black leather outfit. The sun glinted dully on the blued metal of the automatic pistol she was holding loosely in her right hand.

'Oh!' Marina sat down suddenly on the thick bed of pine needles. 'My God, Katerine . . . You scared us half to death! What on earth are you doing here?'

Katerine giggled. 'Just practising,' she said. Her left thumb went up to her mouth. 'Come and see.'

Marina scrambled to her feet, and they followed Katerine into the wood, Jean feeling more and more nervous as the light faded below the high canopy of ancient trees.

After a short walk, however, they reached a clearing, and Katerine stopped. She expertly put a fresh clip of ammunition into the weapon, stood with her feet apart and slowly raised both arms straight out in front of her. Four more shots rang out in quick succession. Jean watched Katerine slowly put the gun down, and saw the glow of pleasure the girl experienced while she was shooting. With a growing feeling of dismay, and her ears still ringing from the shots, Jean followed Katerine and her mother across the broken ground towards the target, a life-sized figure propped up against a tree about forty yards away. When they reached it, Jean saw a cluster of small holes around where the heart would have been; the target was a life-sized photograph of Katerine's sister Ilona, stapled to a long rectangular piece of plywood.

'My God, Katerine!' said Marina, staring at the target. 'Why . . .?'

'Why Ilona?' Katerine's husky voice got harsh. 'For a bunch of reasons, *Mummy*, some of which you know . . .' She giggled, and put her thumb up to her mouth again. 'I'll need to make a new one, I suppose.' She gazed at her mother with a curious, vacant, fixed stare.

Jean looked at the gun Katerine was still holding. 'Is that an automatic?' she asked, breaking the silence. Katerine giggled again. 'Of course,' she said, holding it up. 'It's a .38, and most of them are automatics.'

Marina didn't say a word to Jean on the ten-minute walk through the trees and across the fields back to the castle. She strode along, pale as a ghost, obviously very shaken and frightened by what she had seen.

Jean felt quite shaken herself as she drove back towards Perth; the incident with Katerine had put the other events of the afternoon out of her mind, and she struggled to recollect them all and put them away in the right niches for future reference.

My God, what a weirdo, that Katerine! Jean thought, using
terminology she knew her daughters would have employed.
And, as Doug had pointed out, the girl was just the same age
as Lisbie . . . But when she contrasted Katerine's scary
antisocial behaviour and bordering-on-psychotic personality
with Lisbie's open, affectionate nature and easy friendliness,
she felt a wave of renewed affection for her second daughter,
and wondered what could have made Katerine turn out the
way she had. Maybe it was something hereditary, something
Calum might have a colour for on his family tree . . .

And what would happen to the title when Calum died, Jean
wondered. She knew that both the girls were Honourables, but
would the Earldom of Strathalmond be automatically
extinguished on Calum's death? Would it be reinstated if and
when Ilona had a son? Mulling over those thoughts, Jean put
a Horowitz tape in the cassette, and soon the fluid, magical
notes of a Chopin sonata spread through the car. Jean's sombre
mood translated into thoughts about death and mortality; she
touched the side of the tape player; it was quite beyond
understanding how that long strip of plastic tape in the cassette
immortalized both Horowitz' virtuosity and Chopin's genius
. . . Would science ever develop any other kind of immortality,
one that the individual himself could participate in and enjoy?
It seemed only fair . . .

As she drove along the winding, almost deserted roads back
towards Perth, her mind drifted back to Katerine; she imagined
her following Graeme's Porsche down the road in her little
MG, parking it by the oil spill she'd made earlier that evening,
then, with a torch in one hand, sashaying in her sexiest way
down to the overturned car, her automatic in her hand, intent
on doing maybe the sexiest thing she'd ever done . . . Jean
shuddered, and tried to laugh at her own imaginings. The
Horowitz tape lasted almost until she got back to the surgery.

Chapter Fifteen

Douglas Niven woke up next morning with his head full of the Graeme Ferguson case. He cautiously got up on his elbow and started his preparations to slide quietly out of bed. He was eager to get to work and start the process which he confidently expected would end up with Denis Foreman in the dock, accused of murder. Cathie turned towards him, warm, sleepy, and affectionate. 'Gie's a hug first, Douggie, afore you go . . .'

Doug patted her absently on the shoulder, his mind full of other things. 'That's nae a hug,' said Cathie, putting her arms around him and pulling him down beside her. 'I need a REAL hug! . . . For a start,' she went on once he was inescapably in a horizontal position. With an inner sigh, Douglas abandoned his thoughts about computer fraud and turned his full attention to Cathie.

About an hour later, Constable Jamieson came into Doug's office to find his chief about to make his first phone call of the day. Doug's hand stopped over the phone.

'Well?' Making love always made him irritable, especially in the mornings, and a number of the people who worked closely with him had begun to wonder whether there might be such a cause-and-effect relationship.

'Inspector Garvie wants to talk to you, sir, as soon as you come in.'

'Well, I'm in. Tell him he can come down.' Garvie's narcotics section was directly above on the fifth floor. Jamieson looked at the phone, then at Doug, who snapped at him, 'Go up the stairs, Jamieson. You need the exercise.'

While Jamieson went clumping off on his errand, Douglas

phoned Sam Braithwaite at Crossman Securities. He was on another line, the girl told him.

'I'll hold,' said Doug, irritated.

He was still holding when he heard Inspector Ian Garvie's steps outside. There was a perfunctory knock on the door and he marched in. Douglas slammed down the phone and glowered at his visitor. Garvie was a large, gritty-looking man with short, almost crewcut pepper-and-salt hair, a thick, muscular neck and an aggressive, heavy-jowled chin which was naturally tilted at a challenging angle. Ian had a very simple attitude to law enforcement; until Bob McLeod finally ordered him to remove it, Ian flaunted a sticker on the back of his family car; he'd picked it up in the States, and it showed three flashy drug dealers on a yacht, and the words *Nuke the Bastards!* written below it.

'Who bit *you* in the arse?' he asked Doug, sitting down heavily in the visitor's chair.

Doug shrugged. 'I could spend half my life waiting on the dam' phone . . . What do you want?'

Ian moved his bulk on the chair, and Douglas noticed again what good physical shape he was in. 'I want the people who killed Graeme Ferguson,' he said softly. Ian had a way of looking at a person while making a low whistling between his teeth which could make certain people very nervous.

'You in a mood for revenge?' Douglas sat back and the top of the chair hit the wall. Another small flake of plaster fell from the groove worn in the wall by hundreds of similar contacts.

'Are you kiddin'? I don't give a rat's ass for him or any of them . . .' Ian had returned a few weeks previously after being seconded for a deliriously happy three months to a very tough narcotics unit in Miami, Florida, and was now full of new ideas and vivid transatlantic expressions. 'That bunch of peddlers Graeme was mixed up with . . .' Douglas could feel the pent-up anger in Ian, 'they've more than doubled the drug traffic in Scotland over the last eighteen months,' he said. He took a wooden match out of his pocket, sharpened the end and started to scrape the inside of his right ear with it. His eyes didn't leave Doug's for a second, except once to examine the end of the match. 'I was counting on Ferguson to deliver them to me, lock, stock and bloody barrel . . .' Ian got up and pounded a ham-like fist into his open hand. His face was red with frustration. 'I know who they are, those peddlers . . . I know what they eat for breakfast, who they sleep with . . . But I can't get enough proof to satisfy even McLeod, let alone the courts. I tell you, Douglas . . .' Ian sat down again, his eyes glowing like hot coals. In Miami,' he pronounced it *My-amma*, 'there was a group of narcs who used to go out together, off duty, couple of times a week. They took the law into their own hands, those boys. No reading their rights to those scumbag dealers, no sir . . .' Ian's tough grey eyes flickered over Doug.

'Did you ever go out with them?' Doug's eyes were full of envy; one could never do anything like that in Scotland; everything had to go by the book and nine times out of ten, however well-prepared and however tight the case was, the guilty escaped. In fact, the guiltier they were, the more likely they were to get off scot free, thanks to the high-priced lawyers they were able to hire.

Ian hesitated. 'Between you and me . . .?' Doug nodded. They had been friends for a long time. 'Yes, I did. Three times . . .'

'What did you do?'

'We kicked in some pretty expensive doors, ruined a couple of cosy evenings . . . The third night, we sank a big yacht full of the bastards, five miles out beyond Key Biscayne, near enough for them to see the lights of Miami, but a lot too far for them to swim. One of our guys was a scuba diver . . .' Ian leaned forward, his eyes gleaming. 'Doug, did you know you can make a limpet mine in your own kitchen from a magnet, a couple of feet of wire, a coffee can, a half-pound blob of Semtex, a Timex watch and two AA batteries?'

'You should become a Scoutmaster, Ian. How many of them got away?'

'Not a single one. We were in one of these motorized rafts, and we took care of the only three guys who surfaced. Struck by floating debris, that's what the coroner said, but even he knew better. They were all having a big party below, then kaboom! and she went down in less than a minute.'

'Wow!' Doug was impressed, but his sense of fair play came to the fore. 'How could you be sure they were all drug dealers?' he asked, troubled by the bloodthirsty story. 'How about wives, girlfriends, guests . . . How about the ship's crew?'

Ian ignored the question. 'That one sortie did more to cut down on drug traffic in the Miami area than anything the MPD or the Feds had ever done. I tell you, we had those drug cats running scareder than shit when they heard about this freelance team of agents that was operating . . .' Ian got up again and his lips came together in a hard line. 'God, I'd like to be able to do that here . . .'

'Well, you can stop reminiscing . . . This is Perth, not Miami. Meanwhile I think we may have a lead . . .' Doug told Ian about his unsatisfactory conversation with Mrs Ferguson the day before.

'The thing is, she called again, later. I wasn't home, and when I called back, she sounded really angry and wouldn't say a word. I think those drug lads must have put the bite on her, and she was too scared to say anything.'

Ian shrugged. 'Those boys know all the tricks . . . But maybe we could do a sting operation.'

'You'd have to clear it with Bob McLeod,' said Doug. 'What works in Miami might not . . .'

'What did you tell her?'

'Mrs Ferguson? Nothing. I asked her one question, whether they'd told her where and when to take the money, and she said no. So that means they were just softening her up, and they'll get back to her in a day or two. We're going to put a tap on her phone, but we can't get official permission to do that until tomorrow at the earliest. Only if it's a national emergency, the man said when I told him we needed it now . . . Then we'll set up a drop for the money . . .'

'Are you kidding? *You*'ll set up a drop? What do you think these boys are? A bunch of amateurs? Infants?' Ian hit his forehead with the heel of his hand, a blow which would have

knocked most people cross-eyed. 'If you think you can fool
them that easy, it's just as well you're not in my section . . .
We've tried all that kind of games and more, but they have
more money and more backup than we do.'

'And maybe they're smarter, too,' smiled Doug, not at all
delighted that Ian thought him so naive.

'Probably . . . You want to do a joint venture here?'

'If you promise to change our nappies regularly,' replied
Doug, still smarting. 'And if it's OK with the management.'

Ian's eyes narrowed and brightened simultaneously. Next
to actually kicking front doors down and blowing holes in the
bottoms of boats, Ian was happiest when he had a strike in
mind, and was sitting down to plan it.

'OK,' he said, pulling his chair up a few inches so that he
could write on Doug's desk. 'Here, let me have the pad . . .
and let's see if we can't do it this way . . .'

'Just one thing,' said Doug. 'They didn't kill Graeme.'

'Of course not. Why would they kill somebody who owes
them money unless there's no chance of getting it back? What
they would have done, if he'd upset them enough, would be
to kill him *after* he'd paid up . . .' Ian stared at Doug, his
pencil in mid-air. 'Do you know who did kill him?'

'White collar crime, it was,' said Doug, sitting back again
and sounding rather portentous. 'Computer fiddling . . . I
don't expect you're familiar with that kind of stuff.'

'About as familiar as you are,' said Ian. 'So don't try to
bullshit me. Now, let's get back to our combined operation
here . . .'

Chapter Sixteen

Sam Braithwaite came out of his interview with Denis Foreman feeling very uncomfortable indeed. Just after they'd got started the secretary said there was a call for Sam, from a Mr Douglas, which was the name Doug had said he'd use if he ever had to call him. But he must have jumped, or gone pink or something, because Denis had fixed him with that calm, direct look that seemed to see right through him, or so he thought.

And Denis's words were disturbing, to say the least.

'We're going to reassign you, Sam,' he said. 'Now that Graeme's gone, I don't think our group'll be working in international currency any more. He was lucky, but it's really too risky, in the long term . . .'

Sam waited; there had to be more coming.

'Yes, right . . . As of today, you're going to be working directly for me.'

Sam's face broke out into an entirely spurious grin of pleasure. Denis put his hands through his thick curly brown hair, and it sprang back in position as if it hadn't been touched. 'Your first assignment, Sam, will be some tidy-up work. Graeme's operation took up a huge amount of space in the computer mainframe memory and, as his assistant, you know more than anyone about the records . . .'

'Except you,' thought Sam. 'You knew enough about the system to put together a really masterful fiddle . . .'

'So, Sam, I'm going to put you in charge of going through the entire computer file and make a *summary* of the year's foreign exchange transactions.'

'Summary . . .? How detailed do you want it to be?'

'Just enough to have an overview of the operation for the records. We don't need the details of the actual transactions; as I said, they're using up a lot of computer memory, and we need that space.'

'Right you are, Denis.' Sam grinned cheerfully. 'When do you want me to start?'

'What better time than the present?' Denis flicked an invisible piece of lint off his elegant cuff. 'And, by the way, Sam . . .'

There was something in Denis's voice which made Sam's diaphragm flutter.

'I want you to know that I consider this a *very* important assignment. I'm going to be keeping a close personal eye on your progress, Sam. If you do it *exactly the way I expect you to* . . .' Denis put only the slightest emphasis on the last words, 'And I'm sure you will . . . It'll greatly help your chances of a very substantial raise and promotion in this company. Sam, I'm talking about a week or two from now, in time to get your photo in the annual report.'

'Terrific, Denis. You can count on me. I'll get started right away.'

Sam's head was in a turmoil as he left Denis's office. In the space of a few minutes he had received a new assignment, a warning, and been offered a very substantial bribe.

Sam's step down the stairs was flat-footed and thoughtful; he had some very important decisions to make, and he had to make them fast.

'Don't forget Mr Douglas,' said the ever-smiling Miss Arnold as he passed her desk. 'He wants you to call him back . . .'

But Sam, on the very last step of the stairs, had already decided that the best way of insuring his future was not to talk to Doug Niven again.

'Well,' asked Fiona, 'how do you like it?' She was feeling excited and nervous; it was the first time that Robert had been inside the cottage.

'It's terrific,' he said, bouncing up and down on the single bed, and looking around at the small chest of drawers, the mahogany bedside table with a brass lamp on it. Next to the bed was a small bookcase with several dozen paperbacks and some back copies of a management magazine she subscribed to. 'I'll help you to put up some new wallpaper, if you like. Those big red flowers are fine, but there's too many of them . . .' In fact both rooms in the cottage had the same design of wallpaper, and once one noticed and thought about it, the pattern did start to look a bit oppressive, particularly as the rooms were very small.

Fiona sat close beside him on the bed. 'I feel so *free*, finally living in my own place!' She put her arms around Robert's neck. 'There's nobody telling me what to do, nobody else waiting for the bathroom, nobody saying don't talk so long on the phone . . . It's really great!' Her eyes were shining with her new-found freedom. 'But honestly, Robert, do you *really* like it?'

'Yes, because now we can finally be together,' Robert said in a curiously stilted way.

Fiona laughed. 'And aside from that, we'll be able to cook just for ourselves, and have our friends over . . .'

Robert's glance went to the front door. 'Did you lock it?' he asked. He sounded very nervous.

'Of course,' said Fiona, getting up off the bed. 'I always do; otherwise it wouldn't be safe . . .' She turned her head and smiled at Robert as she drew the curtains.

'Ilona?' The voice was loud but lacked assurance. It took a moment for Ilona to recognize it.

'Oh, Roderick . . .' After her initial surprise, a wave of unpleasant memories came back.

'I was thinking . . .' Roderick swallowed. 'Seeing as how . . . I thought you might like to go out to dinner, or something . . .'

Ilona took a deep breath. 'I don't think so, Roderick, but it was nice of you to ask.'

'Maybe it's too soon? I mean too soon after . . .'

'Yes, it certainly *is*.' Ilona's emphasis would have been unmistakable for most people.

'Perhaps in a week or two, then?' Roderick gave a brief laugh to cover his uncertainty.

'I don't think so Roderick . . .' Ilona was about to put the phone down when she had an idea. Maybe she could do something for her sister . . .

'Roderick, you know perfectly well I couldn't . . . not after Graeme . . . it just wouldn't be right,' she said, her voice sounding sensible and friendly. She paused for just long enough. 'But did you know that Katerine *really* likes you?'

Roderick took a deep breath. Katerine! That sexiest of all the little chicks he'd ever seen! To think he'd never even thought of her.

'Well, there's nobody quite like you, Ilona,' he said, but the tone of his voice gave him away.

When Ilona put the phone down, she felt pleased with herself and disgusted with Roderick. Still, it was all in a good cause, and for all she knew, much good might come of it. She smiled and set off slowly along the mirror gallery, hardly noticing the countless reflections that accompanied her slim figure. As a child, they had fascinated her; she'd played games there, quietly, trying to trick the reflections into not noticing a tiny movement she'd deliberately make . . . Passing the door to Katerine's apartment, Ilona could just hear the phone ringing inside, and she smiled to herself again.

Roderick put down the phone, an unattractive flush on his face. To think he hadn't thought of Katerine himself! He shook his head; he must be getting old, or something. That had been really nice of Ilona; there weren't many girls who'd be as understanding and thoughtful. And he *had* made a mistake phoning Ilona; it was a lot too soon after Graeme's death to try on something like that. If things didn't work out with Katerine, he could always get back to her, but later.

Roderick picked up the phone again, and dialled Katerine McAllister's private number which Ilona had given him. She was delighted to hear from him. A couple of minutes later, he put down the phone, all happy and excited. He pressed the buzzer on his intercom.

'Elizabeth, would you come through, please?'

Meanwhile, he thought, he could put in a little practice with Elizabeth; she was pretty, and very young . . . He knew just how to handle *that* kind of bird.

Chapter Seventeen

'New patient,' said Eleanor. 'A wee bairn. It looks all right
– it's probably just the mother who's anxious . . .'

Jean shook her head but said nothing. It always annoyed
her when Eleanor made comments like that. Jean and Helen
agreed that if she were given a chance, Eleanor would quite
happily take over the practice and dispense advice in all
directions; she'd never let a little thing like ignorance stand
in her way.

'One of our families?' asked Jean.

'No. They moved here just a month ago . . . He's got a job
on the railway.'

'Did you get the history? Details of the pregnancy, birth
weight, all that?'

'I didn't have time,' said Eleanor defensively. 'I had a lot
of other patients who came in all at the same time.'

'Well, you can get the information on the way out,' said
Jean. 'But it's a help to have them before I see a new
patient.'

Eleanor gave a little shrug, and Jean felt annoyed; maybe
it was time for Helen to talk to Eleanor again about her
attitude. There were times when Jean was very glad Helen was
the senior partner and therefore handled disciplinary problems.

Jean crossed the reception area towards her office; there was
a worn place in the carpet that would need to be fixed.
Somebody could easily trip, and nowadays people were starting
to sue over that kind of thing, even in Perth. The child's
mother, a well-dressed, attractive young woman, sat in the
patient's chair near the desk. She was pale, with big dark eyes,
high cheekbones, pale makeup and dark hair drawn back in

a severe style. The baby was on her lap; he looked about five
months old, Jean thought.

'Alan's been acting sort of . . . sluggish, I suppose you'd
say,' said the mother, whose name was Freda Muncie. She
didn't seem very concerned. 'He had a cold two weeks
ago, and he just didn't seem to get completely better.' She
smiled apologetically at Jean. 'I'm probably wasting your
time . . .'

Jean examined the baby, checked his throat, listened to his
little chest. Everything seemed to be all right; he did seem a
bit lethargic, but he didn't have any neck stiffness that might
suggest meningitis, he made the right kind of goo-goo noises
for his age, his lungs were clear, and his heart was beating away
perfectly. There was no sign of inflammation in his throat.
Jean hesitated before handing the baby back to his mother;
something, some tiny point about the baby that she had seen
but not recorded in her mind was disturbing her. 'You're
probably right,' she said, looking at the baby's face for a clue,
but there was none to be seen. 'Sometimes it takes a while for
them to get over a cold . . .'

Freda's face showed her relief. She stood up, and tucked
the blue blanket around the child. 'Thank you so much, Dr
Montrose,' she said. 'I feel much better, and so will Arthur.
We were worried . . . it's a big load off my mind.'

'Let me know in a few days if he's not all better.'

Jean watched Freda go to the door, and felt just a little
unsure of herself. There was nothing she could put a finger
on . . . No, she decided, that child's perfectly all right. She
put him out of her mind and called for her next patient.

At ten o'clock next morning, long before Doug got his phone-
tapping order, Marjorie Ferguson got the phone call she was
dreading.

'Write this down,' the voice said. 'Ready . . .? Travellers'
Motel,144 Dyce Road, second on the right after the roundabout
at Dunblane.' Looking at it now, Marjorie couldn't recognize
her own writing. A motel . . . 'First go to the bank,' the man
had said, 'leave the car outside, double parked if you have

to.' She was to take the money in used notes, tens and twenties. The bank would give her a bag if she asked for it, and it would come with a padlock. She was to hold the bag in her right hand, put the bag in the back, get into the car and drive directly to the A9; no stops, no shopping. When she got to the motel, she was to park in the handicapped parking space, next to a white Escort estate car. There would be a piece of red tape tied to the tip of the extended radio antenna. The front driver's side door would be open. She was to drop the bag on the floor, close the door and then leave immediately. If the white car wasn't there, she was to go home, and she'd hear from them again.

'Do it right, Mrs Ferguson,' the man said, 'and there'll be no trouble, none at all. Don't tell the police or anybody else,' the voice went on, very softly, 'and don't make any phone calls after this one.' She would be followed, he told her, and if she didn't do exactly what they said, it would be the worse for her and for Roderick. When Marjorie put the phone down, she found that she was trembling all over.

A moment later, the phone rang again, and Marjorie almost jumped out of her skin. It was Roderick.

'What's the matter with you?' he asked. 'You sound as if you'd just seen the devil.'

'No, I'm fine, Rod,' she said, her voice bumping into the words.

'What's for dinner?'

'Oh . . . Plaice . . . It'll be late today, I'm awfully sorry, but I have to go out . . .'

'Yuk! Mother, you know I don't care for plaice. I'll eat out, so don't bother . . . You're going out *now*?'

'In just a few minutes, Roderick . . .' Marjorie was stammering with apprehension, and barely knew what she was saying. 'I have to deliver something in Dunblane . . . a place called the Travellers' Motel . . . I'll explain when I get back.'

'Well, drive carefully . . .' There was something odd about Roderick's voice, but she couldn't have said anything to upset him . . .

After putting the phone down, Marjorie hurried to get her

purse and passbook. Luckily there was enough in her savings account to cover the £20,000 they said Graeme owed them.

If the teller was surprised at the amount she asked for, she made no sign. She put it all into a grey canvas bag for her, locked the padlock and gave her the key. Marjorie hurried outside to where she'd left her car in a no-parking area. Luckily the traffic wardens hadn't come by, and Marjorie swung out into the traffic, narrowly missing a cyclist who swerved and shouted at her through the open window. Marjorie was well into the High Street when she realized that she'd left her distance glasses at the bank, and she almost panicked. She hated driving, and let Roderick drive her around whenever possible, but she couldn't drive without her glasses. Everything looked blurred, and she couldn't tell how far away things were. But she couldn't go back to the bank . . . The man had given her specific instructions. The sun was shining, and that helped her to see; she could make out the cars reasonably well, but they still appeared rather suddenly in front, then sped off to the side. A grey shape moved in front of her, a pedestrian. Marjorie slowed, but with her difficulty with distances, she was almost on top of him when she saw him jump and disappear from her field of vision. She made it to the Glasgow road without further incident, but getting on to the A9 she went into the outside lane directly in front of a large foreign lorry which left black rubber tracks for over twenty yards, and only the driver's skill kept him from going off the road. Marjorie, totally unaware of the near-disaster she had caused, concentrated on the road. Vehicles would abruptly come into her field of vision and disappear, or cross in front of her . . . The white line was a relief, because she could see that quite well, but the kerb was more difficult, and a couple of times she found herself driving with two wheels on the verge without realizing she was off the road. Everybody was driving so fast . . . She could hear the sound of horns behind her, and the great big coloured blobs kept suddenly appearing and rushing past on her right, sometimes making a wind so strong that she knew they'd come far too close.

By this time Marjorie was so nervous that she hardly knew

what she was doing; she must have pushed or turned something because the windscreen wipers went on and she couldn't think how to switch them off. In desperation, she pulled off at the side of the road, switched everything off for a few minutes while the traffic went hurtling past her. She could hardly breathe, she was so scared, but the thought of those evil men coming after Rod spurred her on. The rain started, just a drizzle, soon after she started up again, and for a few minutes she thought it was just her vision getting worse, then she realized what was happening and put her wipers on. Luckily Marjorie knew the road quite well, but the God of fools and little children must have been watching over her, otherwise she'd never have made it unscathed as far as the big roundabout in Dunblane. By the time she got to the Travellers' Motel, she was weeping with exhaustion and fear, and once she'd got into the handicapped parking space she simply couldn't move for several minutes, she was so shaken. The white Escort was there, with a little red flag at the end of the antenna, just like the man had said. Marjorie didn't see the other car, parked further down the line, nor did she see the man sitting in the driver's seat, wearing dark glasses and looking straight ahead of him. Marjorie almost fell getting out of the car, but she put the bag into the white car as she had been instructed and got back into her own vehicle. A few moments later a big man with red hair came up, opened the door of the white car and took out the bag. He didn't even glance at Marjorie's car, and headed back towards the motel. Her heart beating fast, Marjorie got out of her car and started to walk. A few minutes later she was back and weeping again with fright and tension she drove slowly out of the motel's parking lot. She hadn't driven a mile before she realized she'd never make it back to Perth. The red and yellow sign of a petrol station came up on her left, and she drove in. There was a phone booth outside, and she fumbled for change in her purse. She called Roderick, but he wasn't in the office, and Elizabeth didn't know when he'd be back. The only other person Marjorie could think of to phone was Douglas Niven, and she was frightened to call because she'd delivered the money without telling him. She'd been too scared of what Rod would say or do to her if she talked to him again without his permission.

After standing indecisively for several minutes in the phone booth, she realized that if she wanted to get home alive, she *had* to call Douglas Niven. She had some trouble getting through, and by the time she did, there was no change left in her purse. To her surprise, Douglas was just as nice as could be, after she explained. Almost in tears again, she told him about the awful drive, the money, the white Escort . . .

Doug put his hand over the mouthpiece. 'Call Inspector Garvie,' he whispered urgently to Constable Jamieson. 'Get him on the blower. Get back into your car, Mrs Ferguson,' he said, 'and don't move from there. I'll come and pick you up as soon as we've finished at the motel.' All Marjorie understood was that she would not have to make the drive back to Perth. She went to the toilet at the back of the garage and, weeping with silent relief, compulsively started to wash her hands.

'Yes, we have a Task Force designation, so we have jurisdiction a' through the Region,' said Ian Garvie, sitting in the front passenger seat of Doug's police car. He had his head down, working the radio power switch on and off. The radio was full of static, and he thought there might be a bad connection.

It had taken only a few minutes to mobilize his group. Ian clicked on the radio microphone in his hand and told his team to call in; after a short delay, both cars identified themselves. One was fifty yards behind him, and the other, with Constable Jamieson and two men from the narcotics section was just coming out of the garage.

'You got your boys together fast,' said Doug, getting into top gear.

'Och, we're used to moving fast,' replied Ian, his eyes glowing with a fierce anticipation. 'Not like your people. Jamieson wanted to phone his mother and tell her he'd be late for supper . . .' Ian held on to the grab handle on the dashboard and grimaced as Doug ignored a stop sign and turned right across the traffic at the junction of York Place and Glasgow Road.

A few miles from Dunblane, Ian called the local police on the radio and told them there was going to be a raid on the motel, but they should stay out of the way until it was over.

Doug, manoeuvring his way at high speed through the traffic, heard the crackling sound of angry voices at the Dunblane end, and Ian switched off. 'They don't like it when we go into their territory,' he said, then added as an afterthought, 'Tough shit.'

'You realize they probably won't have any drugs there, don't you?' said Doug, glancing over at Ian.

'Just keep your eyes on the road, my man . . . That's what happens most of the time; we get a lead, do the raid, find nothing. So we have to get them on something else . . . Blackmail, extortion, resisting arrest, assaulting a police officer, we can arrange one or all of the above. Oh Jesus . . .'

Douglas was passing a string of traffic and just managed to get back into his lane in time.

At the roundabout, Ian called in his two other cars, and asked Doug to slow down for a minute until they caught up.

'Unit one will take the rear entrance, and put a man to guard the white Escort,' said Ian. 'Unit two, position your car across the entry road with all lights and flashers on. Jamieson to cover the rear exit; everybody else except the drivers to join us at the front door.

'We all go in together,' he said on the radio, as all three cars turned into Dyce Road, one after the other. 'We want this operation clean and fast . . . Good luck all!'

Doug pulled up at the entrance with a squeal of brakes, and Ian was out and running before the car had stopped. Ian crashed through the door, with Doug right behind him. 'Police! This is a raid!' said Ian even before he reached the desk. The receptionist, a young girl with thick glasses and thin fair hair, stood up, panicked. Doug grabbed the register while Ian went to guard the main corridor.

'Room one one two!' Doug shouted to Ian; he snatched the spare room key off the rack, and the two of them sprinted down the corridor, followed by three men from Ian's squad.

'It's the only room with two men registered,' said Doug, panting.

'It'd better not be two priests going to a seminar,' replied Ian, who was in better physical shape. He banged hard on the door of room 112; there was no answer. Doug fumbled with the door key; it stuck, and Ian grabbed it, taking a few anxious seconds before he got it to turn. Out of the corner of his eye Doug saw the lobby door open far behind them; the manager stood in the opening, watching nervously from a safe distance.

Finally Ian got the door unlocked, kicked it hard and went in, his body in a crouch, his gun outstretched in front of him, grasped in both hands. Doug, unarmed, came in right after him.

There was nobody there. Nobody alive, that was. Ian ran into the bathroom, took a second to look behind the shower curtain, then came back slowly into the room, putting his gun back in his pocket. Two men lay sprawled, one on the floor and the other face down on the couch, a large red stain spread on the fabric under his head. There was a grey canvas bank bag open on the low table in front of the couch, with a pile of paper money beside it.

Chapter Eighteen

'All right Mrs Ferguson, here we are . . .'

The police car drew up outside Jean Montrose's surgery, and Doug Niven got out, leaving the car double-parked with the motor on. He opened the back door and helped Marjorie Ferguson out. She was still so shaken that she had difficulty walking without stumbling, so Doug helped her gently up the three steps and along the short path.

Eleanor saw them come in, and pretended to be busy behind her desk. She didn't like the police coming around the surgery, and she particularly didn't like Doug Niven.

Jean came out of the little room they used for urinalyses and other lab tests.

'Jean, would you take a look at Mrs Ferguson here?' asked Doug. 'She's . . . well, she's had a bit of a shock . . .'

'Yes, of course. Come on into the office, both of you,' said Jean. 'Eleanor, would you bring in Mrs Ferguson's folder? And some tea for everybody.'

Eleanor's lips tightened, but she went over to the filing cabinet without comment.

It took a few minutes and a cup of strong, hot tea before Marjorie was able to speak, and then she started to shake as if she had the ague.

Doug briefly told Jean what had happened, about her drive to Dunblane. And then he'd had to tell Marjorie about what he'd found in the motel.

'I'll call Roderick for you,' said Doug, trying to be helpful. 'He can come and fetch you home . . .'

'No!' said Marjorie, suddenly coming to life. 'I can get home

by myself. And *please*, don't tell Roderick about this . . . He
. . . He'd be very upset . . .'

Douglas stood up. 'It'll be in the papers, you know, Mrs
Ferguson,' he said quietly. 'So even if he didn't see it on the
telly this evening, he'd know by tomorrow morning.' He
glanced at Jean. 'I'll be on my way, then,' he said. 'Maybe
I'll stop by later . . .' That, of course, meant that evening at
her house.

Jean checked Marjorie, and found that she was suffering
from exhaustion and the effects of fright and anxiety.

'It's nothing that a good night's sleep won't cure,' she told
Marjorie encouragingly, but privately Jean suspected that her
problems might be harder to cure and might well last longer
than overnight.

Marjorie raised her eyes, and shook her head.

'It's too much responsibility for me to carry,' she said. 'You
don't know what it's like, being all alone . . .' Marjorie's
shoulders started to heave.

'You're not alone, now, Marjorie. You have Roderick . . .'

Marjorie raised her eyes. 'Other people have husbands to
help them when they're in trouble . . .' She told Jean about
her terrifying drive to Dunblane, and how she'd had to wait
for an hour and a half in her car in the Esso station, too scared
to move. 'Well, my husband's still alive, but he might as well
be dead . . .'

She talked on about her husband, about his drinking, how
he'd abandoned them.

'He had to go into an institution, didn't he?' asked Jean.
That, to her mind, didn't really constitute abandonment. 'Is
it near here? I mean, near enough so you and Roderick can
visit him?' Jean made a note in Marjorie's folder.

'He's at the Abbotsford Clinic . . .' Jean had heard of it,
a private mental home near Edinburgh that specialized in long-
term alcoholic patients. 'Anyway,' Marjorie went on tearfully,
'*he* got himself into that state. Nobody forced him to drink
like that . . .'

'Was it really a huge amount?' asked Jean sympathetically.
'It must have been very difficult for you, with the children

and everything.' Jean realized that Marjorie wanted to talk about this long-suppressed problem. With sorrowful indignation, Marjorie told Jean how much her husband drank on a day-to-day basis, and her answer astonished even Jean, who was used to complaints about husbands who drank too much.

The tea seemed to have settled Marjorie down and, after talking for another ten minutes or so, she said she felt strong enough to go home. Jean decided not to give her any kind of sedative, but instead got Eleanor to call a taxi to take her home. One of Ian Garvie's men had driven her car back from Dunblane, and by now it would be back outside her house.

After Marjorie had gone, Jean sat in her chair, thinking hard for several minutes before going through to see who was in the waiting room. The whole business of Graeme Ferguson's murder seemed to be spreading into all kinds of surprising directions, and with a feeling of alarm, Jean realized that even now it wasn't over yet. Not by any means.

That evening Jean made spaghetti Bolognese, a favourite in the Montrose household; quick, easy to make, and filling enough to satisfy everyone.

The meal had barely started before Fiona started to tease Lisbie. 'I hear there's somebody rather interested in you at the office,' she said. 'It's all over town . . .'

To her own great annoyance, Lisbie blushed a bright red. She didn't want to talk about it, but in fact, there was the beginnings of something there . . . just a friendship at this point, that most likely would never lead to anything . . .

'Leave your sister alone, Fiona,' said Steven wearily. 'It's terrible that I can't have an intelligent conversation with your mother without you interrupting . . .'

Fiona opened her mouth for a retort, but Jean got in ahead of her.

'How do your curtains look, dear?' At the weekend, Jean had made a set of curtains for Fiona's cottage from a bolt of blue-and-white flowery cotton material she'd bought at the Home Stores.

'They're lovely, thanks, Mum. Robert was just saying how
nice they were.'

A snort came from Steven. 'I'm delighted *he* likes them,'
he said. 'Has he moved in there, or what?' There was no
mistaking Steven's angry tone.

'No, of course not, dear,' said Jean. 'Now, as this is the
first time Fiona's been home this week, could we all try to be
nice to each other, just this once?'

The doorbell rang as they were finishing the meal. Fiona
was piling up the plates, and Jean was about to take the
spaghetti dish into the kitchen.

'That's likely Doug Niven,' said Jean. 'Lisbie, would you
open the door?'

'Why does he always have to come when we're in the middle
of supper?' asked Steven, putting his napkin on the table.

'I suppose he just eats faster than we do,' replied Jean
placidly. Steven stared at her for a moment, then shrugged
his shoulders and went off upstairs so that he wouldn't have
to speak to Doug. It wasn't that he didn't like him, it was just
that the evening was a time to spend with his family. Almost
at the top of the stairs, he stopped, turned to see Doug coming
in to the hallway, and went down again.

'Doug, I know what's the matter with you,' he said, stopping
halfway down the stairs and grinning at the policeman. 'It's
time you and Cathie had some kids.'

Doug looked at him, astonished. 'Evening, Steven. Why
should we have kids?'

'They'd keep you home at night,' replied Steven, and went
back upstairs, followed by Doug's slightly puzzled gaze.

'Steven's had a hard day,' said Jean, coming out of the
kitchen, 'and so have I.' From Jean's tone of voice, Douglas
knew that although he was always welcome at the Montrose's
house, tonight would not be a time to linger too long.

'Was Mrs Ferguson all right?' he asked. 'I was worried about
her.'

'I sent her home in a taxi,' replied Jean. 'She was shaken
up by that drive down to Dunblane. Can you imagine, driving
all that way without her glasses? It was only later she realized

she could easily have been killed. And then hearing about those two men . . .' Jean stopped and looked steadily at him. 'You don't think she . . .'

Doug looked at her with astonishment. 'Mrs Ferguson? Why on earth . . .'

'She's very protective of Roderick,' said Jean. 'And with him wanting to be in politics, the publicity would be very bad for him.'

'My God,' breathed Doug. 'I never thought . . .' He got half out of his chair, then sank back into it. 'I was thinking we could take her in to check for gunpowder residues on her hands, but if she knows enough to shoot those two men, she'd know how to get rid of the residues . . .'

'Did you find the gun?' asked Jean.

'No. But we think it was the same size that killed Graeme Ferguson.'

'I don't think she's a realistic suspect,' said Jean. 'Her eyesight, for one thing . . . And anyway, she's just not the sort.'

'These drug-related crimes are becoming a real problem, specially around Glasgow and Edinburgh,' said Doug, moving restlessly in Steven's green chair. 'You may not believe this, but some of our higher-ups wouldn't mind if those drug people just killed each other off, then we shouldn't have to waste our time on them . . . Of course you'd never hear any of them actually *say* that out loud, though.'

'Do you really think that Graeme's was a drug-related death? He was earning a lot of money at his job, and it seems a bit radical to kill him just because he was a bit late paying them off.'

'At this point, Jean, I honestly don't know. The narcotics people here knew about Graeme; in fact they were very disappointed when he was killed; they'd been hoping he'd lead them to the big boys.'

Jean just shook her head. There were so many possibilities now, it was dizzying. She glanced at the clock.

Doug didn't miss the look. 'Well, I just thought I'd stop by,' he said, heaving himself out of the chair. 'I'd better get

myself back home. And,' he grinned at Jean, 'you might tell
Steven I'll discuss his suggestion with Cathie.'

'That went off rather well, don't you think?' Calum
McAllister, Earl of Strathalmond, put the half-gallon bottle
of Glenmorangie back in the cupboard where they kept drinks
and glasses for visitors. The office in the farm administration
building was where he met with visiting agriculturalists,
government inspectors and livestock buyers. Sometimes Bert
Reynolds, the livestock manager, would have been happier if
Calum left him to do the bargaining, but on certain occasions
the prestige of Lord Strathalmond's name was a big help. This
morning they had been negotiating with a group of Americans
for the sale of sperm from Mains of Targ, their prize-winning
Aberdeen Angus bull, and the Mid-Western farmers couldn't
keep their eyes off his Lordship.

'Aye,' replied Bert calmly; he was a man of few words. He
put the glasses in the sink and washed them out before putting
them upside down on the draining board. There was something
bothering the boss, Bert was pretty sure of it. It probably had
something to do with that Ferguson boy's death, because there
were no problems with the farm.

'You'll lock up, then,' said Calum, heading for the door.
The Range Rover was outside, and he climbed in. He really
preferred to walk, feel the wind on his face and the mud of
the land on his boots, but most days it would simply take too
much time. Calum drove with both side windows open.

The gravel scrunched under the tyres as he pulled out into
the service road. There was a late summer calm over the
countryside which touched the white fences with a clear glow,
and dappled the massive trunks and thick, mature foliage of
the horse-chestnuts separating the fields. Calum felt no pride
that everything he could see belonged to him; it was a trust,
a commitment which had been handed down to him. His
father, the eleventh Earl, from whom he had also inherited
his strong sense of responsibility and family honour, liked to
tell Calum that their family was like a long river; each one of
them successively responsible for the next stretch, and what

they did during their stewardship determined the course and size of the river, maybe for ever.

How was he doing? He turned the corner, and looked back at the spotless white farm administration building he'd just left. They now kept all the stock breeding records there, all the computerized planting and livestock data for the entire estate. *He* had initiated that, and put it all together . . . Beyond the buildings was a part of his renowned Aberdeen Angus herd, sleek and well-fed in their glossy black coats; his grandfather had started it, but he, Calum, had enlarged it, and by careful breeding had improved significantly on the measurable characteristics of the animals.

Yes, Calum thought, as his Range Rover came into the shadow of a clump of trees, he was reasonably satisfied that his stretch of the river had been well husbanded.

Past the trees, the road made a right-angle turn into a wide unpaved courtyard, bounded on the right side by the old brick wall of the stables. Calum drove past the high arched entrance, decorated above with the large built-in brick coat-of-arms of the Strathalmond family, a shield with a claymore on the left side and three lilies on the right. *Puritatis defensor* . . . Still holding on to his train of thought which he wryly recognized was verging on the obsessive, he thought about the family motto. It wasn't an easy task, these days to defend his family's integrity; he'd had to fight off a few attacks on the family honour, and he felt he'd done that in true crusader style.

Thinking about that, Calum felt a wave of gratitude for Ilona; what a splendid young woman she was! She'd loyally backed his decisions, even when they'd been personally difficult for her. He felt truly proud to be her father. Ilona was the link between the generations; she was the one who kept him up to date, the one who kept him abreast of what was going on at the castle, even if sometimes that didn't make the happiest of news . . . And she'd taken her recent loss on the chin. She was a brave girl, Ilona, worthy of all the long history of courage and integrity in the Strathalmond family. And she had developed a surprisingly good grasp of the principles of estate management; Ilona was tougher than she looked, he recognized that, and wouldn't be one to let any obstacles get in her way. It was really surprising, he reflected, that a woman with Ilona's burning desire to be worthy of her place as future head of the family, should have such poor taste in men. Still, Calum felt confident that the stewardship of the next stretch of river would be in thoroughly capable and honourable hands.

Caught up in his reflections, Calum turned the sharp corner at the end of the stables a little too fast and the back wheels of the Range Rover slid, kicking up a small cloud of dust. With Ilona's son, assuming she bore one, Calum hoped the ancient patrilinear title of the Strathalmonds would be restored. His lips tightened momentarily. It was hard enough planning for next year, let alone for the next generation.

Cole was waiting for him as the vehicle pulled up outside the service door.

'You may be interested to know, your Lordship,' said Cole, holding out a folded copy of the *Perth Courier and Advertiser*, 'that there have been two further deaths, possibly connected with that of Mr Ferguson . . .'

Calum took the paper and read the report. 'Very interesting,' he said slowly, 'but I'm sure you realize there is no connection whatever between this . . .' Calum flicked the paper with the back of his hand, 'and Graeme's death.

Cole's astonished eyes followed Calum as he strode briskly along the corridor towards the haven of his genealogy room.

PART THREE

Chapter Nineteen

Jean woke up in the middle of the night, thinking about Freda Muncie's baby. There *was* something the matter with him; it was his eyes, the way they moved, as if he couldn't focus or concentrate . . . and by this age, he should have been able to do that. Jean moved restlessly, and Steven mumbled and turned away from her. She looked at the faint green luminosity of the alarm clock. Ten minutes to five. Maybe he had an eye defect of some kind, maybe a congenital one . . . Freda, the baby's mother, seemed perfectly normal, but of course that was no guarantee. Jean peered at the clock again; it was hard to read, and she'd been known to get up an hour early. No, it was almost five, no mistake. It wasn't worth trying to go back to sleep, although there was nothing she could do about the Muncie baby at this time in the morning. Well, she might as well get up and make herself some tea. And there were some scones in the bread tin, and some homemade strawberry jam that Steven's mother had brought last week from Turriff . . . Jean moved her legs over to the edge of the bed, then swung them down slowly, trying to get out with a minimum of disturbance.

In the bathroom, Jean brushed her teeth, scrubbed her face and looked in the mirror; she was not impressed. She looked pale and tired, and that matched how she felt. And there was a bit more grey at the sides of her hair . . . Enough more so that moving a curl over didn't quite cover it up the way it used to. Fiona had been making comments about it, too. Well, Jean supposed, rubbing some cream into her face, it was finally getting time to talk to Rosie, her hairdresser, about it.

A touch of lipstick, and a quick dab with the blusher brush

on each side . . . Jean remembered her mother's acid comments the first time she'd ever experimented with cosmetics and appeared all resplendent at dinner. Her mother had stopped serving and stared coldly at her. 'Have you ever heard the expression, *painted slut*, Jean?' she asked her daughter in a cutting tone. Jean was ten years old at the time, and answered, quite logically, 'But I'm just a painted *girl*, Mother.' Her mother had not been amused by that, any more than by anything else Jean ever did.

Jean switched the bathroom light out and headed silently for the stairs. The second step creaked loudly under her foot. Twelve years they'd been there, and she still sometimes forgot about it.

All was quiet in the kitchen. Outside, everything was dark; through the window she could see a small clump of Mr Forrest's sheep. They had been joined temporarily by a pair of old horses belonging to a neighbour; the two nags always stood close together, immobile, and made strange, grunting and sighing noises in the night.

Jean had forgotten to put away what was left of the spaghetti sauce; she took a wooden spoon and scraped it all into a bowl, tore off a piece of plastic film and covered it before putting it into the refrigerator, on top of a plastic box of left-over rice. They really were going to have to get a bigger refrigerator; Fiona's leaving hadn't made any difference to the amount of space they needed. Jean wondered how Fiona was doing; she'd gone out to see the cottage, and it was nice enough, but at the back of her mind Jean wondered if Fiona felt that Steven had driven her out of her own home. There was nothing Jean could do about Steven's dislike of Robert; she'd certainly tried. Jean wondered if she would have had the same reaction if she'd had a son; would she have disliked any girl he really got serious about?

The first glimmer of daylight was starting to come through the window, and Jean almost dropped the tea-pot when she heard a scratching at the window right by her head. It was only Alley, their marmalade cat sitting on the outside windowsill. Fiona always maintained that her name was 'Allez!' for *Scram*!

but then Steven would pull on the outer corners of his eyes
and say it was '*Allee* same to him *what* they called the cat . . .'
That was in the old days, when Steven and Fiona were still
talking to each other . . .

Jean opened the door and, as usual, Alley rushed in as if
she were being hotly pursued by a pack of ravenous German
Shepherds. Jean poured the water into the tea-pot, then opened
a tin of Friskies with the new electric opener Steven had brought
home a few days before. Steven couldn't resist gadgets; there
were so many food processors, electric stirrers, coffee grinders
and espresso machines in the kitchen that there was barely
enough room to cook.

That baby, Alan Muncie . . . Jean felt annoyed that Eleanor
hadn't filled in the *new patient* sheet when the child had come
in; it was the inflexible routine that it should be completed
before any new patient was seen. It probably didn't matter,
anyway, unless the child had had some birth injuries or lack
of oxygen during delivery that could have damaged its brain.
Or maybe he'd had too much oxygen; Jean knew that could
cause eye damage to newborns. Now then, Jean, she said
sternly to herself, this is all in your imagination; that baby
seemed perfectly all right *while you were actually examining
him*, so it's unlikely that you've discovered something seriously
wrong with him at 5 a.m., when he's happily sleeping at home.

Jean looked at the clock and wondered for a moment
whether Steven would like an early cup of tea, but she was
pretty sure that he would rather sleep. Depending on what was
happening at the glassworks, Steven, who was the manager
and part owner, usually got in to the office between nine and
ten.

Alley, having devoured the Friskies as if she hadn't been
fed for a fortnight, lapped at the saucer of water, licked her
lips, then twirled around Jean's legs, rubbing herself against
them, silently asking for more.

'That's it, Alley,' said Jean, cutting a scone in two. 'You
got a whole tin, and anyway it was the last one.' The homemade jam was high on the shelf behind her, and being rather
short, Jean had to climb on a chair to reach it. The jar was

wrapped in paper, with a label bearing a printed heading 'From the kitchen of' and below that, in old Mrs Montrose's precise script, the date and description of the jam. She was a wonderful old lady, in her eighties now, benign, white-haired . . . Steven said she hadn't always been benign, not by any means. When he was a child in Turriff, and he'd done something to upset her, even in the middle of winter she would make him stand in the tub naked and turn on the cold shower until he was blue and shivering and barely able to stand up. Now, of course, she was a wonderful, loving old lady.

Jean's own mother had done things exactly opposite; she had carried out her stint of motherhood with astonishing grace and patience, but was now the scourge of the nurses in the private nursing home on Barossa Lane.

Lisbie appeared at the kitchen door, wearing a cotton nightie, her eyes barely open. 'You look like a zombie,' said Jean. 'When did you get home?'

'About two,' replied Lisbie, but she wasn't going to say any more about the evening. When Fiona was living at home, the girls usually went out together and, between the two of them, Jean always had a pretty good idea about what was gong on.

'Tea?' she asked, the pot poised over Lisbie's mug.

'No thanks,' said Lisbie. It might have been just the early morning, but Jean had a strong impression that Lisbie had something on her mind, and was trying to decide whether she was going to talk to her about it.

Lisbie decided not to. 'Do you want the bathroom first?' she asked.

'No, dear, I'm all done.'

Lisbie headed towards the stairs and slowly started to go up. Jean's concern for Lisbie increased for no obvious reason. There was something going on there . . . Oh, for heaven's sake, she told herself. Here you are diagnosing who knows what in a well baby, and who knows what else with your daughter . . . It's time to get to work.

She left a note on the hall table for Mrs Cattanach, her cleaning lady, asking her to wash the china in the display cabinet in the living room. Normally Jean would do that delicate cleaning herself, but Mrs Cattanach did it as well or better and had never broken anything.

When Jean got to the surgery, the first thing she did was to look at little Alan Muncie's *new patient* sheet. He had been a normal delivery, seven pounds eight ounces, and was seven weeks old when his parents formally adopted him. Still feeling anxious, Jean asked Eleanor to phone the Muncies and ask them to bring the baby in.

Helen came in, dressed as if she were going hiking in the Trossachs, with a dark green windbreaker, a plain tweed skirt, thick socks that reached up to her knees and boots that Jean had heard clumping on the path long before Helen reached the door.

'I'm away round the North Inch,' she said. 'I just stopped in to see if there were any messages.'

'Helen, I'm glad I caught you . . .' She told her about the Muncie baby.

'They're bringing it right over,' said Eleanor from behind her desk.

'*It* is a *he*,' replied Helen sharply. 'I'll wait.'

When the Muncies arrived, Freda was accompanied by her husband Arthur. Both seemed concerned and scared by the abrupt summons to the surgery.

'There's just a couple of things Dr Inkster and I want to check on Alan,' said Jean. Her friendly and cheerful manner seemed to relieve them. 'If you'd both like to sit in the waiting room, we'll take Alan with us.'

Jean picked up the baby and brought him in to the examining room. He seemed more listless this morning, and his arms were floppy, although it was obvious he could move them all right.

'The kid looks perfectly all right to me,' said Helen in her booming voice, after watching Jean examine him. She was anxious to get out to the North Inch.

Jean passed her hand quickly in front of Alan's face; he did blink, but the reflex seemed delayed . . .

Shaking her head, and thinking she was making a right fool of herself, Jean picked up the ophthalmoscope.

'Would you turn off the light, Helen?'

Helen obliged while Jean adjusted the scope, then leaned forward and looked into the back of Alan's eye. She didn't see very much for a few moments, then her grip tightened, and she took a sharp breath. She didn't say anything, but turned to Alan's other eye. Again he didn't flinch at the bright light shining on his retina. Jean narrowed the beam to look at the macula, the most sensitive central part of the retina, then went back to the first eye.

'Well, girl, what are you seeing in there?' Helen's voice showed her restlessness. 'A peep show?'

'Take a look,' said Jean very quietly. Helen took the ophthalmoscope and adjusted it to suit her own vision before bending over the baby.

'Oh, my!' she breathed, then quickly checked the other eye. 'Both of them,' she said, straightening up. 'It's on both sides, the "Cherry-red Spot".' Helen frowned. 'They don't look Jewish . . . I mean the parents . . .'

'He's adopted,' replied Jean.

'We'd better go and talk to them,' said Helen.

'Let me go over his CNS first,' said Jean. She checked Alan's reflexes and muscle tone; everything confirmed the diagnosis.

Slowly, Jean picked the baby up and went to the door. The Muncies jumped up, their anxiety showing clearly on their faces.

'I'm afraid we have some bad news for you,' said Jean, as gently as she could. She put the baby back in Freda's arms. 'We think Alan may have a congenital condition called Tay-Sachs disease . . .'

Freda caught her husband's hand and held tightly on to it.

'What is that?' she asked. 'Is it serious?' Her face had gone pale, and Jean made her sit down.

'It causes severe mental deterioration,' replied Jean carefully. 'And it also affects the vision . . .'

Freda started to cry quietly.

Arthur put his hand protectively on her shoulder. He was angry. 'They should have told us,' he said. 'We adopted the baby in good faith . . .'

'They seemed all right,' said Freda, looking up. 'I mean the girl and her boyfriend. They were very young, just kids, still at school . . . but neither of them were crazy or anything . . . Didn't you say it was inherited?'

'Yes it is,' said Helen. 'But often it doesn't show up in previous generations because it's a Mendelian recessive.'

Arthur and Freda both looked at Jean.

'That means the parents can carry the gene without suffering from the disease,' said Jean.

'Is there any treatment? Can we do anything for him?' Freda was looking at Alan as if he'd suddenly grown another head.

'No, I don't think so.' Jean knew that she was no expert in congenital neurological diseases. 'But it's important that we get the diagnosis confirmed. We'll get you an appointment to see the neurologist in Dundee.'

'What shall we do?' asked Freda desperately, looking at Jean. 'We can't . . .'

'Let's take one step at a time, Freda,' said Jean firmly. 'When you've been to Dundee and seen the specialist, we'll sit down and go over your options, all right?'

The Muncies went off silently, Arthur carrying the baby, and Freda leaning heavily on his arm.

Jean and Helen remained standing in the examining room. Then Helen went off towards her own office, after giving Jean a strange, penetrating look. 'I don't think I'll go to the Inch today,' she said. 'I think it's time I reviewed my knowledge of congenital diseases.'

Chapter Twenty

'Aye, it's a sair fecht a' thegither,' said Doug reflectively. He was sitting on a lounge chair next to Cathie in their tiny garden, and with one corner of his mind he was enjoying the fine display of red and pink roses that grew in the far corner of the brick wall. 'I hiv three deid bodies, and I believe that it was one pairson that killed them a', but I've enough suspects to fill up the entire Perth unemployment office.'

Cathie leaned forward and picked up the tea-pot; she always knew to a second when the three-minute infusion period had elapsed.

'Well, Douglas, remember what Jean Montrose asked you that time when that Stroud mannie got burned up; who has most to gain; "Who hated him enough?" '

'Cathie, this time it's no a matter of hate — nae with the two druggies, onywye.'

'Then maybe it's hate with Graeme Ferguson and gain with the two others, or the other way around. Here's your tea . . . it's a bit full, dinna spill it.'

'For God's sake, woman!' cried Doug, hastily putting down the hot dragon-decorated china cup. 'Why can we no' use cups wi' handles? If the heathen Chinese want to burn *their* fingers, it's up to them . . .'

'The cups came free with the tea-pot,' explained Cathie patiently, 'but that was only because I ordered the tea-pot with the tea.'

Douglas stared at her.

'It's not just gain and hate, Cath,' he said after a moment. 'You have to think about things like jealousy . . .' A brief vision of the tiny-skirted Katerine McAllister flickered before him. 'Or fear of exposure, things like that . . . There's a lot of things the Wee Doc doesn't know about crime because she's never come across it.'

'Aye,' said Cathie, shaking her head, 'Nae doubt. But she makes up for that wi' her common sense, Douglas Niven, and dinna you forget it!'

'I'm going to use my old mug,' said Doug, eyeing the fragile-looking Chinese cup with suspicion. He went inside and came out with his chipped cream-coloured coronation mug. It was so old and worn that the oval-framed portraits of the Duke of Edinburgh and Queen Elizabeth were faded and barely recognizable.

'It holds a proper amount, too,' he said, filling it, 'not like them wee Chink cuppies . . .'

'Maybe it was Ian Garvie and his men that killed the two in Dunblane,' suggested Cathie darkly, just to tease him. Doug had told her about Ian's reported exploits in Miami.

'No way,' replied Doug loyally, although the thought had crossed his mind. 'Ian knows that even if they do things like that in Miami, it's no the way to do things here . . . It's no the *Scottish* way.'

'Maybe he killed Graeme Ferguson too,' went on Cathie with the faintest trace of sarcasm in her voice.

'Maybe you're right,' said Douglas, putting down his cup. 'Ian's a frustrated man, Cath. He's not getting any real results the way he has to work . . . I mean within the system . . . I think he's developed a what-d'ye-call-it, a *vendetta* against a' them druggies.'

'Douglas Niven, you know I was just joking . . . What about that broker man you were telling me about, I forget his name?'

'You mean Denis Foreman?' Douglas shook his head. 'Aye, him, and then there's Lady Strathalmond, and that feel girl of theirs, Katerine, and her father too . . . Even Marjorie Ferguson − I can't even rule her out because she was the last one to see those two men in the motel . . .

'That's what I was saying, Cath. There's just too many people that could have done it.'

'Well, Douglas,' said Cathie sensibly, 'you're just going to have to narrow them down to the one who did do it.'

She started to gather up the tea things, and put them on a gold-coloured metal tray. She grinned at him. 'And there's another suspect you forgot to mention, Doug; Mr Cole, up at the castle.'

Ilona knocked on the door of Katerine's apartment.

'Who is it?' The reply was muffled, as if Katerine had her head under the bedclothes. The sound of rock music coming from inside made the door vibrate.

'It's me,' said Ilona, keeping her voice calm, although she knew Katerine couldn't hear her over the crashing sound of bass drums. She turned the knob and opened the door. Katerine was lying on her bed; she turned on her side and crushed out the fag-end of a cigarette in an ashtray on the bedside table. The sweetish smell of marijuana hung all over the room.

Ilona came in, went over to the stereo and turned it down. The flashing lights dimmed; she went over to the bright red satin couch and sat down facing her sister.

'Mother told me about your shooting practice,' she said.

There was a long pause.

'So?' replied Katerine. Her thumb was half in her mouth and she was sitting up on her bed, watching Ilona with a faraway expression.

Ilona's lip trembled. 'Why were you shooting at a picture of me?'

Katerine giggled. It was not a nice sound. 'Like Mum said, I was practising.'

Ilona folded her hands. She knew that if she waited, Katerine would start talking because she couldn't stand silence.

'I may use a different method, actually,' said Katerine, thoughtfully. She took her wet thumb out of her mouth for a moment and looked at it.

'You see, sister dear . . .' Katerine snuggled back down on the pillows, but her eyes didn't move from her sister for one second. 'I know all about you. First you and Denis, then you and Rod, then you and Graeme. And I know exactly what you're doing and why . . .' She giggled.

Ilona's eyes opened wide, and her hand came up to her mouth.

'You weren't *ever* in love with Graeme — you just used him as a patsy, and set him up with Mother . . . He never knew it although I told him again and again, even that last evening when he was here . . .'

Ilona's eyes flashed angrily. 'If you'd stop smoking pot and do something useful with yourself, Katerine, you wouldn't get so many stupid ideas. Why don't you learn something about the estate? About animal husbandry? Plant genetics, anything?'

'And he didn't really care for you, either, not *really*.' Katerine was high as a kite, and probably hadn't even heard Ilona's words. She giggled again, quite inappropriately. 'Why didn't you see him to the door, that night, huh? *I* went to the door with him that last evening . . . Why didn't *you*? Because you'd had a fight over me, and he'd told you . . .'

Ilona went swiftly up to the edge of Katerine's bed, and Katerine moved quickly away from her.

'I was on the phone, Katerine, when he left,' said Ilona, 'and he said he'd let himself out. He laughed and said you'd probably be waiting on the stairs or by his car to catch him, as usual . . .'

'Yes I was.' Katerine's eyes were like black holes in her face, and she couldn't keep the hatred out of her voice. 'And a couple of minutes after he'd gone, when I was talking with Cole, we heard your car start up and go down the drive . . . COLE heard it too . . . That's when you went down the road to shoot him, you . . .' Katerine called her sister a foul name. Ilona gasped, and quick as a flash, hit Katerine across the face with the back of her fist, hard enough to split her lip. Katerine fell back on the bed; she wasn't wearing any underwear beneath her tiny leather skirt. Katerine put her hand up to her face and looked at the blood on her fingers. Surprisingly she started to laugh, then she started to sing, in a husky, tuneless voice, 'I did it all for you, Denis . . .'

Ilona tried not to show the disgust she felt, and was going

to say something to try to cool off the situation, but when Katerine started to laugh again, she gave up and left the apartment. The crazy sound followed Ilona down the corridor back to her apartment.

The next day was Thursday, Jean's day off. It wasn't a particularly convenient day to have off, but Helen, as senior partner had always taken Wednesday, and Tuesday was always too busy in the surgery. Jean started her preparations early in the morning, because she wasn't sure when she'd be back. Strangely enough she had wakened up again thinking about little Alan Muncie, and the terrible dilemma his adoptive parents were in. It turned out that some months before, when the Muncies were living in Aberdeen but about to be transferred to Perth, their neighbours' daughter Sarah, aged fifteen, was about to have a child, and the parents were desperate. Her boyfriend, the son of a local banker, was sixteen. Sarah was bright, and had been planning to go to law school. Early in her pregnancy, she'd talked to a nurse about an abortion, and had been told very sternly that she had no right to take the life of an unborn baby, and the message had stuck. In spite of her parents' entreaties, she decided to have the child, but agreed to have it adopted. The next-door Muncies were the perfect couple; and the fact that they were moving away helped. It was all arranged in the most friendly way; Freda Muncie was at the hospital and held Sarah's hand when the baby was born, and the Muncies took him home.

But now . . . What could they do? The outlook for the baby was miserable; he would go completely blind and would be mentally defective for the rest of his short life. He'd had his first convulsion while being examined by the neurologist in Dundee.

Jean was thinking about the few options open to the Muncies when her mind went back to her conversation with Marjorie Ferguson, and she decided that very moment how she was going to spend her day. With the kind of schedule Jean had, it meant a good deal of reorganization; she had to meet Lisbie for lunch before going to the Mall to buy some clothes for her. Lisbie was unable to decide on clothes by herself, and always went either with Fiona, who had an excellent dress sense, or with her mother who in addition had a quick eye for a bargain.

Lisbie was very silent at breakfast, and Jean worried that she was disappointed about their cancelled lunch.

'Oh, no, Mum, we can get the clothes this weekend,' Lisbie said.

Jean watched her daughter over her bowl of rice crispies, and admired the way she looked. Quite obviously there was something on her mind. Jean knew she'd hear about it soon enough; Lisbie had never been very good at keeping secrets.

'You're going to be late,' said Jean, looking up at the clock on the dining-room mantelpiece. 'My car's behind yours . . . I'll go and move it.'

Lisbie didn't finish her cornflakes, and didn't eat any toast. She gulped down her coffee and stood up, putting her napkin on the table. She was feeling excited and nervous about going to the office.

After Lisbie had gone, Jean rushed around the house, tidying up and putting clothes in the laundry hamper for Mrs Cattanach. She laughed at herself - it was really a bit silly tidying up for Mrs Cattanach, who came twice a week to do just that for her.

Finally she was ready; she brought up a cup of tea for Steven, who sat up in bed for it.

'I won't be back until this afternoon,' she said. 'Probably late. There's some haddock in the refrigerator, Lisbie knows how to make it . . .' Jean remembered that out of habit, she'd bought enough for four of them. 'Maybe Fiona'll want to come home for dinner. There's just enough if she wants to bring Robert.'

'Well,' said Steven, 'if he comes, he can have my share because I won't stay in the house.'

'Come on, now, Steven,' protested Jean, 'that's just . . .' She changed her mind and got up off the bed. There was no point starting an argument now.

Five minutes later, with the road map on the passenger's seat beside her, she set off down Argyll Crescent in her white

Renault, past the quiet semi-detached red sandstone houses
with their well-tended front gardens and tidy driveways. It was
still early and most of the cars were still there, windscreens
cloudy with dew. At the bottom of the road, Jean stopped to
allow traffic to go by, then turned left. She looked at the little
clock on the dashboard; it would take her a couple of hours
or so to get to the Abbotsford Clinic.

Chapter Twenty-one

Douglas stood opposite Malcolm Anderson in the autopsy room. Two of the four stainless steel tables were occupied by the victims of the motel shooting. On one of the other tables rested the battered body of a small child who had been struck by a milk truck while running across the road to his mother.

Douglas recognized the body in front of him; it was the red-haired man whom they'd found spreadeagled on the floor in the corner of the motel room.

'This one was close up,' said Anderson. He was wearing a long, white, rubberised apron from which the numerous bloodstains had been imperfectly and repeatedly scrubbed. He pointed to the head, picked up the shoulder furthest from him and lifted the body so that Douglas could see the entry wound at the top of the neck, just below the hairline. The man's red hair was thinning over the vertex, and the scalp showed white and waxy. In a few places, the hair was matted with blood, and was almost black. There was a thin black rim of gunpowder around the entry wound, which was small and took Doug a few moments to find.

'The body is that of a middle-aged adult male,' said Anderson, speaking into the microphone suspended above the table. He picked up one arm and lifted it. '. . . who shows a minor degree of residual post-mortem rigidity and dependent rubor consistent with the noted time of death. Distinguishing features include . . .' He paused for a moment, his eyes scanning the naked corpse. '. . . a well-healed scar in the left groin, and an absent left testicle. The distal phalanx of the right index finger is missing; the impression is of an old traumatic amputation. A small, well-healed scar measuring three centimetres in length is present below the right nipple, probably traumatic rather than surgical in origin . . . numerous freckles are noted on the back and shoulders, and several Campbell de Morgan spots are present on the abdomen . . .'

Doug listened, still fascinated after attending many autopsies on crime victims. It was quite amazing how much Anderson's trained eye picked up; sometimes he saw things that Douglas couldn't see even after Malcolm pointed them out to him.

'The face is mottled, edematous, with numerous haemorrhages and lacerations consistent with exit wounds of skull fragments . . . The right orbit is shattered, and . . .' Anderson probed the area with a pair of large forceps, '. . . the eye is missing.'

He looked over at Doug. 'Some puir housemaid's going to find that eye hanging off the ceiling lamp, back in that motel,' he said, grinning.

Doug was just able to return the grin.

While Brian Thompson, the technician, was engaged in the difficult task of opening the skull without further disturbing the contents, Malcolm Anderson and Doug went over to the next table. The body was that of an older man. 'You see the grey hairs on his chest?' asked Anderson. 'It's nae like heid hair — You dinna see grey on the chest until they're over forty-five, usually. Pubic hair goes grey even later . . .'

He tapped the microphone. 'The body is that of a middle-aged male . . .' He droned on while Douglas tried to observe all the details Anderson mentioned. This one had been shot in the middle of the chest, probably from several feet away. In the motel room, Doug had looked for burns or gunpowder fragments on his clothing, but had found none, although there was a good chance the lab would find some powder residues.

Anderson went back to the other table which held the red-haired man. 'The killer must have shot that one first,' he said. Doug had followed him. Brian had the scalp flapped forward over the face. It was meaty red on the inside, with haemorrhages and pieces of skull attached to it where he hadn't been able to separate them. 'He probably shot him from the

doorway, and then came over, made the second man, this one,
lie down and then shot him in the head . . .'

Douglas nodded. That was more or less how he had
figured it himself. Unexpectedly, he visualized a couple of
narcotics police coming in through that door . . . or maybe
just one.

'Gangland stuff, this,' Anderson was saying, 'or it could
just be somebody who watches *Miami Vice* a lot . . .' The
sound of the power saw set Doug's teeth on edge; Brian was
busy cutting through the ribs on either side of the older man's
breastbone.

'Do you think we'll get a bullet out of either of them?' asked
Douglas. 'The ballistics should be interesting . . . I'm thinking
of the Ferguson case.'

'You think it could be the same killer?'

'Could be . . . The bullets might help us to figure that out.
We didn't find any in the motel.'

'This one's all fragmented,' called Brian. He'd found a few
tiny pieces of bullet inside the chest of the older man.

'We'll X-ray both of them,' said Anderson, 'but I doubt
whether there'll be enough to give you any worthwhile ballistic
info. Sorry.'

'Well, it's not your fault, Doc,' replied Doug, getting ready
to leave. 'I'll ask the forensic lab if they can do anything with
the pieces. Meanwhile . . . I just have to go back and start
checking alibis all over again.' He paused, thinking about how
boring that was going to be, and turned back to face Anderson.
'How would you like to trade jobs for a week or two?'

Before Anderson had time to reply, Douglas looked over
at the older corpse's gaping chest, half full of dark blood and
black, jelly-like clot, with the triangular piece of breastbone
and rib ends lying where Brian had propped it up against the
side of the body, kept from sliding to the floor by the raised
edge of the stainless steel table.

'Ugh, forget it,' he said, and walked out.

Anderson grinned and shouted after him. 'It's a nice clean
red-apron job, with union wages and all benefits . . .!'

*   *   *

Sam Braithwaite sounded very uncomfortable when Doug phoned.

'No, I've been busy . . . Actually everything's straightened out . . .'

It took a certain amount of persuasion to get Sam to meet him in the upstairs lounge of the Isle of Skye Hotel, where they had met the first time. Doug got there first; he waited for ten minutes and was about to phone when Sam appeared, gangling and reluctant, and slid into the booth opposite Doug.

'What are you for?' asked Doug.

'Glen Grant, a double,' said Sam automatically, but he wasn't really paying attention. Doug got up and went to the bar and placed his order, trying to decide how to approach Sam, who was obviously regretting his previous openness about the financial manipulations that had been going on in his office.

When he came back, Sam's fingers were drumming on the table. 'Look,' he said, before Doug had a chance to sit down, 'This is a small town, and I really don't like being seen talking to a Detective Inspector . . .'

Douglas sat in the booth and raised his glass 'Slàinte mhathr,' he said in the traditional toast, correctly pronouncing it 'Slange-var'. Sam raised his glass, but didn't smile.

'What's been happening with Denis Foreman?' asked Doug. 'Last time . . .'

'That was last time,' interrupted Sam quietly, turning his glass around between his hands. 'It's all sorted out now.'

Doug sat back and waited for an explanation, but none was forthcoming. Sam stared at his drink, a stubborn expression on his face. After a minute or so, Sam raised his head. 'I have a very good job at Crossman Securities,' he said. 'And I'm getting married in a couple of months . . .' His voice trailed away. 'Also I'm in line for promotion,' he went on after a pause, 'so you can see why I don't want to rock the boat at this point in time.'

Sam seemed to have straightened out a lot of questions in his mind, Doug thought, and didn't want to look at these decisions too closely.

'Look, Graeme's dead, and there's nothing I can do that's

going to bring him back.' Sam's voice was flat, defensive. 'What I told you was going on at the office is over; I made a mistake about that. Anyway, the data's all gone, so nobody could ever prove anything . . . I've decided just to get on with my job, and put all that behind me. Denis Foreman is a great boss, and not involved in anything illegal . . .' Sam stared stubbornly at Doug.

Slowly, Doug got up from his seat. 'Sam,' he said, 'if you can live with yourself, if you can condone the kind of scam you told me about the last time we were here, I'm disappointed and sorry for you as a human being. Do you realize there may be murders involved here too?'

Sam laughed, a strained, harsh laugh. 'You're all wrong there, Inspector, if you think Denis was involved in that. The day those two men were killed, Denis and I went down to London for a seminar. We took the nine a.m. plane from Edinburgh and didn't get back until late that night. You can check it out . . .'

Doug sounded more upset than he felt; he'd never really expected that anything would come from Sam, and in every investigation like this there were bound to be a number of dead ends. Sam was just another amoral Thatcherite yuppie, the kind that was so common these days, lacking any kind of social or personal conscience. All they cared about was making a lot of money as fast as they could, and to hell with everything and everybody else.

Outside the hotel, Doug saw Sam's blue BMW parked next to his undistinguished department vehicle, and felt a strong urge to scrape his car key along the BMW's shiny length.

Anyway, as Sam had so rightly said, Perth was a small town, and that worked both ways. Sam had better not get caught parking in the wrong place . . . An idea struck Douglas as he unlocked his car. Sam was still in there, he always drank doubles, and he'd already had two . . . Driving out of the parking lot, Doug called the police dispatcher on his radio. There might be a DWI coming out of the Isle of Skye hotel soon, he told him, driving a dark blue BMW, registration number F64 7RP . . . With a sense of grim satisfaction, Doug headed back towards the station. His colleagues on the uniform side knew him well, and a nod was as good as a wink any time.

'Come in, and close the door, Elizabeth.'

Roderick Ferguson was feeling very pleased with himself; he had gone out the night before with Katerine, and on the basis of that heady experience, he'd decided to ask Bill McDonald of the election committee if she could work as a trainee with his publicity manager. At this point Roderick felt sure Bill McDonald would be the local candidate, and Bill McDonald, who made all the decisions, would be delighted to have a representative of the nobility on the team.

So at this point everything was going as well as it possibly could for Roderick, and now he even had Elizabeth as an additional source of fun and games. He watched her turn and close the door. She had both hands full of the papers she was bringing in, and had to push the door closed with a swing of her hips. The movement, trivial though it was, excited Roderick enormously; Elizabeth had a really nice shape, and when she came back towards the desk with the papers, he made a motion indicating that she should bring them round to his side of the desk.

'Now, let's take a look at those,' he said. His hand came casually round her waist. Elizabeth tensed for a second but didn't move away. 'The letter to Parkins and Snell, where is that?' His murmured voice told her that he couldn't care less where the letter was, but she searched through the pile. Roderick's hand slid down to the roundness of her hips, and stayed there for a few moments, without eliciting any resistance.

'Oh, Elizabeth,' he murmured, 'I don't know what it is you do to me . . .'

Elizabeth, feeling excited and embarrassed at the same time, smiled shyly. She couldn't get over how nice Mr Ferguson was being to her, especially as she'd only been working for him for a few weeks.

Roderick pulled her a bit closer to him, and smiled up at

her. He was really good-looking and sexy, she thought, and so strong and decisive about everything . . .

'I don't know if I should be getting so attached to someone who works for me . . .' said Roderick, beginning to breathe a little faster. 'But there's something about you, Elizabeth, that turns me on totally.'

'I'm sure you say that to all the girls,' murmured Elizabeth, not thinking for a moment that he would. He was far too nice, far too much of a gentleman.

'Oh, no, I swear . . .' Roderick turned his chair and pulled Elizabeth down on to his knee. He had unbuttoned the top button of her blouse when the phone rang again in the outer office.

Chapter Twenty-two

Jean Montrose, admittedly not the best map-reader in the world lost her way a couple of times but after getting instructions at an Esso station five miles out of Edinburgh, she finally found her way to the Abbotsford Clinic. It was about ten miles south of the Edinburgh city limits, off the A702 on a quiet country road, with the misty grey-blue Pentland Hills sloping gently up in the distance. The clinic had evidently once been a country house, and had been converted, maybe during the war, when many big country houses were used as convalescent centres. Jean drove slowly through the open gates and along a dusty drive. There were a number of grey-white prefabricated one-storey buildings on each side of the drive, giving the place the look of run-down military barracks. The main house was flat-fronted, built of great blocks of yellowish sandstone, flaking in parts on the façade. Jean drove into the dusty parking area in front of the building and left her car in one of the two visitors' spaces. So far she had seen nobody, and walked across the gravel towards the entrance. There was a white sign with red lettering that said MAIN RECEPTION, and Jean went up the three wide steps and through a glass swing door. Inside was a foyer with large black and white square tiles and, opposite the door, a wood-panelled booth with a glass front. It was unoccupied. Jean went up and knocked on the glass, and after a few moments, an inner door opened, and a woman came out, pink faced, with small, watery eyes and untidy short white hair. She was wearing a grey dress with a tiny floral pattern; it almost reached her feet.

'My name's Jean Montrose,' said Jean. 'I called your Dr Patel this morning about a patient here. He's expecting me.'

'Name?'

'Jean Montrose,' repeated Jean. 'Doctor Jean Montrose.'

'Oh, I'm sorry, Doctor,' replied the woman. 'I'll get him right away.'

Dr Patel was short, straight-backed, with big dark eyes and abundant glossy black hair swept back in a high bouffant style. He was dressed in a blue suit, with the shiniest black shoes Jean had ever seen. He marched smartly across the tiled floor and stopped several feet away from Jean, put his hands together and bowed.

'So pleased to welcome you to the Abbotsford Clinic, Doctor,' he said, sounding very formal. 'May I invite you to partake of tea?'

Jean smiled her nicest smile. 'No, thank you very much, Dr Patel, not now, but perhaps we could sit down for a few minutes after we've seen the patient?'

'Of course. Mr Ferguson is exercising in the garden at the present time, if you will follow me . . .'

He turned and marched towards the corridor he had come from, and Jean hurried after him. They went down a long bleak corridor past the doors of the administrative offices, then made a right-angled turn to the left up to a glass-fronted door that led outside. Dr Patel opened the door and stood aside to let Jean past. Outside, in the grounds behind the main building, the sun was bright and hazy, and Jean scrunched up her eyes in the glare. There were maybe a couple of dozen patients scattered around, some sitting on benches, a few in wheelchairs, some just standing, looking over a low wall at the straggly flower beds. The whole impression was as if the scene had been staged; there was an aura of stillness all around, as if life had slowed almost to stopping point. The people on the benches, both men and women, stared, immobile, into the distance, and Jean was uncomfortably reminded of the scene in *The Sleeping Beauty* where all the court retainers were frozen in suspended animation.

'He's over here,' said Dr Patel leading the way along a wide path towards a group of three wheelchairs lined up together, facing the house.

'Mr Ferguson, you have a visitor,' said Dr Patel bending over the nearest chair and speaking loudly. The man in the wheelchair, was gaunt, grey-faced, with irregular patches of stubble on his face. His hair was grey, long and looked as if it had been cut by someone without any training.

'Good morning, Mr Ferguson,' said Jean, facing him. Mr Ferguson's blank expression didn't change, and he didn't seem to notice her presence. A large blanket was wrapped around his knees, and his long hands lay on top of it. Every few moments, he moved his hands in a jerky, sudden fashion. Then, with what seemed to be a great effort, he focused on Jean's face and drew his lips back in a snarl that surprised and shocked Jean. She stepped back, and Mr Ferguson, in sudden excitement, tried to get out of his wheelchair, but fortunately he was tied in and after a few moments of struggling, he relaxed, and seemed to collapse back into it. He resumed his apathetic stare. Jean tried again to converse with him, but without any success.

She turned to Dr Patel. 'Does his family ever come to visit him?' she asked. Maybe Mr Ferguson did better with someone he recognized.

'Never,' replied Patel in his clipped, sing-song voice. 'He had a sister who used to come, but she stopped visiting several years ago.'

'Maybe this would be a good time for that cup of tea,' smiled Jean, taking a last look at Mr Ferguson. She tried to imagine what he must have looked like on his wedding day, young, all dressed up in a morning coat and smiling, with Marjorie hanging happily on to his arm . . . Her mind boggled with the effort.

'Of course. We shall have tea.' Dr Patel marched off down the path, looking neither to right nor to left, and Jean followed after him. Dr Patel paused to speak to the woman in the reception booth, then led Jean into a small room opposite. It was used for consultations, he informed her, and they sat down there. The white-haired woman brought in a tray with tea and biscuits and placed it in front of them on the low table.

'A very sad situation, Mr Ferguson,' said Dr Patel putting

together the palms of his hands. 'Which demonstrates to us all the ravages of alcohol on the human frame.' Jean had the impression that he had used that phrase many times before.

'Is he on medication?' asked Jean gently. Without asking, she poured tea for both of them. He took neither milk nor sugar, and held his cup very gracefully, with his little finger extended.

'Nearly all our patients are on medication,' Dr Patel replied.

'That must make them much easier to deal with,' said Jean. but Dr Patel missed the irony.

'Yes, indeed,' he replied. 'Otherwise we'd never get staff to stay.'

'To come back to Mr Ferguson,' said Jean, suppressing her dismay, 'was he more or less like this when he first came here?'

'I wasn't here at the time, Dr Montrose, but I understand from his chart that he was very agitated, with episodes of acute excitement, for which he needed restraint and medication. He was given sodium amytal initially for the acute phase, then was maintained on paraldehyde. That's how we used to treat most of our chronic brain-damaged alcoholics when they first come in.'

'Yes, of course,' said Jean, sipping her tea. 'Is that what most of your patients are suffering from?'

'Yes.' Dr Patel smiled, a rather prim smile, and recrossed his legs, keeping his knees neatly together. 'We have some chronic schizophrenics, some are mentally retarded, others recovering from nervous breakdowns, but, yes, the majority are indeed suffering from the ravages of alcoholism.'

Jean put down her cup. 'Well, thank you so much for letting me see Mr Ferguson,' she said. 'I hope I didn't take up too much of your time.'

Dr Patel stood up and put his heels together. 'Of course not. Mr Ferguson seems to be very popular these days, actually. Last week there was a Dr Beaumont came out to see him, from Edinburgh, I think, and now your own good self . . .'

Dr Patel accompanied Jean to the main door. 'Well, Doctor Montrose, it was truly a pleasure to have the opportunity to welcome you to the Abbotsford Clinic . . .' He came out and stood on the steps, very erect and formal, and watched until Jean had driven off.

On the way home, Jean put a cassette into the player, a new recording of Vaughan Willams' 'Fantasia on a Theme by Thomas Tallis', but her mind was not on the sweeping, evocative music. She hated having to go to psychiatric institutions, and they always left her with a heavy sense of guilt and sadness. How many people, she wondered, were condemned to live out their lives in these awful inhuman places, medicated, drugged out of their minds so that the attendants wouldn't have too much trouble dealing with them? And of course the general public, if it was interested at all in the fate of its most unfortunate members, only had the vaguest idea of what these places were really like, and what went on there.

Jean had some other business to do in Edinburgh, and as usual took the opportunity to look in at the medical library and take out some books before returning to Perth, so it was late afternoon by the time she drove back up Argyll Crescent. Fiona's car was parked outside the house, and Jean smiled sympathetically. Poor Fiona; living by herself apparently wasn't turning out to be quite as wonderful as she'd expected; she went to work every day, and came home to a house that was clean only if she'd cleaned it, tidy only if she'd done the dishes and made her bed. Not only that, but Fiona was basically a social person who had always depended on her family's support.

Fiona heard Jean's car and came running out to meet her. 'Would you help me take in those books?' said Jean, pointing to the back seat; she wanted to make sure she treated Fiona just as she always had, and not as a visitor to the house.

She looked at Fiona walking back into the house in front of her, and tried to dismiss the worry she felt. Her daughter, normally slim and pretty, had lost a little weight, and there wasn't the usual vivacity and sparkle in her walk.

When the phone in Roderick Ferguson's outer office rang, Elizabeth broke away to answer it. To her, Roderick, a partner in the firm, had always had Olympian status, and the thought that he might be interested in her as a person, and not just as a secretary, made her feel quite breathless. Her hand was not entirely steady when she put the call through to Roderick.

'It's Mr McDonald again, from the election committee . . .'

Roderick smiled quickly at her through the open doorway and grabbed the phone. Elizabeth watched his face as the pleasure spread across it. She felt so happy that things were finally going better for him; he'd been so sad and upset when his brother had been killed.

'Ah, yes, Bill . . .' Roderick was saying. He sat straight up in his chair 'Yes, thank you . . .'

This time, Bill's voice was quite different from the hectoring tone he'd employed when he'd come to see him in the office; now he sounded genuinely friendly, almost deferential.

'The death of those two drug dealers will do you no harm,' he was saying, 'no harm at all. In fact, you'll gain from it. It shows that here in Perthshire we're not about to tolerate people like that.'

Roderick tried to interrupt, but Bill went on. He was used to rolling right over interruptions. 'I don't know the whys or the wherefores of what happened in Dunblane,' he said, 'and I don't want to. The fact is that the public is tired of the drug problem, and they welcome the deaths of people like that. And certainly from the point of view of your own involvement, you are now looking as clean as Mother's laundry. Congratulations; we're having a meeting of the election committee at the end of the week, and I confidently predict there'll be some good news for you after that.'

'Thank you, Bill . . . I must say . . . Yes, thank you indeed.' He glanced at Elizabeth standing in the doorway, and decided that this was not the moment to talk to Bill about Katerine.

When he put down the phone, Elizabeth could see that Roderick's face was flushed with delight, and she came into the room, smiling and feeling very tender and proud at his obvious pleasure.

'What is it the other girls call you?' he asked when Elizabeth

came back into the office, and he put his hand on her hip again.
'Don't they have some kind of . . . pet name for you?'

'Oh, everybody calls me Lisbie,' replied Elizabeth. 'Except
you . . .' She moved abruptly; Roderick was getting very bold.
'I *like* it when you call me Elizabeth.'

Chapter Twenty-three

The killing of the two men in the motel had attracted more than local attention; probably, they said around police headquarters, because they were simultaneous. 'Can you imagine the uproar if there had been three of them?' grumbled Douglas, sitting in his office.

'I wish there had,' replied Ian Garvie. 'Or even better, a round dozen of the buggers.'

Douglas was feeling hugely relieved because the nagging doubt about Garvie's possible involvement in the deaths had been disposed of once and for all. And that was thanks to the attention the national press had given to the double murder.

Two days after the momentous events in Dunblane, a long distance call from Carlisle had been put through to Douglas, who picked it up in his office.

'I'm looking at today's *Daily Express*,' said the voice. 'There's a photo on page three of the Travellers' Motel in Dunblane . . .'

'Would you give me your name, sir?' asked Doug, and at that moment the phone made a single beep, indicating that the call was being made from a phone booth, and in ten seconds he'd be cut off unless more money was put in.

'I was there, leaving the motel . . . Oh dear, I don't have any more change . . .'

'Give me your number to call you back, sir,' said Doug quickly, but at that moment the call was terminated.

'Damn!' said Doug, looking at the receiver. It had sounded as if the man might have something interesting to tell him.

Five minutes later the phone rang again. The caller was back on.

'Before you say anything else, sir, please give me the number you're at, in case we get cut off again.' Douglas's voice was cool and even he'd learned years ago that the more important the occasion, the more important it was to remain calm and in control.

'I was at that motel,' said the voice, after giving the number, 'And I almost got killed there.'

Douglas said nothing, but held on tightly to the phone. Constable Jamieson came in and started to say something, and Doug angrily waved his free hand at him to shut him up.

'Not by getting shot . . .' went on the voice. His voice was deep, and Doug thought he sounded like an actor or a radio announcer. 'I was crossing the parking area to get to my car, and a car came barrelling down between the rows and I just had time to get out of the way.'

'About what time was that, sir? And if you could give me your name . . .'

'Rick Archibald. It was about three fifteen . . . I had to get to Carlisle that evening early, so I was leaving. I got a good look at the car, but I didn't get the licence number because I had to dive between two cars. It turned the corner and was gone before . . .'

Three fifteen — that was ten minutes after Marjorie Ferguson had delivered the money.

'What kind of car was it, sir?'

'It was a Jaguar, a Sovereign, maybe a year old, very clean, silver with red upholstery . . . There was an AA and an RAC badge on the front, and two oblong fog lights with black and white chequered covers . . . Oh, and the front right tyre had a thin white sidewall,' he went on. 'I didn't see the left side.'

'Not bad observation for someone who's diving for his life out of the way,' said Doug, suddenly suspicious.

'Well, Inspector, I happen to be a police artist with the Northumberland force. I'm trained to pay attention to details, and I have a pretty good memory . . .'

'Did you get a view of the driver? Even a glimpse?'

There was a pause, and Doug worried they might be cut off again. 'It was a man,' he said, 'that's about all I can tell you.'

'Could you recognize him?' persisted Doug. 'Look, let me call you back . . .'

Doug did call Rick Archibald back, and got him to agree to make a formal statement at the Carlisle police headquarters; they would fax a copy on to him. Meanwhile, Doug got Archibald to agree to travel back to Perth if necessary, to identify the vehicle and look at photos, but Rick wasn't anxious to come back. His ex-wife lived in Dunblane, and the only reason he'd gone there was to see his lawyer.

Douglas put out a bulletin describing the Jaguar, and had it sent around, but he knew that the likelihood of tracing it was slender; it was probably a stolen vehicle which would either be found abandoned, or resprayed and sold through one of the stolen-car organizations.

'I hear from our people in Glasgow that the drug network down there is seriously concerned about those two men,' said Ian Garvie, stretching out his muscular legs. 'Apparently it wasn't done from within the system.'

'Are there any local Dunblane or Perth operators who would have got upset having those men in their territory?' asked Doug.

'How would they know? They were just passing through. They weren't trying to do any business there . . .'

Douglas scratched his ear. 'I'm trying to get a tie-in with the Ferguson killing,' he said, 'but the only thing I can find in common is that they were both probably done with .38 automatics.'

Ian shrugged. 'Big deal,' he said. 'That's like saying two people are both German because they've got blond hair.'

There was an aura of perpetually suppressed anger about the man, thought Doug. Being in the drug task force must be a thoroughly frustrating job, even worse than his. The druggies were smart, ruthless, well organized, had plenty of money, didn't have to abide by any rules, and didn't have to waste their time filing incident reports or pacifying cynical and unfriendly media.

'Who knew they were there?' said Ian. 'Apart from Mother Ferguson, of course.'

'Maybe she told somebody . . .'

'Her son, possibly.'

'Do you know if anybody else was after them, Ian? If some of the Glasgow boys wanted to eliminate them, it would be maybe tidier to do it outside their own territory.'

'It's certainly possible. I've asked our people to check on that, but so far there's no hint of internal trouble involving them.'

Ian stood up. 'I have to go. I'll tell you if anything more comes through on the wire. Meanwhile don't take any wooden nickels.'

Doug stared at him.

'It's an American expression,' said Ian. 'It means don't let anybody fool you.'

'Awa you go,' retorted Doug. 'I hope you're nae as feel as you're ugly-looking.'

As soon as Ian had gone, Doug sat back and thought about who else might have known of the two men's presence in the Travellers' Motel. Whoever it was must have been told by Marjorie Ferguson, unless somebody from their end had followed them up from Glasgow . . . That was certainly possible, considering the amount of money involved. But the money had been left there in full view on the table, untouched.

Roderick Ferguson . . . His mother might easily have told him that she was going to Dunblane, and he could have followed her down, but Doug knew he'd have to be very careful with him. After all, Roderick wasn't just a local lawyer, which would have been bad enough, but very likely to become an official candidate for Parliament.

The phone rang; it was Malcolm Anderson to tell him that each man had been killed with a single bullet, and that both bullets had struck bone and fragmented. They were sending the pieces in a sealed container to the forensic lab in Dundee.

'We got all the bits, I think,' said Anderson, 'so they should be able to tell you the calibre and the type of round, but that's about all. They won't tell you what weapon was used, or even if it was the same one that killed the Ferguson boy,' said

Anderson. 'And by the bye, while I'm on the phone, do you want to play a round of golf this afternoon?'

'Thanks, but some of us have work to do,' replied Doug. 'Anyway you know I don't play golf.'

'Aye, I ken that fine,' said Anderson, with a short laugh. 'I was just rubbing it in, what a fine job I have.'

That evening, dinner at the Montroses was almost like the old days; Steven in particular was quietly delighted to have Fiona back, even if it was only for a meal. Fiona had brought her laundry and put it in the washer; she had no facilities in her cottage except for the kitchen sink.

At the end of dinner, Fiona asked Jean if she could stay over in her old room. 'If it isn't already being used for something . . .' Fiona always tended to make a drama out of things, and brought tears to her own eyes with her question.

'No you can't,' chipped in Lisbie, her eyes big. 'We're using it as a storeroom now, and it's full of stuff.'

Shocked, Fiona raised her eyes to her mother who was smiling at her. 'She's teasing you,' said Jean. 'Of course you can stay. As long as you like . . .'

Normally at this point Fiona would have grabbed something off the table and hurled it at her sister, and out of habit Jean quickly scanned the table in front of Fiona to pre-empt any assault. But Fiona didn't move; her expression didn't even change, but the tears receded back into her eyes.

It wasn't just Lisbie who was having problems, there was something going on with Fiona too, Jean was sure of it. And if she followed her usual pattern, she'd first talk it over and straighten it out in her own mind with Lisbie, and then in the fullness of time, she'd come and talk about whatever it was with her and Steven.

Today the girls decided to do the clearing and the washing up together, so their parents went into the living room, Steven to watch TV and Jean to catch up with the medical reading she needed to do.

Fiona took over the organization of the task as if she'd never been away. 'You put the dishes on the trolley, and I'll put away the inside things,' she said. Lisbie, as usual, was quite content to do as she was told.

There was hardly enough room in the narrow kitchen for both of them, so Fiona stood in the doorway and passed the dishes in to Lisbie who started to wash them.

'Aren't you going to put in some soap?' Fiona eyed her sister.

'Oh, I forgot,' said Lisbie, reaching for the plastic container of dishwashing fluid. She squirted a long, white jet into the water running into the sink, making it foam up. 'It's funny, having you back.'

'Can you reach me a dishtowel,' asked Fiona. 'And put the dishes over here where I can get to them.'

Without saying anything, they both automatically checked for the sound of the TV on the other side of the hatch which opened into the living room. It was quite loud enough to ensure they wouldn't be overheard.

Fiona opened the conversation. 'I hear something about you and that Roderick Ferguson,' she said. 'I hope it's not true because everybody says he's a slimeball.'

'He is NOT!' replied Lisbie, blushing bright red. 'He's a really nice man, and anyway we're not . . .' Lisbie turned her head so that Fiona wouldn't see her embarrassment.

'You're not WHAT?' asked Fiona loudly after a long pause. 'You've gone back to not finishing your sentences again.'

'We're not . . . anything,' mumbled Lisbie. 'Anyway, why don't we talk about you for a change?'

'Not just yet, we don't,' said Fiona grimly. 'How old is he?'

'A bit over thirty, I suppose,' said Lisbie, knowing what was coming.

'Thirty!!! God almighty, girl, what is it with you? You go from Neil Mackay who was just a boy at school, straight to this al' manny . . .'

'He's no an al' manny,' retorted Lisbie. 'And he's a very *young* thirty, well, thirty – something . . . And anyway he's really very nice,' she went on, vigorously scrubbing the dishes in a circular motion. 'And he's going to take me to dinner and the theatre in Edinburgh on Friday, so there!'

'Have you told Mum?'

'No, and I'm not going to, either,' replied Lisbie defiantly. 'It's nobody's business except mine . . .' her expression softened, '. . . and Roderick's.'

'You make me sick,' said Fiona loudly, watching her. 'He is BAD NEWS, everybody says so. Are you listening to me?'

The sliding door of the hatch opened and Steven's face appeared. 'Everything all right?' he asked, his eyes going from Lisbie to Fiona.

'Fine, Dad,' said Fiona. 'D'you want to help?' She took a dishtowel off the hook and held it out to him. The hatch closed.

'Now we've talked about me, we can talk about you,' said Lisbie.

'Wait till we get downstairs,' replied Fiona, her voice becoming very quiet.

They put away the dishes and wiped the counter and Lisbie found that the cat's dish hadn't been washed, so she did that, and then they were done.

Fiona opened the door to the basement and led the way down the stairs, feeling more and more scared as she thought about her problem.

The bed was unmade, but it only took a minute for the two of them to get the place looking like its old self, except for the posters, which she had taken to the cottage with her when she moved.

Fiona lay back on the bed, looking sad. Lisbie sat cross-legged on the floor looking up at her sister and waited.

'I've just had the worst few days of my life,' Fiona blurted out, and the tears came back into her eyes. 'I thought I was pregnant, and I don't think I love Robert any more.'

Lisbie's eyes grew big and she put a finger up to her lower lip.

'Oh my,' she said. 'What are you going to do?'

Fiona sat up. 'It was just awful, because the first night I was there in the cottage, he slept with me . . .'

Lisbie's eyes went to the floor. This was really embarrassing stuff.

'. . . I spent the whole night awake, because, well, it hadn't

been great, you know, and it's the most uncomfortable thing
trying to sleep with somebody else there. You can't turn, and
you can only stretch out in one direction.'

Lisbie started to pick at a piece of cuticle on her thumb.
She felt really out of her depth with Fiona talking about this
kind of thing.

'And his parents gave him hell for staying out all night . . .
Although he's certainly not a child any more either. They said
that if he wanted to do that sort of thing he'd have to move
out.'

'What about . . .' Lisbie choked on the words, '. . . being
pregnant?'

'Oh . . .' Fiona fell back on the bed again. 'Well, you know
my period's always right on time, practically down to the hour.
I hadn't even been thinking about it, then suddenly I realized
it hadn't come. I checked the calendar just to be sure . . . it
was a day late, and no sign of anything . . .'

'Hadn't Robert . . .' Lisbie blushed again, and looked at
the floor.

'Hadn't he WHAT?'

'Well, hadn't he used anything . . .?' Lisbie was mortified
to be asking her own sister about such things.

'Well, no. I suppose there wasn't time . . .' Fiona grinned
briefly.

'So what happened?'

'Well, it was four whole days late. I thought I was going
to croak. Can you imagine how Dad would have reacted, if
I came home and said, Hey, Dad, guess what? I'm going to
have a baby!'

'Well, you could have got . . .' Lisbie's voice faded.

'An abortion?'

Lisbie nodded.

'Well, for one thing that costs money, and I'm broke, with
the cottage and everything. Mum would have lent me the
money, I know that, but she'd also have told Dad . . .'

'Why should you have to pay?' asked Lisbie. 'Isn't that why
we have a National Health?'

'The waiting list for abortions is over a year, now,' said

Fiona. She waited for Lisbie's reaction to her joke, but Lisbie just said it would be terrible to have to wait that long.

'You *can't* wait that long for an abortion, you dummy!' shouted Fiona.

'Oh,' said Lisbie after a pause. 'Oh . . . I see what you mean. But still, you could have had one, even if Mum had told Dad about it. In this day and age . . .'

'Yeah, sure. You tell that to Dad.'

'But you're getting married anyway,' said Lisbie, puzzled. 'You could just have been a bit . . . premature, right?'

'Oh Lisbie, that's really the worst of it. You see, he loves me, and all he talks about is what we'll do when we're married . . . But now I'm not sure . . . And it's supposed to be in just six weeks . . .'

'Why don't you put it off for a while to think about it?'

'I can't . . . He'd be too upset. And you know how nice he is about everything, I just couldn't bear to. And anyway, I suppose I really love him, maybe . . .'

Fiona turned face down on the bed. Lisbie came over and stroked Fiona's hair and gently rubbed the back of her neck and shoulders. She felt awkward and totally distressed; Fiona had always been the decisive one, always knew what to do, and was never unsure about anything. And now, here she was, having made all kinds of decisions that led only in one direction, and suddenly she wasn't sure if she was doing the right thing.

'Well, Fiona,' she said softly, admiring the cut of Fiona's hair, 'I'm not sure if I'm doing the right thing either.'

Chapter Twenty-four

Next morning, Jean was in even more of a rush than usual, and she had a whole lot of unscheduled things to do in addition to her normal work. There was a meeting with the Muncies and the social service lady to arrange for the institutional care of their baby Alan, whose condition was deteriorating. And then she had the well-baby clinic, which had originally been shared between Helen and herself, but was gradually taken over by mutual agreement by Jean, because she really liked it and the young mothers felt very comfortable with her.

'You've had a couple of kids yourself,' Helen said in her brusque way. 'I can deworm puppies, but that's where my genuine interest in paediatrics ends.'

Jean looked at the list of phone calls she had to make; Helen and she had long ago agreed to make a formal log of their phone calls, especially long-distance ones, and Jean had tried, but, somehow with her, the numbers always landed up on the backs of envelopes and rarely made it to the notebook Eleanor kept for that purpose, so at the end of each month, Jean had to rake around in her handbag for the pieces of paper, many of which had additional information such as quick recipes or shopping lists.

Dr Beaumont . . . she might as well start with him. Jean found his number in the registry of specialists, and fortunately caught him just before he went to do rounds at the hospital. While she was talking to him, she had to put a finger in her other ear to drown out the noise of the babies and their mothers in the adjoining waiting room.

Eleanor came in just as she put the phone down, bringing a cup of tea and two digestive biscuits. 'There's fourteen of them out there,' she said in a reproving tone, as if Jean should be already half-way through the clinic.

Jean's next call was to Roderick Ferguson, and he answered the phone himself. Jean, who had expected to talk to Lisbie first, had to swallow a mouthful of biscuit rather quickly, but when he heard what she had to say he promised to come in that afternoon.

'I'll just need a few minutes of your time, Roderick,' said Jean, trying to sound as businesslike as possible. She nodded with mild irritation at Eleanor who had again poked her head through the doorway.

Eleanor went back to her desk. She had heard on the grapevine that there was something going on between Lisbie Montrose and Roderick Ferguson, who although an up-and-coming lawyer and politician, was not too highly thought of in some circles in town, and was considered a rather dangerous womanizer. And he was so much older than the impressionable Lisbie . . . Good for Jean, she thought. He needs to be told by someone like her.

Douglas Niven decided to go home for lunch; he was feeling irritable and swamped by all the possibilities in the Ferguson case, now compounded by the deaths of the two drug dealers. His boss, Bob McLeod, had told him, after they'd discussed the entire problem, to treat them as one case. Doug was also instructed to liaise closely with the Drugs Task Force, which suited Douglas just fine. They had more facilities and more leeway; he could at least try to get some of the travel and communications costs on to their budget.

He called home before leaving the office, and decided to walk, as it was a clear day, and crisp for the time of year.

He pushed the bar on the door that led to the back yard of the station, where the police garage and storage area were. Steve Webb, the garage foreman, was looking under the bonnet of one of the patrol cars, and straightened up when he saw Doug coming towards him.

'You still want to buy that Porsche?' Steve pointed with his thumb at the crumpled red vehicle sitting in the car pound, lined up with four other traffic casualties on the other side of the chain-link fence. 'The insurance man was here yesterday, says it's a write-off. He'd let you have it for not much . . .'

Doug stared at the car. It was back on its four wheels again, and apart from the crushed top and some deep scrapes in the bodywork, was looking pretty good. But Doug was wishing the metal could talk, that it could tell him what had happened in the minutes after it hit the oil patch, skidded off the road, turned over, and slid into the undergrowth.

'Aye, it's a real fine vehicle,' he said finally. 'But what would everybody think, if a poor Detective Inspector like me was to drive around in that kind of a car? They'd say I was on the take, right?'

'Well, my lad, there's no chance of people thinking that with that old Austin you drive,' grinned Steve. 'In fact, it gives the force a bad name. Everybody thinks you bribe the MOT man to get your certificate.'

'I'll tell you what,' said Doug. 'I'll just get one of those bumper stickers that says "My other car is a Porsche" and put that on the back of the Austin, OK?'

They both laughed, and Doug went on his way, feeling less grumpy.

For no more reason than it was a fine day and he needed to stretch his legs, Doug decided to go the long way home and take a stroll along the river bank. He turned the corner and walked down Atholl Street, busy with lunchtime traffic. At Rose Street he crossed over to walk along the edge of the North Inch park, and left the pavement to walk on the grass. It was nice not to hear the sound of one's feet all the time . . . Just ahead of him was the statue of Prince Albert, as always covered with streaky white tributes from his loyal pigeons, and just as Doug was about to turn left before the bridge to join the riverside path, he happened to look across the road. There was the group of offices, set back by a small cobbled courtyard. On the left was Crossman Securities, where Graeme had worked, and where Denis Foreman and Sam Braithwaite still were. Next door was Roderick Ferguson's office, and Doug recognized Lisbie Montrose's little Morris Minor parked in front of the nearest house; he knew the car well from all the times he'd been up at the Montrose's house.

Doug stopped suddenly, and a woman pushing a pram ran into him from behind. He barely heard her apologies; next to Lisbie's car was a new Jaguar, silver in colour. And through the back window, he could see that it had red leather upholstery.

Fog lights, he thought, fog lights with chequered black-and-white covers, and a whitewall tyre on the right . . . Doug crossed the road at an angle, as if he were heading for the museum. He turned right down North Street; from there he could get a look at the front of the car over the low wall.

Sure enough, it had the two covered fog lights, the thin white stripe on the right front tyre, plus the AA and RAC badges that Rick Archibald, the police artist, had described so well.

About half an hour later, long after Doug had continued on his way, the door of the office opened, and Roderick Ferguson came out, taking a set of car keys out of his pocket. He was dressed very nattily in a lightweight grey pinstripe suit and looked every inch the successful lawyer and potential Member of Parliament. He got into his Jaguar, backed out of the parking space and turned to head for Jean Montrose's surgery.

Eleanor looked curiously at him as she showed him into Jean's office. He was certainly a good-looking man; no wonder Lisbie had become interested in him. Well, by the time Jean Montrose had finished with him he wouldn't be looking so smug.

And in fact, fifteen minutes later, when he emerged from her office, Roderick was looking far from smug. His face was quite pale and dejected-looking and he went straight out the door without even answering Eleanor's polite goodbye.

By five p.m. Jean was finished with her work, and felt a great wave of tiredness sweep over her as soon as the last patient had gone out through the door. She sat there, tired to the bone, feeling every muscle in her body sagging with exhaustion. What a day! She heard Helen's door slam, and then she came in, holding a piece of paper in her hand, and flopped down in the patient's chair.

'My God,' said Helen, echoing Jean's thoughts, 'what a day!' She gazed at Jean for a moment. 'You look pooped yourself, my girl.' She took a deep breath and smacked the paper down on Jean's desk. 'Take a look at that,' she said grimly, 'and see if it doesn't make your bowels twist and groan.'

The letter was a computer-generated missive from the local Health Board; it informed them that their practice had a higher than average prescription rate, as judged by the weighted average of similar medical practices, and their per capita costs were 11.35 per cent higher than a statistical analysis had predicted. If these costs were not brought down within the next fiscal accounting period, the letter went on, the principals might be held liable for the additional costs, which would be automatically withdrawn from their remuneration.

'I don't believe it,' said Jean. 'I know that you don't overprescribe, and you know that I don't.'

'I think I know what it is,' said Helen slowly. 'I have three patients on home dialysis, and we both have a few patients who have to be kept on high doses of chemotherapy. That's what's skewing our costs, I'm sure.'

'What do they want us to do? Let them die?' Jean's tiredness made her more angry than she normally would have been. 'Those bureaucrats, what do they know about medicine or taking care of patients? You know, Helen, I'm so tired of being bossed around by those people, told how to practise medicine by folk who don't know the first thing about it. All they know is how to read balance sheets, and I'm telling you, Helen, I've just about had enough of it. Steven makes plenty for all of us . . .'

'Now, Jean, take it easy.' Helen had always been better at dealing with administrative problems of this sort than Jean; she was able to approach it with detachment, as just another aspect of the practice which had to be dealt with, in exactly the same careful way as the clinical problems.

'I'll just write them a letter explaining the situation,' she said placidly. 'It probably won't make any difference, and they'll send down a couple of highly paid inspectors who can barely read and write, and *they*'ll threaten to close us down, and then we'll hear no more about it because a couple of months from now they'll have had a change in policy. It's all part of the way we have to practise medicine these days.'

Jean glowered. 'Well, I think it's a disgrace. If only they'd have the sense to fire all those useless people, those health parasites, and let us get on with our job, it would be better and cheaper for everybody, particularly our patients.'

'Health Parasites! Jean, I really like that term. I'll start my letter, "Dear Health Parasite . . ." '

'Then we'd both be out of a job' replied Jean, smiling, then her anger flared again. 'How is it that in Maggie Thatcher's capitalist society, we have a Communist health service, run by a bunch of ignorant Commissars?'

Helen eyed her partner and grinned. 'It's getting to be Valium time, my dear . . . Jean, why don't you take the rest of the afternoon off and go home?'

Jean looked at her watch, which showed almost six o'clock in the evening.

She stood up. 'Helen,' she said with quiet emphasis, 'you can take your afternoon off, and you can shove it in your ear.' Then she went out, picking up her cardboard box full of records and letters; she would be working on these until late that night.

Chapter Twenty-five

Jean stopped at Marks and Spencer's on the way home to buy some food for dinner. She paused by the oven-ready pre-stuffed chickens, but these took an hour and a half to cook, so she settled for a bag of frozen prawns. She already had a tin of marinara sauce on the shelf at home, and the whole thing, including the spaghetti, would only take about ten minutes to prepare. On impulse, she picked up a box of garlic bread; that could heat in the oven while the spaghetti was cooking. Perfect. Steven would like that. Then she picked up some grapes and a bottle of white wine for her mother; Jean felt very guilty because she hadn't had time to visit her for two days. She'd look in at the nursing home during lunchtime tomorrow.

At the checkout counter Jean smiled at the clerk. 'They're keeping you busy today, Elsa, aren't they?'

'Aye, fairly,' answered Elsa, putting Jean's groceries in a bag. 'My mither's coming doon to see you the morn, she's got an infection on her hand, where she burned it . . . Do you remember, a while back, when it was so hot and she was making chips?'

'Yes, I certainly remember. That must have been the hottest time we ever had in Perth.'

'Here's your charge card, Dr Montrose . . . If you'll just sign there . . .'

Jean hurried out, going like a little tank; Elsa watched her, and said to the next customer, smiling, 'Do you see her go? There's naebody like that Dr Montrose.'

Fiona came home for dinner again, and afterwards Steven suggested they all go to the cinema; they were showing *The Dead Poets' Society* and he'd heard it was a good film. Jean and Lisbie had decided to spend the evening writing out wedding invitations, but Fiona jumped at the opportunity to avoid doing that, and didn't even ask if Robert could come with them, much to Steven's relief. Fiona was very quiet and seemed scared but hadn't said anything to her yet. Jean felt sad and apprehensive about her elder daughter; to her mind, this was no way for a girl to be feeling six weeks before her wedding day.

After the film, which was showing at the theatre on High Street, Lisbie suggested that they go and have an ice cream.

'Well, I don't know,' said Jean. She sighed and patted her tummy, but the others persuaded her without too much difficulty and soon Jean was tucking into a chocolate chip ice cream twice the size of her fist.

It was well after eleven by the time they got back in the car, and the High Street was almost deserted. Steven, who was driving, decided to go home through some of the quiet back streets, mostly because he liked driving at night. The car liked it too, he said. The main streets were lit with the reddish glow of mercury arc lamps, but as the Rover crept through the smaller side streets, the lights became dimmer and less frequent. They went down Cready Street, a long street which had been widened at the expense of the pavement, which was now just wide enough for one person to walk down. They passed Singh's Indian grocery store and to their surprise, the lights were on, although they couldn't see through the window.

'Dad, there's something wrong there,' said Fiona, her voice sharp. 'Mr Singh *always* closes sharp at eleven . . .'

'He's probably just counting his money,' replied Steven. 'You worry too much.'

'No, Dad. Please, I just have a feeling there's something wrong there . . .'

'Oh, don't be so silly.' Steven negotiated the turn at the end of the road. He sounded irritated, but out of the corner of his eye he saw Jean staring at him.

'It wouldn't do any harm to drive around again,' Jean said, almost apologetically. Steven sighed and went around, and slowed when they came abreast of Singh's shop.

'Oh my God,' said Fiona, who was nearest, peering out through the window, 'the door glass is broken . . .' They all saw the star-shaped hole. Steven, shaken, pulled up a few yards down the street.

'We'd better go and get the police,' he said.

'Mr Singh could be dead by then,' said Fiona. 'I'm going in . . .' And before anybody could say anything to her, she opened the car door and was out, running back along the street.

'Damn!' exploded Steven, undoing his seat belt and jumping out after her. He had almost caught up with Fiona when she pushed the door of the shop open and ran in, with Steven right behind her. Then they both stopped dead in their tracks. Mr Singh was sitting in a chair in the narrow space behind the till, pale as a ghost, with blood running from a cut in his forehead down his face. Standing next to him was a young man of about twenty, filling a plastic bag with money he was taking from the drawers of the old-fashioned till. The bag was already half full of bottles evidently taken from the open liquor cabinet behind him. He looked up at Fiona and Steven, a glazed, vacant look on his face. Steven didn't hesitate for a second; he picked up the nearest movable object, a jar of sweets, off the counter and hurled it at the man, who ducked, and the jar smashed into the cabinet behind him. Then, very fast the man put the bag on the counter and vaulted over it towards them. With the heel of his free hand he struck Steven a hard blow in the chest that made him stagger back and fall between two aisles, pulling some groceries down on top of him. Fiona stood there, paralysed, unable even to scream. The man pushed her roughly aside, ran out of the door and into the street. Outside, he hesitated for a second, then made a fatal mistake. He turned, away from the bright lights of the main street to his right, and started to run in the opposite direction towards Steven's car. Jean, who had turned in her seat to keep an eye on the shop, saw what was happening.

'Hold tight!' she said quickly to Lisbie, who was sitting right behind her. Jean put her hand on the doorhandle, and just as the robber came parallel to them, running full tilt with his bag down the narrow pavement, Jean pushed the door open and he ran straight into the edge of it with a force that rocked the car and almost took the door off its hinges. All the air came out of him with a whooshing noise and he fell down without another sound. Jean put her hand on the horn and kept it there, and within moments a small crowd had gathered.

Leaving the man in the not-too gentle hands of the locals, Jean ran back towards the shop with Lisbie in close pursuit. As they went in, a police car came slowly around the corner, lights flashing. Inside the shop they found Fiona helping her father to his feet and Mr Singh still turbaned, still bleeding, and still sitting on his chair as if he'd been hypnotised.

After one quick look at him, Jean told Lisbie, 'Go out there and tell the police to call an ambulance.' Then, after making sure that Steven was not seriously hurt, she took a handkerchief from her bag, put some pressure on Mr Singh's forehead, and in a few moments was able to stop the bleeding.

'It's all right, Mr Singh.' Jean spoke reassuringly to him. 'It's not very serious, just a cut, and it's stopped bleeding now . . .'

Mr Singh stared straight in front of him without answering, his blue Sikh's eyes apparently seeing nothing. Steven came over, still wheezing and breathless, and tried to talk to him, but Mr Singh seemed sunk in a catatonic stupor.

After the ambulance had come and gone, and the police had secured and closed up the shop, Jean got everybody back in the car and drove home. Steven was shaken but had escaped with only a few minor bruises, and Fiona was suffering mainly from the shock of the incident. Hardly a word was spoken, and once they were home they all went silently to bed. Steven started to shiver almost as soon as he got into bed, and Jean hugged him quietly until he fell asleep.

Douglas' immediate instinct after seeing the Jaguar was to go back to the station, get a warrant for Roderick Ferguson's arrest, then go back to pick him up. But his common sense prevailed over his enthusiasm and instead he wrote down the Jag's number to put it through the computer as soon as he got back to headquarters. He was just assuming that it belonged to Roderick, and he quailed briefly at the thought of the scene if he marched in with his warrant and found that the car belonged not to Roderick Ferguson but to one of his law partners . . .

Doug turned around and went back, crossed the street, in his mind tipping his hat to Albert, who surveyed him with good-natured contempt, and continued his walk around the park, his head whirling. Roderick Ferguson . . . That was going to be a tricky situation; he was a lawyer, and beginning to be a public figure. He, Douglas Niven, would have to develop the most water-tight case ever, or he would be out of a job in no time at all. He certainly couldn't go just with the car; a defence lawyer would eat him alive on that. He could just imagine the cross-examination;

'Inspector, do you happen to know how many silver-grey Jaguars were built in 1990? Have you established the location of all the others during the period in question?'

He was still trying to decide what his next step should be when Doug found himself opening the front door of his house.

'Well, did you stop off for a drink, or something?' asked Cathie from the kitchen. 'It's almost supper time.'

'Not funny,' said Doug. 'Wait till you hear this . . .'

Doug liked a solid lunch, and Cathie had warmed up some beef stew from the day before, and added a great dollop of mashed potatoes and a pile of peas that looked like an arsenal of small green cannonballs. In between mouthfuls, Doug told her about his discovery.

Cathie was astonished. 'I wasn't going to vote for that Roderick Ferguson anyhow,' she said.

'That's not the point,' said Doug sharply. 'I have to find a way to nail him. I *know* he did that motel job, and if he did, he probably killed Ferguson too, but I have to be able to prove it.'

'He's not much of a man,' said Cathie reflectively. 'If you go after him, and let him know you know, you can probably scare him enough so that he'll crack and give himself away.'

'That's just what I was thinking,' said Doug. 'Do you have any ketchup? Those peas are like rocks.'

Chapter Twenty-six

The next morning about eight, before anyone had left the house, there was a loud ringing at the Montrose's door. Surprised, Jean went to answer it, and when she opened the door, standing on the top step was Mr Singh in a sparkling fresh white turban, carefully trimmed beard and immaculate dark grey suit. There was a small, tidy dressing over the cut on his forehead. He looked thoroughly impressive, and was carrying a huge box with a big ribbon around it. His son stood respectfully on the step behind and below him.

'Oh my goodness,' said Jean who, luckily, was dressed. 'Do come in, both of you!'

Mr Singh marched in, followed by his son, and Jean led them into the sitting room, keeping her fingers crossed that it was presentable. She installed Mr Singh on the sofa with his son; the box was placed at the father's feet. Soon the rest of the family came down, and Jean offered her guests tea, which was ceremoniously accepted.

After the first sip Mr Singh cleared his throat. 'I am here for two purposes,' he said in a deep, musical voice, 'first to thank you all for saving my life last night . . .' He raised his hands at Steven's objection. 'But I am here principally to formally release your daughter Fiona from her betrothal to my son Robert.'

Robert looked at the floor.

'We have talked about this much of the night,' Mr Singh went on. 'Robert will be taking over my shop now, and we do not think that to be the wife of a humble shopkeeper is proper for your daughter. And it is dangerous . . .' Mr Singh put his hands together in a prayerful pose.

'Have *they* talked about it?' asked Steven, astonished.

Robert slowly raised his dark eyes to Fiona, and saw surprise turning to relief in her face. So did Steven, Jean and Lisbie.

'This . . .' Mr Singh patted the box, 'is a token of our gratitude and also to acknowledge the termination of the betrothal.'

He's a real businessman, thought Steven. He's making sure there's no misunderstanding. He was about to say that there was no need for any gift when he felt Jean's firm grip on his wrist. She wasn't looking at him, but he heard her as loud as if she'd stood on the table and shouted at him. Keep quiet, she was saying. Smile, but please, just don't say anything.

Mr Singh got up followed immediately by Robert, who, with a very sad expression, put out his hand to Fiona. After a moment's hesitation, she took it, and to his astonishment, Steven saw that she was trying very hard not to laugh.

As soon as they were gone, Fiona and Lisbie rushed back into the sitting room to open the box. Inside were two packages, one heavy and one light, and below that was a huge selection of jars and containers of exotic Indian food. Lisbie pulled out a big green pottery jar of candied ginger, followed by tins of spices and a wooden box made like a crate which contained the best tiny-leaved Darjeeling tea.

'Let's see what's in the packages,' said Lisbie, grabbing the heavy one.

'Hey, whose *betrothed* was he anyway?' protested Fiona, pulling it away from her. She ripped open the tissue paper and pulled out a large bronze model of the Taj Mahal. The two girls looked at each other silently for a second, then fell into each other's arms, exploding with delighted laughter.

Jean and Steven came back into the room, wondering what was so hilariously funny, in time to see Fiona unwrapping the other package which contained a dark blue velvet box with the name of Perth's leading jeweller on it. Inside was a string of exquisite matched pearls with a diamond-studded clasp and Fiona's laughter suddenly stopped. She stood up, fighting back tears, and went over to put her arms around Steven and Jean. Lisbie got up quickly and joined them, and for a long moment they all stood there silently hugging each other, for the first time in many weeks feeling that they were a family once again.

With the morning mail, Doug received a large flat cardboard envelope with DO NOT BEND written all over it. Inside, Doug found a remarkable painting of a recent-model Jaguar, with a note from Richard Archibald, the police artist who had almost been run down at the Travellers' Motel in Dunblane. 'It helped me to remember when I painted it,' Doug read, 'because there were a couple of additional things I hadn't even realized I'd noticed . . .' The couple of additional facts were that there was a circular yellow tag in the lower left corner of the windscreen, and that the passenger side windscreen wiper didn't retract fully. Doug sent Constable Jamieson to look at Roderick's Jaguar and see if these items matched.

'The yellow sticker is a parking permit for the Craigie Hill Golf course,' Jamieson reported fifteen minutes later on his radio. 'And that windscreen wiper blade is stuck about a quarter of the way out.'

Douglas promptly called a conference with the Drug Task Force and they all met an hour later in the small conference room on the fifth floor. Chief Detective Inspector Bob McLeod was there too, ostensibly to give advice when asked but also to keep what he considered Doug's excessive zeal within bounds. There was an almost palpable atmosphere of excitement in the room after Doug outlined the case against Ferguson; the policemen felt like a posse taking up their positions around the encampment of a dangerous outlaw.

'That's terrific,' said Ian Garvie. 'Actually, we've got absolutely nothing on Roderick Ferguson from the drug standpoint, not even a suspicion. On paper, he's as clean as my conscience.' He grinned at Douglas.

'Nor do we, aside from this,' said Doug. He pointed at the painting which he'd pinned up on the noticeboard so they could all examine it.

'Have you accounted for his movements the afternoon those two lads were killed?' asked Bob.

'No. I was hoping to have a bit more ammunition before

gong to see him,' replied Doug. 'Talking about which, by the way, he has never had or applied for a gun licence.'

'Why do you think he killed them?' Bob took out his pipe and a watered-silk tobacco pouch. 'Would he have left the money? It was all still there, you said. It hadn't been touched.'

'Well, he'd have known he'd get it back, or rather his mother would,' replied Doug slowly, 'and I think that's an argument against him. If it had been some other faction inside the drug scene, they'd have taken the money, nae doubt.'

He looked across the table for confirmation, and Ian nodded.

'No,' went on Doug, 'I think he did it to silence two men who could have blackmailed him about his brother's drug involvement. And not just for money, but for all kinds of favours if he became an MP . . . As a Parliamentary candidate for this area, Roderick has to be squeaky clean.'

'You say there's absolutely no indication that he was into drugs himself?' Bob was feeling very sceptical about the whole thing, and the idea of going after an important local figure on a murder charge made him very nervous indeed.

Ian Garvie shook his head. 'Who knows? Maybe he had a snort from time to time. All I can tell you is that there's nothing on the books, and none of our people have heard of him being involved in any kind of drug activity.'

Douglas wasn't feeling too comfortable himself; if he put his foot in it in this particular case, it would be a lot harder getting it out again.

'Maybe you can get another ident on the vehicle,' suggested Bob. The smoke was coming out of his pipe like a chimney, a good indication that he was concerned. 'Did anybody else see it at the motel?'

'No. We asked the desk clerk. There was a fair amount of coming and going that day, and she didn't look outside. She's not too bright, that girl, she can barely see over the counter and wears thick glasses . . .'

The men in the room grinned in sympathy; for some reason crucial witnesses often seemed to be blind or mentally defective or both.

Doug went on, 'I got the guest list and we're going through that, but we haven't turned up anything useful so far.' He sat back in his chair and looked over at Bob. 'I'm going to need a search warrant for his house; there was no weapon at the scene, and we might be able to find it at his home.' Bob looked acutely uncomfortable at the thought of searching the next local MP's house, but he nodded weakly.

'Ian's going to be in charge of the search,' went on Doug, 'and while that's going on, I'm going to be interrogating him in his office . . .'

Constable Jamieson came into the room, late, and both Bob McLeod and Doug eyed him with disfavour as he sat down.

'As I was saying,' said Doug, 'I plan to interrogate him, and at the same time let him know that we think he killed those two men. I'll be very careful,' he said, looking at Bob, who was now almost hidden in a pall of blue smoke. 'I won't give him any grounds for complaint. But from what I know and what I've heard, he sounds like a rather flashy but gutless individual. I think he'll fall apart under the strain, and we'll be right there to pick up the pieces.'

Bob stood up. 'Just don't you forget,' he said emphatically, pointing the stem of his pipe at Douglas, 'if you mess this up, it won't be just *your* head that'll roll.' He looked around the room at the others hoping they would get the message.

After he'd gone, Ian shook his head. 'He just wishes you'd pick less important suspects,' he said, grinning in the way people everywhere grin about bosses. 'He wouldn't be happy even if you'd caught the lad standing over the bodies with a smoking gun in hand, and twelve Wee Free clergymen volunteering to be witnesses.'

'He'll put his own head in the noose,' said Doug confidently. 'I mean Roderick. You'll see.'

When Jean came in to the surgery the next day, there was a message for her to call Marina, Lady Strathalmond, as soon as possible. Jean was in a hurry, as usual, and didn't get around to returning the phone call until about an hour later.

'It's about Katerine,' said Marina sounding anxious. 'She's

not well. She didn't look well at breakfast, but you know how she is.' Marina sighed. 'Anyway she has a bit of a fever, I think, because she's flushed and hot-looking.'

Jean asked a few questions, then suggested some aspirin, and told Marina to bring her daughter in the next day if she wasn't better. But on and off for the rest of the morning, the two women came back into Jean's mind, the mother and the daughter; Jean had many serious problems to worry about, but she was feeling more and more apprehensive about the events that had led up to the murder of Graeme Ferguson and then the two drug dealers.

Back in Roderick Ferguson's office, Lisbie was worried by Roderick's appearance when he came back in after seeing Jean. He was pale, dishevelled looking, and gave her a really strange look as he went straight into his inner office and closed the door. Lisbie had to run some errands around the office and do some Xeroxing, and when she came back from one of her forays about an hour later with a folder full of papers she was astonished to see Doug Niven coming upstairs with Constable Jamieson.

'Is Mr Ferguson in, Lisbie?' asked Doug, sounding more formal than usual. 'Because we'd like a word with him, if that's convenient.'

'Have a seat,' replied Lisbie. 'I'll see if he's free.' She put the folder on her desk, knocked softly on Roderick's door and went in.

'Two gentlemen to see you,' said Lisbie, lightly, 'Inspector Niven and Constable Jamieson.' It was not unusual for police officers to visit different members of the firm in the course of their duties, so Lisbie was not prepared for Roderick's response. His jaw slackened, and the left side of his face began to twitch nervously until he rubbed it hard with his hand. A strange look spread across his face like an infection, and he glanced momentarily at the window as if it might afford him an avenue of escape. Then his shoulders sagged, and without looking at Lisbie, he said in a resigned tone, 'All right, then, send them in.'

Astonished and scared, Lisbie opened the door for Doug and Jamieson, who had already got up from their chairs. Lisbie closed the door behind them. She was already deeply concerned about Roderick; he'd come in looking like death warmed up, and at this point Lisbie was sure that something really terrible was happening, and her gentle heart went out to him.

'I hope we're not interrupting you,' said Doug, coming into the room.

'Do sit down,' said Roderick, indicating two chairs opposite his desk. He had quickly pulled himself together from his momentary loss of aplomb with Lisbie. 'What can I do for you two gentlemen?' He looked pointedly at his watch.

'We won't take too long,' said Doug, putting his briefcase down by his legs and settling in to his chair as if he were prepared to stay there all afternoon. 'We'd like to talk to you about last Tuesday, which, as you may recall, is the day two men were shot to death in a motel in Dunblane.'

Roderick said nothing, but Doug could see the panic close beneath the surface. Roderick looked as if this was just the latest in a series of catastrophes, and knew that this one was going to break his back. The left side of his face started to twitch nervously again, and Roderick's hand came up abruptly to cover it. He's going to keel right over, thought Doug with contempt. He really preferred an opponent who had a bit more spunk to him.

'Well?' said Roderick, gently rubbing the side of his cheek.

'Would you mind telling us your exact movements on that Tuesday?' asked Douglas in the slow, methodical voice which was designed to irritate people like Roderick Ferguson. He glanced over at Jamieson to make sure he was taking notes.

Roderick's hand came down hard on the desk. 'Are you suggesting that I killed these men?' asked Roderick, his voice unnaturally loud. 'Because I can tell you right now . . .'

'I'm not suggesting anything of the sort,' interrupted Doug without making it sound like an interruption 'and as a lawyer, I'm surprised I need to tell you that.'

Roderick laughed, but it was a sound near hysteria, and he passed his hand through his already rumpled hair. He's done that a few times this morning, guessed Doug, watching Roderick's nervous movements. He must have known we were coming to visit him.

'Sorry.' Roderick's laugh was higher-pitched than he wanted. 'I've been under quite a strain recently, and . . .'

'Of course,' said Doug soothingly. 'That's all right. You were going to tell us about your movements last Tuesday.'

Roderick shifted in his chair. 'Let's see . . . I had breakfast at home . . .' He broke off. 'Do you want me to start at the beginning?' he asked with a touch of sarcasm 'I brushed my teeth a few minutes before eight . . .' He paused, expecting Doug to tell him to start at when he got to the office, but Doug just looked at him without expression. He knew that in this kind of person truculence was just a stage in the process.

'I had two eggs and two rashers of bacon,' went on Roderick trying to maintain his brash demeanour, but his voice didn't match his expression.

'At what time was that, sir?' asked Doug. Although Jamieson was taking notes, Doug ostentatiously took out his own black notebook, slowly undid the elastic band around it, and flipped over several pages before he found one that was entirely suitable. Then he patiently searched about in his pocket for a pencil. Meanwhile Roderick stared at him, and Jamieson watched impassively. He'd seen his boss do this on several occasions, and it rarely failed to infuriate the interviewee, although Jamieson was never quite sure why Doug went to the trouble.

Douglas licked the tip of his pencil. 'You were about to tell me at what time you had two eggs and the rashers of bacon,' he said, writing. He looked up. 'I assume you also had toast and coffee, sir?'

'Oh, for God's sake!' said Roderick. That was about eight fifteen. My mother will vouch for that, I'm sure.' His voice was high again, reflecting a mixture of petulance and fear.

He's losing his rag, thought Jamieson, astonished, because to him, the questioning had not seemed in the least threatening. It didn't occur to him that Doug had carefully manoeuvred Roderick into the state of mind he wanted him in.

Trying to beat Doug at his own game Roderick described in detail the events of the morning, but was somewhat vaguer about the afternoon, and very quietly, Douglas zeroed in.

'After lunch at the Theatre restaurant with . . . let's see . . .' Doug turned back a page, 'with Mr William McDonald, you were joined for coffee by Miss Katerine McAllister . . . That wouldn't be the *Honourable* Miss McAllister, would it?'

'Yes, it would,' snapped Roderick. 'She's going to be helping me in my election campaign.'

I bet she is, thought Jamieson, suppressing a guffaw. And I know just how . . .

'And after lunch?'

For some reason, the sight of Doug's blunt-pointed pencil poised over the paper infuriated Roderick.

'Do you both have to take notes?' he asked. 'Wouldn't one be enough?'

'And after lunch?'

'I came back here to the office.'

'Did you make or receive any phone calls?'

Suddenly Roderick understood the slow, painstaking speech, the pencil-licking, the double set of notes. Douglas Niven was just plain *stupid* . . . He sat up in his chair; it was time he took command of this situation.

'Yes, I made several phone calls, but I don't keep records of these, only long distance ones.'

Then Roderick decided to take a risk, but one which, if it came off, would get him once and for all out of trouble. 'My secretary can tell you I didn't leave the office all afternoon,' he went on, his voice careless. 'I probably went to the bathroom and to our legal library a couple of times, but I didn't keep records of that either, not knowing you'd be asking.'

'At what time did you leave the office, Mr Ferguson?'

Roderick's hesitation was only momentary. 'About five thirty,' he said.

'Did you bump into any of the cleaners?' asked Doug, and Roderick looked startled, but relaxed almost immediately. 'They don't come in on Tuesdays,' he said.

Doug got up, went to the door and opened it. 'Miss

Montrose,' he said, sounding very formal, 'would you mind
stepping in here a moment?'

Lisbie came in, wide-eyed. 'Mr Ferguson tells me you can
confirm that he was here in the office all Tuesday afternoon
. . . Is that so?'

Constable Jamieson's portable radio crackled, and he held
it to his ear. Roderick strained to listen, but didn't hear
anything he could understand. Then Jamieson wrote something
on his pad and passed it to Doug, who read 'Nothing
incriminating in the Ferguson house.'

He looked back at Lisbie, who was looking at Roderick in
a puzzled kind of way. Roderick was staring at her as if he
were trying to tell her something.

'Tuesday was my afternoon off,' she said.

'Of course,' said Roderick, smiling. 'I completely forgot.
I'm so sorry . . .' Lisbie looked at him, puzzled; she felt that
somehow she'd let him down, that he'd expected her to say
that yes, he'd been here all afternoon. To her surprise she felt
tears starting to form in her eyes.

'Thank you, Miss Montrose,' said Douglas, watching her.

'So it's just your word against mine,' said Roderick after
Lisbie closed the door.

'Not entirely,' murmured Douglas. He picked his briefcase
up, pulled out the painting of the Jaguar and passed it to
Roderick.

'That picture was made from memory by a talented police
artist who you had the misfortune to almost run down while
you were leaving the Travellers' Motel,' said Douglas, reaching
over and taking it out of Roderick's hands. 'Extraordinarily
detailed, isn't it? Down to the badges, the yellow sticker and
the windscreen wipers . . .'

'He must have done that from a photo,' said Roderick, after
staring at the painting for a long moment. He was obviously
very shaken and had difficulty pulling himself together. 'You
know it as well as I do, Inspector; that picture would never
stand up as evidence in a court of law.'

'We have an affidavit,' replied Doug, standing up,
'concerning the manner in which this painting was made. Now,

Mr Ferguson . . .' Doug put his hands on the desk and leaned forward, coming in for the kill. 'I realize that you acted under considerable provocation. Your mother had been threatened, and so had you, and it's evident that you were under great strain and anger when you went down there. Also, you knew these were two desperate men, and I have no doubt that they threatened you. To have killed these men, these two criminals in self-defence would certainly get a sympathetic response from a jury . . .'

Doug leaned forward over the desk, and seemed to get about a foot taller. 'The alternative to your co-operation, Mr Ferguson, is that we prosecute the case with everything we've got.'

For a second, Roderick wondered how he could have thought this man stupid, and only a few minutes ago. Doug went on in his relentless voice. 'We would take the position that this was a cynical, calculated double murder in order to save our reputation and your hopes of becoming an MP.'

Roderick licked his lips. He felt overwhelmed and hopeless, and his voice was barely audible. 'I need time to think about this,' he said.

'No problem,' said Doug, feeling the sparkle of victory rising like champagne in his veins. 'I'll come over to your house this evening at . . .' He looked at his watch. 'At nine exactly. I'll expect you to make a statement to us at that time, which we will record, and if you wish to have a lawyer present that will be fine.'

A faint smile passed over Roderick's face. 'I don't think a lawyer will be necessary,' he said. He stood up, and leaned momentarily on the desk for support. 'We'll see you at nine then.'

'You might want to pack a few things,' said Jamieson, speaking for the first time. 'I mean tonight. A toothbrush, stuff like that.'

When Lisbie came into the office a couple of minutes after Doug and Jamieson had gone, Roderick lifted his head up from the desk.

'I'm so sorry,' she said, her heart going out to him. She came around the desk to comfort him but he recoiled from her. 'No, Elizabeth,' he said. 'It's . . . it's time you went home. And don't lock the door,' he said. 'I . . . have a client who's coming later . . .'

Feeling immeasurably sad, Lisbie slowly left the room and went back to her desk. She put the cover on the typewriter, switched the phone so it would ring in his office, picked up her handbag and looked at his closed door. She hoped he would be all right . . . She didn't like leaving him like that, so sad and depressed, but he'd told her to go.

Very quietly, Lisbie opened the door on to the corridor and closed it quietly behind her, remembering his instructions not to lock the door. She tiptoed down the corridor as if she were leaving the bedside of a seriously ill friend.

Chapter Twenty-seven

Dinner was different that evening at Strathalmond Castle. Far from her usual sulky self, Katerine was bright, with a brittle, febrile liveliness, but she remained just as vicious as ever.

'How was your lunch, dear?' asked Marina. Cole was at the sideboard with his back to them, filling the soup plates from the heavy silver tureen on the sideboard, one big ladleful for each Copenhagen plate.

'Awesome!' replied Katerine. She shot a swift glance at Ilona. 'I'm going to be in charge of publicity for Rod Ferguson's campaign. He'll make a wonderful Member of Parliament, don't you think?'

'I'm sure he will,' replied her mother. 'Cole, would you turn the lighting up, please? It's like a night-club in here.'

'Yes, madam.'

Doris, the maid, came around the table, and carefully deposited a soup plate on each rectangular Carrickmacross lace placemat. Above her, the glow from the dozens of lights on the chandelier increased, and the silver on the table and the sideboard sparkled with an elegant, muted lustre. The table they used *en famille* was a square, heavy pedestal piece of dark walnut and of uncertain origin; under the vast crystal chandelier it looked tiny and temporary.

'Serve from the left, Doris,' said Marina in a bored tone, 'and clear from the right. How many times do I have to tell you?'

Cole glowered silently at Doris.

'Rod was so funny at lunch,' went on Katerine. 'He told me he even asked you to dinner . . .' She glanced spitefully at her sister across the table, and giggled. 'He is such a *compassionate* man, always putting the feelings of others before his own personal preferences.'

Calum, who had come in late, and for whom Marina had delayed the meal, looked expressionlessly at Katerine. 'Are you feeling better? Your mother said you had a fever.'

'I'm fine, thanks, Daddy,' replied Katerine, but under the sparkling lights, her mother could see that she was still flushed and her eyes had a feverish shine to them.

There was a tension in the air, a tension they all felt but could not identify or pin-point its source. Marina sat at the end of the table nearest the door, opposite Calum.

Again it was Katerine who broke the silence. 'I was listening on the radio on my way home,' she said in a conversational tone. 'And I heard that they've had a big break in what they're calling the drug deaths.' She looked around the table. 'They're expecting to make an arrest any moment.' Her father kept on eating; his thoughts seemed to be far away. Marina remained silent, and Ilona stared at her plate.

Katerine jumped up and threw her full wineglass on the middle of the table where it exploded with a crash. The red wine formed a spreading irregular stain on the white tablecloth, as if someone had been shot in the chest.

'Don't any of you care?' she screamed, leaning over the table. 'Don't you realize they *know* who killed Graeme?' She threw her napkin on to the table after the glass, then ran towards the door, stumbling on her high heels.

'Katerine!' Calum's voice cracked like a whip. 'Come back here this instant and sit down!'

Katerine stopped. The authority in Calum's voice was overpowering; it made her turn and come slowly back to her pace.

Cole, who had been standing at the sideboard, came smoothly into action. Within moments he removed all the plates and glasses, the bowl of flowers from the table, and placed them on a small serving stand to his left.

'This won't take a moment, your Lordship,' he murmured. Deftly he picked up the corners of the tablecloth and swept it away with the broken glass. Two minutes later, a fresh tablecloth was in position, and the plates, glasses and cutlery were back on the table.

'Normally I wouldn't have allowed you to return after that outrageous behaviour,' said Calum sternly to Katerine. 'But these are not normal times. I have something very important to tell you all . . .' Out of the corner of his eye he saw Cole heading discreetly towards the door. 'Cole, I'd like you to stay and hear this too, although there's no need for us to keep Doris.'

Afterwards, there was a strained silence around the table, broken only by an occasional anguished sob from Katerine. Cole stayed in the shadows near the sideboard, but his expression was unusually tense. He glanced at the clock, estimating the time to the next news broadcast.

Doug reported to Bob McLeod, his Chief Inspector, and gave him a blow-by-blow account of what had transpired at Roderick Ferguson's office.

Bob was astonished. 'I'd have thought he'd defend himself a bit better than that, him being a lawyer and everything,' he said, puffing on his pipe. 'It sounds as if he gave up without a struggle.'

'Not at all, sir,' said Doug, not wishing to have his triumph minimized. 'He's a very canny man, and he's covered his tracks very well. Garvie's group found nothing at his house to incriminate him . . . But I think that we got him with that car painting — there wasn't much he could say about that.'

Bob could think of several things that Ferguson could have said, but he held his peace.

'I'm coming with you tonight,' he said.

'You want to take over the case *now*?' asked Doug, surprised and offended.

'No, man, no . . . Dinna get yourself in a lather. I'll stay in the car and keep an eye on things. I'll take my own car. Use channel forty-four, all right?'

'Yes sir,' said Douglas, relieved. Some Chief Inspectors he knew would have taken over the case at this point, without any regard for who'd done the work, just to garner the publicity and the kudos.

There was a feeling of suppressed excitement at Police Headquarters; none of Doug's or Ian's people went home, and they all had a hurried supper of sandwiches around the table where they planned the final scene of the drama.

'Why did you decide to take him at home?' asked Ian. 'I'd have booked him there and then — saved us all this flap.'

Doug shook his head. 'That's why they put you into Drugs, and me into Detective,' he replied. 'Psychology, my boy, you've got to think about his psychology. Roddy went home this afternoon in a blue funk, told his mummy what happened, and right now he's working on exactly how he's going to make his confession. I practically told him what words to use . . . Can you imagine, and him a lawyer!' Doug laughed, feeling very pleased with himself. 'So you see, Ian, my lad, if we'd taken him then, he'd have been forced to bluster his way out of it, and then he'd have found we didn't have that much of a case . . .' He glanced at Bob. 'I mean one that would stand up solidly in court,' he added hurriedly. 'We *know* he did these killings, and he knows that we know . . .'

Bob looked at his watch. 'I've told the Super, and he said he'd brief the Chief Constable. So, men, I want you to know the eyes of the world are on you tonight. Not that that matters — it's the eyes of Chief Constable McConnach you have to worry about.' He stood up. 'Good luck, and no screw-ups. All right, Niven?'

'Yes sir,' replied Doug, thinking that he was ready to be a chief detective inspector himself, and would be made one soon, if his run of successful cases continued. 'We'll take him back to the station for formal booking, so we'll meet you back here.'

Bob hesitated at the door. 'What about the, er, press and television? Have you told them what's going on?'

'Just that we expect to make an arrest at any moment,' replied Doug. 'Their presence at the house might have a negative effect on our perpetrator.' He felt totally in control; he'd covered everything there was to be covered; in fact, this was the kind of case they'd probably use in the next generation of police textbooks, perfectly worked out, with the final strike organized and carried out from A to Z exactly as planned.

'All right, men,' said Doug, taking command again. 'Let's go.'

Dinner at the Montroses was not a jolly affair either, that evening; Lisbie was distraught about Roderick.

'You should have seen him,' she said, almost in tears, as Steven served the plaice from the trivet in front of him. 'He was so upset I thought he was going to do something terrible, like kill himself.'

'He's *already* done something terrible,' said Fiona. 'The radio must have meant him, when they said they were about to arrest somebody.'

'He couldn't have done it,' sad Lisbie stoutly. 'Kill his *brother*, and then those two men . . .' Her voice faded. 'Why would he ever want to do anything so horrible?'

'Because he's a horrible man,' said Fiona.

Tears always came easily into Lisbie's eyes, and now they really started to flow. 'How can you say that, Fiona? You don't know him, you've never worked with him . . .' Lisbie's distress was so evident that Fiona got up and went round the table to comfort her sister.

'Can we change the subject, if you don't mind?' asked Steven, firmly putting the lid back on the pyrex dish. He looked at Jean and shrugged one shoulder angrily. It was always the same; he came home from a hard day's work, ready for a bit of peace and quiet and maybe some intelligent conversation about things of general interest. And then, every time, one or other of the girls would totally disrupt the meal . . .

Jean unfolded her napkin and put it on her lap. 'All right, now, Fiona,' she said firmly, 'you can go back to your chair. Lisbie, I'm just glad you didn't get *really* involved with him . . . Now *that* would have been a problem!' Jean tried to sound bright and cheerful to restore Lisbie's sense of proportion, but Lisbie's tears redoubled, and Fiona's lips tightened as she watched her from her own side of the table. She'd just hugged Lisbie, and knew the signs; her sister must have hit the vodka bottle as soon as she got home.

Doug sent Jamieson on ahead with instructions to keep a watchful eye on the Ferguson house, and, just before nine, when Doug turned into Lintock Gardens with Ian Garvie sitting beside him, the headlights picked up the reflectors on Jamieson's car. It was parked discreetly under the overhang of a big ash tree at the end of the cul-de-sac.

Doug drove up to the front of the house, while the squad car which would take Roderick Ferguson back to Headquarters pulled up behind them, just as Doug had ordered.

There were only a few lights on in the house as Doug and Ian walked up the short path and up the stone steps. A shadow appeared for a second on the tulle curtains of the sitting room bow window. On the top step, Ian and Doug looked at each other, then Doug took a big breath and pressed the doorbell. They could her it, echoing unnaturally loud inside the house.

A few moments later, they heard the sound of footsteps, not Roderick's, but lighter and rather shuffling.

The hall light went on at the same time as the outside light; the door opened and Marjorie Ferguson appeared, wearing a pink nightgown with white trimmings and a red belt, carpet slippers and big round pink curlers in her hair. She looked at them in astonishment, and Doug was about to say something when there was a sound behind them and Constable Jamieson came up.

'His car's not here, sir,' he said in a stage whisper.

Taken by surprise, Doug turned back to Mrs Ferguson and asked her if Roderick was home, as they had arranged to meet him here. Doug looked at his watch beginning to wonder if something had gone wrong. It was nine o'clock exactly.

'No,' replied Marjorie, obviously frightened and puzzled. 'He didn't come home for dinner, so I thought . . .' Her eyes widened. 'We're you coming to . . .'

'If he comes, tell him to wait here until we come back,' said

Doug over his shoulder, following Ian back to the car at a trot. He cursed under his breath and glowered at Jamieson. 'You imbecile!' he hissed at him. 'You've been there half an hour and you just now found that his car was missing!'

'You never told me he was supposed to be home,' replied Jamieson, sounding aggrieved. He closed the gate behind him, then had to run to catch up with Doug. 'All you said was to keep an eye on the place . . .'

Doug sat in the driver's seat, looking straight ahead, thinking hard, while Ian watched him out of the corner of his eye.

'He could be anywhere,' said Ian.

'Yes, but I think I know where he is,' replied Doug. Suddenly galvanized into action, he started the car, and with a squeal of tyres made a U-turn, going up on the opposite pavement and scraping the side of the car against the hedge. For Ian, the next five minutes were a jolting, fast-moving blur as Doug hurtled through the streets of Perth, dodging, avoiding traffic until they were on Caledonian Street. Doug zoomed past a patrol car coming out of the Headquarters garage, and Ian saw the driver's shocked expression for a brief second, then they were gone. Doug turned the sharp corner at the junction with Atholl Street; the car slid over to the wrong side of the street, swerved back as Doug twisted the wheel, then sped down the hill towards the park. It was only at that point that Ian realized where Doug was going, and he eased the gun in his pocket.

There was another turn into Charlotte Street, and Ian closed his eyes as they approached. He was momentarily pushed hard against the door, then they were heading straight towards the bridge, but before he got there, Doug slammed on the brakes and the car broadsided across the empty street, pointing at the cobbled space in front of the tidy law offices of Roderick's firm.

'Oh shit!' breathed Doug. 'There it is.'

Ian opened his eyes and saw a silver Jaguar, standing alone, its chrome highlights glinting in the glow of the old-fashioned street lanterns around the parking area.

Doug let in the clutch and parked beside the Jaguar. Ian

peered up at the illuminated facade; there were no lights on in the offices, or at least none were visible from the street.

Behind them they heard a siren and saw the flashing lights. The squad car had followed them, and now stopped in the street, before pulling up with a squeak of brakes alongside them.

'Hey you, what the hell do you think you're doing?' shouted the driver, jumping out of his car, and pointing his flashlight in Doug's eyes before he recognized him.

'You came just at the right time,' said Doug tersely. 'We're going to break in here . . .'

The policeman's eyes grew even bigger. 'You have a warrant?' he asked.

'Don't you worry your head about that, sonny,' said Ian. 'Just come along with us.' Doug ran across the cobbles and up the two steps. He shook the door; it was locked. Ian looked at the door, then to Doug's astonishment, pulled a piece of stiff plastic out of his pocket and slid it between the door and the doorpost at the level of the lock. It clicked and the door was open. The bolts hadn't been fastened. Five seconds later, a deafening sound of alarm bells exploded above their heads, and Doug, already overwrought, almost had a stroke at the suddenness of it.

'Burglar alarm,' yelled Ian, turning to the young policeman who by now was fervently wishing he hadn't taken it into his head to chase their speeding car. 'Take care of it!' he shouted over the din, then ran after Doug towards the stairs. Doug found the light switch, and went up the stairs two at a time, accompanied by the deafening clang of the alarm. Ian took his gun out as he came up behind him. Doug hesitated at the top, then pushed open the first door to the left and switched the lights on in the room. There was nobody there, or in the next one; the offices were comfortably, almost opulently decorated, and deserted. They came to the third door; Doug flung it open and switched on the light. Roderick was there, behind the desk, sitting slouched in his leather chair. His head was tilted back over the top of the chair, and he was staring wide-eyed at the ceiling. There was a red stain on the front of his white shirt, not a very big one, maybe the size of a small saucer. Neither Ian nor Doug could see the hole until they came up close. The gun, a .38 automatic, was lying on the floor a small distance away from his right hand, which was flopped over the arm of the chair, palm upward, the fingers slightly curved, as if he were explaining some point of law to a colleague.

Chapter Twenty-eight

About ten thirty that evening, Doug was able to leave Roderick's law office in the hands of the forensic technical team. Dr Anderson had come and gone, cheerful as ever, the photographer had already packed her equipment and taken her film back to headquarters. An electrician had been summoned and had turned off the burglar alarm. Even the radio people and the lone reporter from the *Courier* had gone, after a brief statement from Doug and a promise of more in the morning. The fingerprint men were still there, dusting everything they could think of, but they were just going through the motions, as Inspectors Niven and Garvie had both unofficially agreed that this was a clear case of suicide. Even Dr Anderson, always cautious about such things, finally agreed, although he made the point that self-inflicted gunshots to the chest were not as common as headshots, as he called them. 'I hope it's the start of a trend,' were his parting words. 'I'm really tired of seeing brains all over the ceiling . . .'

Douglas drove Ian back to Headquarters, although Ian had refused to set foot in his car until Doug promised not to exceed the speed limit, whatever happened. They were both exhausted, and didn't say much on the way back. Doug had radioed the news to Bob McLeod as soon as the burglar alarm had been shut off and he could hear himself speak. Bob sounded relieved; he didn't like the idea of a highly publicized trial, which is what would have happened had Roderick Ferguson lived. In this kind of case, he said, the police always comes out looking worse than the accused criminal.

But Ian was morose. 'We could have got a whole heap more

mileage out of that case,' he said. His three months' stay in
the US had left Ian with a slight accent and a permanently
altered vocabulary. 'It would have shown them we can get the
big, important perpetrators too.'

'He wasn't a big perpetrator, Ian,' protested Doug. 'He was
just a little man who'd bitten off more than he could chew.
Where did you leave your car?' He turned the corner into the
back entrance of the main police station, driving as sedately
as a little old lady going to church.

'Over by the car pound. Want to go for a drink some place?'

'No, thanks, I'd better be going home. See you in the
morning − Bob said he'd do all the meet-the-press stuff
tomorrow, thank God.'

'Yeah . . . I hope he remembers which case he's supposed
to talk about.' Ian unfastened his seat belt, which he had
adjusted more tightly than usual. 'You'd better get ready for
the enquiry,' he said, opening the car door. 'They'll want to
know why you didn't arrest him this afternoon. The way it
is, it's going to look as bad for you as if he'd hung himself
by his braces in jail.'

Instead of driving home, Doug went back up to his office
and wrote out his report. He put the portable radio on, and
sure enough, within fifteen minutes there was a news flash
about the finding of Roderick Ferguson's body. According to
the announcer, no arrests were expected.

Doug sighed, and put his report in the tray to be typed in
the morning. Then he went out, got into his own car and
crossed the bridge and headed towards Argyll Crescent. He
looked at the luminous dial on his watch. Almost eleven thirty
. . . Well, he'd go by Jean's house, and stop if the lights were
still on. They didn't usually go to bed until late.

The lights were on, upstairs and in the living room, so Doug
parked behind Lisbie's Morris Minor.

The hall light went on, and Fiona came running out to meet
him.

'We heard!' she cried, even before she reached his car. 'It
was a special bulletin on the radio, so we knew you'd be coming
over . . .' Fiona gave him a brief, hard hug before putting her

arm through his. They started to walk up the curving flagstoned path.

'This is just like old times,' he said, smiling at her. Doug was feeling very good. Fiona hugged his arm close to her.

'Lisbie's very upset,' she said coming in the door. 'Poor wee thing . . . She went off to bed right after we heard. Lisbie really liked that Roderick, although nobody else seemed to, much.'

'Did they say he committed suicide?' asked Doug.

'They said no arrests were expected, so that's the same thing, right?'

'Fiona, you're too smart by half.'

At the door of the living room, Fiona paused with her hand on the doorknob and grinned mischievously back at Doug. 'Dad was just saying you should have arrested him when you saw him this afternoon.'

Steven and Jean were in the living room; Steven was watching television with one eye and reading a glossy catalogue of West German glass-manufacturing equipment with the other.

'Do you read German?' he asked Doug, looking up when he came in.

'*Nein*,' replied Doug. 'All I know is "*Hinde hoch*!" and "*Schlaffen, schweinhund*!" '

'That certainly dates *you*,' said Steven with a grin.

Douglas looked at the brochure, which showed a new and very complicated-looking model of industrial glass oven.

'Well, they should certainly know by now how to make the best ovens,' he said.

'Come on, Doug, the war's over,' said Jean reprovingly. She was sitting on the other side of the fireplace from Steven, the light from the standard lamp shining down on the cardboard box of NHS forms on her lap. 'Sit down and tell us what happened.'

Ten minutes later, Fiona brought in some tea, then poured out a cup and took it up to Lisbie, who she knew wouldn't be asleep.

'So it's all wrapped up,' said Doug. He was feeling tired but satisfied. 'Graeme had stolen Roderick's girl, Ilona, and that's even according to his own mother, and Roderick went totally round the bend about it. That's why he killed Graeme, out of rage and jealousy, and hoping he'd get Ilona back when the dust had settled. Not only that, but Roderick was implicated in a computer scam Graeme had uncovered and was going to blow wide open the very next day . . .'

Doug grinned, taking the glass of sherry that Steven held out to him. 'I tell you, this is the most open and shut case I ever came across. I just can't imagine why it took me so long to figure it all out.'

'Why did he kill the two drug people?' asked Fiona, who was sitting on the arm of his chair, listening breathlessly to his every word.

'Well,' replied Douglas, taking a sip of his sherry, and feeling a bit self-conscious and professorial, 'Roderick knew they could blackmail him forever, especially if he became an MP. He simply couldn't afford to let them go, especially after his mother had paid them off, which was the same thing as admitting their involvement.'

Jean had sat quietly during Doug's discourse, going through her files, catching up with her patient notes while paying careful attention to what Doug was saying. She put her pen down and spoke quietly. 'Doug, there might have been another reason why Roderick . . .'

The telephone rang in the hall, insistent and shrill. With a sigh, Jean got up and went to answer it.

'They never even consider that she might have a private life,' said Steven, annoyed. 'They'll call any time of the day or night.'

Jean reappeared at the door. 'That was Marina Strathalmond,' she said, a strange inflection in her voice. 'There's something the matter with Katerine, their younger daughter. She has a high fever, apparently, and she's delirious . . .' Jean looked at the clock. 'I suppose I'd better go up there. Doug, I don't suppose you'd like to go for the ride?' There was something in her voice which made both men look sharply at her.

Doug hesitated. 'I should really go home . . . Cathie . . .'

His voice trailed away. 'All right, then. I'll tell her where I'm going, if I can use your phone.'

On the way out to the castle, Jean didn't say very much. Doug was still feeling very pleased about having cleared up the entire case to everyone's satisfaction, and he chatted on about the increasing difficulty of attaining the rank of chief inspector.

'That's the hardest jump,' he said. 'From inspector to chief inspector.' He rolled the last two words around his mouth as if he could taste them. 'And they're slowing down all promotions,' he said. 'Apparently it's not the salaries that bothers them, as much as the pensions they have to pay later.'

'You'll get the promotion, Douglas,' replied Jean, keeping her eyes on the road. 'You're honest and capable . . . what more could they want?'

Doug glanced over at Jean, but he couldn't see her expression in the dark.

'Why did you want me to come up to the castle with you?' he asked, after they had been travelling about twenty minutes in friendly silence.

Jean didn't answer while she negotiated the turn on to the side road where Graeme Ferguson had met his death. She didn't like driving at night because of difficulty judging distances, and tended to go more slowly than her usual brisk daytime clip.

'I'm not really sure the whole case is quite closed, Douglas,' she said when they were on the last stretch of road up to Strathalmond Castle. 'And I think I may need your help up there.'

Jean would not utter one more word until they drove up to the castle, where the floodlights had been put on for her. She pulled up under the portico, and turned off the engine.

'I don't expect any trouble,' she said, very quietly, and Douglas could see that she was gearing herself up for a very unpleasant and possibly frightening task.

'Do you want me to come in with you?' Doug asked. 'If there's any question of your safety . . .'

'No, I don't think so.' Jean turned and pulled her black bag out of the back. 'But maybe you could keep the window down.

Sound travels well in this still air.' Jean smiled in the dark. 'Either I'll come out or I'll send somebody to get you.'

And then she was gone, walking quickly under the *porte cochère* and up the steps. The door opened, and then closed silently. Douglas experienced a twinge of apprehension for Jean's safety, then laughed at himself. What did she have to fear? She was the best-loved and respected doctor in the community, and anyway she'd only come to visit a patient at the home of a peer of the realm . . . Douglas felt in his pockets for his pack of cigarettes. There it was, in his shirt pocket, with that single cigarette rattling around inside. He took it out of the crumpled box, looked at it, rolled it between his fingers, sniffed it, then put it back with a sigh. Then he adjusted the seat, and settled back to wait. He was used to waiting; that seemed to make up a large part of a policeman's job.

Chapter Twenty-nine

Cole closed the door behind Jean. It made a soft, hissing thud, like the door of a safe.

Calum and Marina came hurrying down the stairs; Marina was smiling nervously, and Calum's usual rather bristly military look had been replaced by a gentler air of patrician concern.

'It's so good of you to come out!' said Marina, holding a hand out.

'How is Katerine?' asked Jean, handing her coat to Cole, who disappeared with it.

'Her temperature was 103° half an hour ago,' said Marina. She touched the side of her cheek. 'I put cold compresses on her forehead and her chest . . . But she didn't want them, and threw them off. She's been, well, a little difficult . . .'

'That's not completely out of character, is it?' Jean smiled. 'Well, let's go and see the patient.'

'I'll be in the g-room,' said Calum. He looked at Jean. 'Unless there's anything I can do . . .'

'If he could he'd *live* in his genealogy room,' said Marina when they reached the top of the staircase. She gave a small shrug, and Jean gathered that she didn't have much patience for Calum's hobby. Understandable, thought Jean. He's certainly more interested in his heredity and family tree than he is in her.

Jean followed Marina along the high mirrored gallery. The lights were on; switched from some central location by the ever-watchful Cole, Jean supposed. They came to a door, and passed into a smaller corridor. She hadn't been in this part of the building, and looked curiously at the gilt-framed family portraits and battlescenes closely grouped on both walls. It was oppressive, she felt, all these long-dead people staring out at her from their gilded traps, traps they could never escape from.

Marina stopped at a large oak door at the end of the corridor, knocked perfunctorily, opened it and went in. Jean looked around the gaudy, red velvety wallpaper, curtains and furniture of the sitting room.

'Not exactly our taste,' said Marina, noting Jean's glance. 'But that's how she wanted it . . .' She shrugged again, and it occurred to Jean that there was very little that Marina seemed to be happy about, particularly when it concerned the people she lived with.

Marina stood at the door of the bedroom, and Jean joined her. Katerine was lying, half in and half out of the red-satin-sheeted bed, her nightie up around her waist, her long, shapely legs moving restlessly around. Jean noticed a small tattooed heart, high on the inside of her left thigh. She was muttering incoherently to herself, but seemed to be mostly asleep.

'I'll leave you with her,' whispered Marina. 'She's been . . . well, talking quite a bit, but don't pay any attention, she's just rambling . . . When you're done, or if you need anything, just ring.' She indicated a large, old-fashioned bellpush on the wall behind the bed.

Jean put her bag down on the chair by the bed, and when she looked around Marina had gone. There was a click as the apartment door closed back in the sitting room.

'All right, my girl,' said Jean, half to herself, 'let's see what's going on here . . .'

Katerine moaned something, put her legs into a frog-like position, then put them straight out together. She turned her body towards Jean, and sat up.

'Well, how are you feeling?' asked Jean, smiling. One of the things her patients liked best about her was that Jean gave them her full attention; she listened to what they were saying, noticed how they looked. Katerine must have felt it, because she smiled faintly through her dry lips, then, as if she'd been abruptly wakened from a nightmare, her eyes widened and a fearful expression came into her face. She stared at Jean for a full minute, her lips moving very slightly, but no words came out. Then she turned her head to one side, looked away from Jean and said, in a strange, hoarse voice, 'You know, don't you?'

'Yes, Katerine. I think I do.' Jean put her hand gently on Katerine's arm. 'Do you feel well enough to talk about it?'

'Yeah, OK . . . But I need some water first.' She showed her dried lips and tongue to Jean, who got up, filled a mug at the sink and stood by the bed, watching Katerine drink the water greedily. Jean took the empty mug, returned it to the bathroom, then sat down on her bed again, feeling utterly sick at heart.

Half an hour later, after they had talked and Jean had examined her, Katerine fell asleep, exhausted. Jean put her diagnostic instruments back into her bag, closed it, pushed the ancient round bellpush and tiptoed out of the room.

Marina came along the corridor to meet her.

'I think she has German measles,' said Jean.

'I'm glad it's nothing worse,' said Marina, sighing with relief. 'These days, you never know . . . Jean, would you mind telling Calum yourself? He's been terribly worried about her.'

'Surely. I have to talk to him anyway . . .' Jean's expression was so full of sadness that Marina must have noticed, but she made no sign.

'Good. He's in the g-room, of course. It's like a womb for him, he always retreats there when he's upset. And also when he isn't.'

There was an inflexibly hard look about Marina when she spoke about Calum, and Jean felt increasingly uneasy as she followed Marina's long, spidery steps back along the mirrored gallery, across the balcony overlooking the great entrance hall, and down the east wing corridor towards the g-room.

Marina was about to knock at the door when Jean said to her, 'Of course, I'll need to talk to you too, Marina, I'm sure you know that. And you know what about, I'm afraid.'

Marina drew herself up quickly, and stared at Jean. 'I'm sorry, but I don't have the faintest idea . . .'

'Marina, it's too late for all that, it's just a waste of time. Would you come back in . . .' Jean looked at her watch, '. . . fifteen minutes, so I have a chance to talk to Calum first?'

'Very well, then,' replied Marina haughtily. 'I'll come back here, in exactly fifteen minutes.' She made it sound like a threat.

Inside the g-room, Calum was working at his computer, and jumped up when Jean came in. He came over towards her and took her hand in both of his. 'Doctor Jean,' he said, his eyes full of gratitude. 'It was so kind of you to come out late. But Marina and I were so worried about Katerine . . .'

'She'll be fine,' replied Jean. 'What I mean is,' she added hurriedly, 'she has German measles, and that normally takes ten days to a couple of weeks to run its course.'

'Ah, yes,' said Calum thoughtfully. 'German measles . . . That shouldn't keep her out of circulation too long. Assuming she isn't pregnant, of course.' His eyes bored into Jean's with a fierce intensity that contrasted strangely with his previous worried but amiable expression.

'That's a good point,' smiled Jean. 'Congenital heart disease, eye lesions and mental retardation; I'm sure that with your special interest in heredity, you know about the risks to the foetus when the mother has German measles early in the pregnancy.'

Calum nodded. It was nice to be treated as an intelligent and knowledgeable person; even with his exalted social rank, most doctors he'd come across assumed he was totally ignorant of medical matters.

'Yes, I do know.'

'Well, I took a urine sample and a blood sample, just in case,' said Jean, tapping her bag. 'We'll know by tomorrow.'

'It's terribly important that she shouldn't be pregnant,' said Calum, staring at Jean again.

'Yes. I discussed all that with her just now,' said Jean quietly, but she could feel her heart was beginning to race.

'*All* that?' asked Calum very quietly.

'Yes.' There was a heavy, almost frightening silence.

'Do you mind if I sit down?' asked Jean. 'It's been a long

day, and my legs are tired.' She smiled, and the atmosphere lightened.

'I do beg your pardon,' said Calum, instantly contrite. He pushed a comfortable chair forward for Jean and installed her in it. 'I was so concerned about Katerine that I neglected my duty as a host. Could I get you a cup of tea, or a drink, perhaps?' He went to the bellpush on the wall, similar to the one in Katerine's room.

'A cup of tea would be lovely,' said Jean 'Thank you!'

Calum came back and sat in the desk chair. He pressed a couple of buttons on the computer and the green-lighted screen faded, as did the hum of the cooling fan. 'We don't need that right now,' he said, swinging his chair around to face Jean. 'Now where were we?'

'You were worried about Katerine being pregnant by Roderick Ferguson, weren't you?' Jean tried to cover her embarrassment by searching for a handkerchief in her bag.

'That had crossed my mind,' said Calum drily. 'But now that he's committed suicide, according to the radio, anyway, the risk should be substantially reduced.' He hesitated. 'As I said, it's obviously very important now that Katerine not be pregnant.'

'As it would have been important that Ilona not be pregnant by Graeme.' Jean's lips were suddenly dry, and she ran her tongue over them, but it didn't help.

Calum seemed to stiffen, and he stared hard at Jean.

'Yes . . .?' he said, slowly.

'Graeme Ferguson,' said Jean. She cleared her throat. 'It's really interesting how you and I started from entirely different premises and arrived at exactly the same conclusions about him.'

'I'm sorry . . .?' Calum looked genuinely puzzled.

'Well, you were checking him out from the point of view of a father checking out a potential son-in-law, whereas I got to him indirectly . . .'

There was a knock on the door, and Cole came in bearing a silver tray with a heavy Georgian silver tea-pot and matching sugar bowl and milk jug.

'Shall I pour, your Lordship?'

'I can do it,' said Jean quickly, a little flustered by all this ceremony. 'I always pour at home.'

Calum nodded to Cole, who left as silently as he had come in. Jean watched him receding towards the door; when he walks, he glides like one of those big ocean liners, she thought.

'How do you like yours?' asked Jean. The pot was so heavy her hand shook.

'No sugar or milk, thanks . . .' Calum watched Jean with a smiling incredulity. This is a really unusual lady, he was thinking, and a lot cleverer than he'd imagined.

'Let me tell you how I got started on this,' said Jean. She felt more comfortable with a cup of tea in her hand, and it took care of the dryness in her mouth. 'You'll laugh . . .' She took a sip of tea, and eyed the biscuits. They were all plain digestives. 'It was his mother, Marjorie . . . I can't imagine you had very much in common with your prospective sister-in-law . . .'

Calum waved a dismissive hand. There didn't seem to be much point discussing her.

'Well,' Jean went on, trying not to be too rambling, 'I noticed that there weren't any photos of Mr Ferguson in the house, and she told me about his alcoholism and how he'd had to be sent to a sanatorium . . . I just happened to ask how much he drank, and she told me he sometimes had up to three whiskies a night.'

Jean put her cup down indignantly. 'Now that was ridiculous; maybe it sounded like a lot to her, because she's a teetotaller, but it certainly wasn't enough to make him ill. She told me that towards the end, before she was forced to have him taken away, that he was shaking all the time, and was losing his mind . . .'

Calum got up and went over to the window and looked out over the courtyard, which was still lit up.

'Is that your car down there?' he asked. 'A little white Renault?'

'Yes,' replied Jean, wondering if Doug had stepped out to take a stroll. 'About Graeme's father . . . So I decided to go out to see him at the Abbotsford Clinic.'

Calum came back and sat down again, and Jean noticed that he grasped the arms of the chair so tightly that his knuckles were white.

'And of course,' went on Jean, 'when I saw him, I found that, as I'd suspected, he wasn't an alcoholic at all, but had some kind of neurological disease that nobody had suspected. I phoned Dr Beaumont . . .' Jean paused, and Calum nodded resignedly. 'The neurologist you'd asked a couple of weeks ago to examine Mr Ferguson. Well, Dr Beaumont told me the same thing he told you, that Mr Ferguson was suffering from Huntingdon's Chorea, an inherited disease which usually doesn't manifest itself until the victim is in his early thirties, and nearly always leads to insanity.'

Jean took another sip of tea, and the silence came down in the room like a heavy, black, silk blanket.

'His children, Graeme and Roderick, had most likely inherited the disease, and they were both in their thirties, just about the age when it would start to show up.'

'So that's why Roderick committed suicide?' asked Calum. 'Did you tell him his . . . diagnosis?'

'Yes, I'm afraid I did,' replied Jean sadly. 'I had to. Poor Roderick, he was already showing the first signs. And he was desperate for other reasons, including the fact that he'd killed two drug dealers and was about to be arrested. But, as you know very well, he neither killed Graeme nor committed suicide.'

Calum became very still.

'Graeme . . . I'm sure you agonized about him, Calum . . .' Jean's sympathy showed in her face. 'But he was going to marry Ilona, and as you would say, pollute the family genes . . .'

'She wouldn't listen to me,' said Calum, as if he were talking to himself. 'Ilona inherited her mother's stubbornness, which goes back several generations, possibly to the Habsburgs.'

'So after you heard from Dr Beaumont . . .'

'I realized that our family's genetic pool would be irretrievably contaminated,' said Calum, sitting up very straight. 'And I simply could not allow that to happen.' He paused, and stared at Jean. 'But I'm sure you realize that I wouldn't have killed him for *that*.'

Jean nodded embarrassedly, and looked at the floor.

'The reason he died was because he was having an affair with my wife,' he went on, his voice rock-steady. 'And that, Dr Montrose, I could not tolerate. There's a tradition of honour in this family,' he said, drawing himself up again, 'and a . . . betrayal of this sort could quite obviously not be endured.'

'I'm glad you didn't feel you needed to punish Marina in the same way,' said Jean, still looking down.

Calum shook his head. 'Do you know the Strathalmond coat of arms?' he asked Jean. 'It has a shield *dexter*, and three lilies *sinister* . . . Well, although it was designed over two centuries ago, I consider myself the shield, and Marina, Ilona and Katerine as the lilies. Graeme was the intruder, the attacker . . . not Marina.' His lips tightened and he smacked a fist into his other hand. It was the only display of emotion Jean had seen from him.

'How did you find out?' she asked, raising her eyes. 'She must have been very indiscreet . . .'

'Ilona surprised them in a moment of passion, I regret to say,' replied Calum. 'She was horrified beyond belief, my poor Ilona. I can remember her so vividly, coming in here, weeping, completely distraught . . .'

He stood up and faced Jean. 'Yes,' he said, 'justice was done, old-fashioned justice . . . Graeme was a very fast driver,' he went on. 'And that's a deserted road. There's practically never any traffic on it, except to and from the castle.'

'Was he still alive when you got there?'

'I don't know. I wasn't going to take any chances.'

'Calum, I want you to know that Detective Inspector Niven came out with me tonight,' said Jean, trying to sound courageous. 'He's waiting in my car.'

'I know,' said Calum. 'I saw him; he was leaning up against it, smoking a cigarette.'

'He was?' said Jean in surprise then came back to the topic in hand. 'But why did you feel you had to kill Roderick?'

'He was coming on to Katerine,' said Calum, his lips tightening. 'And her morals . . . well an alley cat would be ashamed of them. And you can guess how much she'd listen to advice. She actually thought that when I said Huntingdon's *Chorea*, I'd said *Career* . . . She hadn't the faintest idea of what I was talking about, and didn't *want* to know.'

'You went down there, then, to Roderick's office . . .?'

'Yes. I occasionally do some business with his firm, so I called and said I had a confidential matter to discuss, and would he mind staying until everybody else had left the office . . .' Calum smiled briefly. 'Roderick was a terrible snob, and would have waited all night to talk to the Earl of Strathalmond . . . I used Katerine's gun. It wasn't traceable; I bought it in the States, years ago, and never registered it . . .'

'I'm so sorry, Calum . . .' Jean got up and took his hand in hers. It felt dry, almost powdery. 'I suppose we'd better get Inspector Niven to come in, now.' Jean felt so tired and sad she could have wept.

'He'll want me to go back with him, I imagine,' said Calum. He sounded quite unconcerned. 'I'll just go and pack a few things.' He got up slowly; his knee seemed to be bothering him a little. 'I fully expected that sooner or later . . . But I must say, I didn't expect *you* to figure it all out.'

He said it with such innocent surprise that Jean almost laughed. But he was right; Jean herself never expected to get to the bottom of the cases she got involved in. She didn't *feel* particularly clever — on the contrary, she spent a lot of time feeling almost criminally stupid. She just had a knack for sorting out certain kinds of problems and figuring out their causes . . . And, of course, when one had the causes, one had the whole story. She never even set out to find who had committed a crime; she amassed facts and impressions just like anybody else, only she put them together differently. It was as if some template developed inside her head, telling her which parts of the story were missing, and which ones had to be found.

They left the room together; Calum closed the door, then sauntered off towards his apartments, and Jean went along

the short corridor back towards the main stairway. Just as she
got to the bottom step, Cole appeared.

'If you're looking for the Inspector, madam,' he said, 'He's
in the kitchen. It was getting cold out there . . .'

On the way back upstairs with Douglas, Jean explained
briefly what had been happening; Doug could hardly believe
his ears. When they got back to the g-room, they sat down
to wait for Calum. A few moments later, Marina ran in, white
as a sheet.

'He's locked himself in the bathroom, and won't come out,'
she said. 'I think you'd better come up.'

Doug was already heading for the door. 'Show me where
it is,' he said. Marina ran ahead, with Douglas right beside
her, and Jean behind.

Douglas pounded on the door; ominously, there was not
the slightest sound from inside. The door was heavy oak, and
built to last for ever. Douglas took a run at it, but only bruised
his shoulder. Finally, Cole had to phone the livestock manager
for help; he lived a hundred yards away, and said he'd be
right over. While this was going on, Jean tried to talk to
Marina, but every few moments she'd go to the bathroom
door and bang on it, weeping, and call out, but there was
no response.

'We all knew,' she said, her voce shrill with anxiety. 'He
as much as told us, tonight at dinner . . .'

Cole and Douglas reappeared, with Bert Reynolds, the
livestock manager, who was dressed in a coat over his pyjama
top and pants. All of them were out of breath from heaving
a big pine log up with them. They lined up, and using the log
as a battering ram, rushed against the door. It splintered, but
needed two more assaults to break it down enough for them
to get through. Doug went in first; he took one look, then,
in a very subdued voice, asked Jean to come in.

Stepping over the splintered remains of the door, what Jean
saw horrified her, but she wasn't surprised. Calum McAllister,
twelfth Earl of Strathalmond, was lying in the half-filled bath.
After cutting his throat he had had time to close the open razor
and place it carefully on the soap dish before he lay back to

die in a welter of the blood whose purity he had tried so hard to preserve.

Jean turned to see Marina; she had come behind her, and was leaning against the doorpost, about to faint. Doug and Cole led her back into the sitting room and sat her down. Jean came and sat with her, holding her hand.

After a few moments, Marina raised her head. 'Tonight at dinner . . .' she whispered, 'he did a terrible thing; he told the girls that it was their fault, because of Ilona's stubbornness and Katerine's . . . whoring, he said . . . They'll never get over the guilt of all this . . .'

Marina started to weep, a hopeless, soft flood of tears.

On the way back to Perth, Jean had to fight back her own tears. If it hadn't been for her nosiness, her fatal compulsion to delve into other people's affairs, Calum McAllister would still be alive now.

Douglas, looking at her profile in the gloomy interior of the car, could see the thoughts passing through her mind.

'He was insane,' he said quietly. 'He'd have probably gone for his wife or children next.'

In the dark, Jean tried to smile. 'I suppose Calum McAllister gave a new meaning to the term "a family man".' She took a deep breath. 'Douglas Niven, this is the last case I'm going to get involved in. I'm a doctor, not a detective, and I'm tired of being the cause of all this grief . . . From now on, I'm going to stick to my work, take care of my family and my patients, and leave all this detecting stuff to you. All right?'

'Of course, Jean, whatever you say.'

They drove on in silence.

'Doug, you knew that Roderick hadn't committed suicide, didn't you?'

Doug cleared his throat but said nothing. Jean could sense his embarrassment.

'The higher-ups wanted to close out the case, I suppose.'

'It was a nice tidy solution, with Roderick responsible for everything . . .' Doug retreated defensively into his seat. 'And we do know he killed those two drug dealers.'

Again there was a long silence. 'Well, maybe God put me here to keep you honest, Douglas Niven.' They both smiled companionably in the dark.

There was hardly any traffic in Perth at this hour, and silence reigned in Argyll Crescent. Jean pulled up behind Doug's car, and he drove off down the hill after a quick, subdued goodbye.

The next time Jean and Doug met was after the Earl's funeral service in St John's church, which they both attended.

Jean was dressed in a conservative dark-blue linen suit with a silk blouse. The girls had wanted to come, so Steven came too, although he grumbled mightily.

Douglas walked back with them to their car.

'Would you like to come back to the house for coffee?' Jean asked him. Douglas was about to make some excuse, but Fiona grabbed his arm. 'Of course you're coming,' she said. 'And I'll ride with you in your car.'

Twenty minutes later when they were all back at the Montroses' house and the Nescafé had been made and served, Jean asked Douglas if he'd seen yesterday's paper. He was listening to something Fiona was saying, and holding the cup of coffee between his knees. Jean gently picked the cup up and put it on the table beside him. She repeated the question, and Fiona went over to talk to Lisbie.

'No,' Douglas replied, 'I did not.'

Jean picked up the newspaper, already opened and folded, and passed it to him. Douglas saw a large photo, in which he recognized Denis Foreman and his fellow worker Sam Braithwaite, both smiling and looking extremely dapper in evening clothes.

'Read the caption,' said Jean. 'I don't have my glasses.'

Doug read slowly, holding the paper up. '*The new head of Crossman Securities, Mr Denis Foreman, and his recently appointed Vice-President, Mr Sam Braithwaite, welcoming the guests at the Annual Ball, held at the Fairleigh Hotel . . .*'

'Well, damn it,' said Doug, tight-lipped, putting the paper down. 'If ever you needed proof that crime pays, and pays well . . .'

'Did you notice who else is in the photo?'

Doug glanced back at it. There was a large, jovial man, also in evening clothes, standing next to Denis. 'That's that political fellow, what's-his-name . . .'

'Bill McDonald,' said Jean. 'But did you notice who's holding on to Denis Foreman's arm?'

'My God,' breathed Douglas, looking. 'Is that . . . who I think it is?'

'Yes,' said Jean. 'Ilona McAllister. Look at her face.'

'She's looking absolutely . . . radiant,' said Douglas, a feeling of total disbelief beginning to creep over him.

'There's a small article to the left of the photo,' said Jean. 'I think you should read that too.'

Reluctantly, Doug picked the paper up again, found the place and started to read; now he was deathly afraid of what he might find there.

'*Successful fiscal year for Crossman Securities*,' he read. '*Mr Denis Foreman, newly appointed CEO of Crossman Securities, stated today in an exclusive interview that last year was their most successful ever, and he gave a good deal of the credit to the late Mr Graeme Ferguson, who had been one of the moving forces in the group. "We'll miss him a lot," stated Foreman, "but his place will be very competently filled by Mr Sam Braithwaite, who has taken over his position as head of a substantially expanded foreign-exchange section."*'

Doug stopped. There didn't seem to be anything out of the ordinary there; it was the kind of thing one could expect these days.

'Go on,' said Jean quietly.

'*On a more personal note, Mr Foreman stated that he had been approached about standing as a candidate for Parliament, but he would not elaborate. "We'll see about that after I'm married," he said. His bride-to-be, pictured above, is the Honourable Ilona McAllister, scioness of the Strathalmond family. Miss McAllister said that she was all in favour of her future husband's entry into politics; apart from running the family estate, she said, she wanted a big family of her own.*

"I've always loved Denis," she admitted shyly, "from the very first moment I saw him . . ." '

'Oh, my GOD!' said Doug, putting the paper down. 'My good gracious God Almighty . . .!'

'The only one who really understood what Ilona was doing was Katerine, although she didn't get it all right,' said Jean. 'I should have guessed; it's not easy to hide stuff from your own sister.'

Doug put his head in his hands. He simply couldn't believe what was screaming through his head.

Jean put her hands rather primly in her lap.

'When you think of it from her point of view,' she said, 'it all makes perfect sense. Just imagine . . . Here's Ilona, a clever, extremely ambitious and capable young woman. She's in love with Denis, but can't marry him because her father is absolutely and adamantly against him, and sees Denis off the premises, so to speak. After a while, Roderick Ferguson comes along, and there's a spark of interest because he's a potential MP, but she soon sees that he's just another wimp. Graeme elbows Roderick out of the way and Ilona's swept off her feet because he's so handsome and debonair, with his fancy car and nice clothes and everything, and before she knows it they're going to get married. *Douglas . . .*'

'I'm listening,' he said, raising his head for a moment from between his hands.

'Ilona realizes he's a spendthrift, a womanizer, and a drug user. She has to get rid of him, but the wedding bells are already ringing . . . Ilona knows her mother and Graeme have something going, so she runs to Daddy saying she found them in bed together. She knows Calum, with all his hangups about pride and honour and all that; Ilona might even have suggested what he should do about it.'

Jean pointed her index finger at Douglas. 'Bang!' she said. 'One down.'

'But what about Roderick?' asked Doug, puzzled. 'Where did he fit in?'

Jean was silent for a few moments; her mind was back in Strathalmond Castle inside Ilona's head planning her future.

'That's when Ilona got the idea of getting back with Denis; after Graeme and Rod, she realized he was truly the love of her life. And she wanted more than anything to be married to a man who was powerful and famous. Do you remember when you interviewed her up at the castle? She said that maybe she'd made a mistake dumping Roderick, as he *might* be the next Prime Minister? She knew very well, after going out with him, that Roderick didn't have it in him, didn't have the talent. But Denis did; he was interested in politics, and smart enough to make it work. And there was unworthy Roderick, who had the local political power structure tied up and working for him. Ilona knew by then about the Huntingdon's Chorea, set Roderick up with Katerine, reported once more to Daddy whose honourable reflexes predictably sprang into action again.'

Almost as if she were taking serious aim, she pointed at Doug again, this time with two fingers. 'Bang!' she said again, softly, 'Two down.'

Jean sat back in her chair with a wry smile, and shook her head; she had to admire the impeccable way Ilona had orchestrated her own destiny.

'And that left Daddy himself,' said Douglas in a hushed voice; he was feeling that the entire case had slipped out of his hands like a djinn, having changed shape numerous times with astonishing speed. 'And he was the biggest problem of all, because he wasn't going to let Ilona marry Denis, not over his dead body . . . My God . . .'

'Right, Douglas. Nicely put. Calum was the last and biggest obstacle, so he had to self-destruct. Once Ilona had persuaded him to tell the whole family what he'd done, sooner or later, the story was bound to come out, through Cole or Katerine or even Marina if Ilona didn't first pass the word out herself. Then poor old Calum would be in such trouble he couldn't stop her marrying Denis.'

'So when *you* found out about it, and the poor guy committed suicide, the whole process was just accelerated,' said Doug, totally astonished and feeling that there was probably *nothing* about this case that he really understood.

'That's really weird. Your being so clever worked entirely in Ilona's favour.'

'I'm afraid so, Doug. I can't tell you how much that bothers me . . .' Jean was feeling so wretched that she couldn't sit still, and stood up and went to the window. The two old brown horses in the field next door were leaning over the fence, the barbs of the wire scratching their necks, but they didn't seem to mind.

Doug's eyes were wide, almost crazy-looking.

'So basically you're telling me that three people who were in Ilona McAllister's way got killed, and there's nothing we can do about it? Jesus! She makes the Borgias and Machiavelli look like Sunday School teachers! Surely there's something we can do to nail this . . . monster?'

'Douglas, Ilona hasn't committed a single crime, but she got *exactly* what she wanted, and there's nothing you could ever pin on her. You'd better get used to that idea, because I have no doubt she and Denis'll be living in Downing Street before you're due to retire.'

There was a long silence, broken finally by Doug.

'I have to go home,' he said. 'I told Cathie I'd be back by noon.'

At the door, Doug turned; he looked as if he had been struck by something heavy moving very fast.

'Jean, you remember on the way back here, the night Calum died? You said you were going to stick to doctoring and stay away from detecting?' He paused, while Jean waited to hear him finish.

'Well, Jean,' he said, 'I most heartily second that motion.'

— C. F. ROE —

DEATH BY FIRE

A DOCTOR JEAN MONTROSE WHODUNNIT

When he sees the horrifically charred corpse of Morgan Stroud, Detective Inspector Douglas Niven isn't sure that there is a criminal case to investigate: at first glance the grisly death seems to be the result of a rare natural phenomenon: *spontaneous human combustion.*

According to the victim's sister, it is simply a manifestation of God's revenge. After all, Stroud had been a very unpopular character: his pupils at St Jude's Academy had often wished the bullying master dead; his estranged wife still bears the scars of his cruel treatment; and fellow teachers George Elmslie and Angus Townes both have axes to grind.

When a second body is found in not dissimilar circumstances, Niven realises he doesn't have the specialised knowledge needed to break the web of silence and superstition, and turns again to Dr Jean Montrose, whose medical expertise and good-natured commonsense finally unlock the gruesome secret of the fiery deaths.

Don't miss the first Jean Montrose whodunnit, *The Lumsden Baby,* also from Headline.

FICTION/CRIME 0 7472 3504 X

A selection of bestsellers
from Headline

FICTION

ONE GOLDEN NIGHT	Elizabeth Villars	£4.99 □
HELL HATH NO FURY	M R O'Donnell	£4.99 □
CONQUEST	Elizabeth Walker	£4.99 □
HANNAH	Christine Thomas	£4.99 □
A WOMAN TO BE LOVED	James Mitchell	£4.99 □
GRACE	Jan Butlin	£4.99 □
THE STAKE	Richard Laymon	£4.99 □
THE RED DEFECTOR	Martin L Gross	£4.99 □
LIE TO ME	David Martin	£4.99 □
THE HORN OF ROLAND	Ellis Peters	£3.99 □

NON-FICTION

LITTLE GREGORY	Charles Penwarden	£4.99 □
PACIFIC DESTINY	Robert Elegant	£5.99 □

SCIENCE FICTION AND FANTASY

HERMETECH	Storm Constantine	£4.99 □
TARRA KHASH: HROSSAK!	Brian Lumley	£3.99 □
DEATH'S GREY LAND	Mike Shupp	£4.50 □
The Destiny Makers 4		

All Headline books are available at your local bookshop or newsagent, or can be ordered direct from the publisher. Just tick the titles you want and fill in the form below. Prices and availability subject to change without notice.

Headline Book Publishing PLC, Cash Sales Department, PO Box 11, Falmouth, Cornwall, TR10 9EN, England.

Please enclose a cheque or postal order to the value of the cover price and allow the following for postage and packing:
UK: 80p for the first book and 20p for each additional book ordered up to a maximum charge of £2.00
BFPO: 80p for the first book and 20p for each additional book
OVERSEAS & EIRE: £1.50 for the first book, £1.00 for the second book and 30p for each subsequent book.

Name ....

Address ....

....

....